Illusions of Love

D0835551

Illusions of Love

CYNTHIA FREEMAN

Pan Books
in association with Collins

First published 1984 by William Collins Sons & Co Ltd
This edition published 1985 by Pan Books Ltd,
Cavaye Place, London SW10 9PG
in association with William Collins Sons & Co. Ltd
9 8 7 6 5 4 3 2 1
© Cynthia Freeman 1984
ISBN 0 330 28820 2
Reproduced, printed and bound in Great Britain by
Hazell Watson & Viney Limited,
Member of the BPCC Group,
Aylesbury, Bucks

Book One

Chapter One

San Francisco was thronged with shoppers in those last days before Christmas. They darted in and out of Macy's and I. Magnin's and Neiman-Marcus with gifts that would undoubtedly be returned in the New Year. But for the moment no one was thinking beyond the holiday. On the corner of Stockton and Geary, Santa Claus tinkled his bell as coins dropped into his small pail, and the smell of roasting chestnuts from a sidewalk vendor filled the air. In spite of the soft winter rain, a children's choir filled Union Square singing 'O Come All Ye Faithful'. People were exceedingly polite as they collided with one another trying to catch the cable car on Powell and Market. Next week would be a different story, but today they apologized, remembering the holy season.

At 6.30 in the afternoon, the office buildings in the financial district were all but deserted. The lights in the Hill Towers Building were being turned off as cleaning ladies closed the doors behind them so that they too could get home and enjoy a mug of hot buttered rum.

Alone in a penthouse office on the forty-first floor, one man sat pensively staring out the window. If there was joy in the world, Martin Roth was unaware of it. He sat in his large swivel chair, consumed with a feeling of loneliness as he watched the early darkness settle over the city. Martin suddenly saw his life in terms as fleeting as the brief twilight. He sighed deeply and continued to stare over the magnificent structure of steel that spread its wings like a giant eagle, connecting Oakland to San Francisco. Although he'd seen it a million times, tonight the size and strength of the mighty bridge left him with a feeling of his own insignificance instead of the opposite, as was usually the case.

No matter how omnipotent we think we are, we have damn little power to control our destinies, he thought. Only that morning he had looked at his life with placid contentment. If his days lacked a certain excitement, they were full, satisfying. Then in a moment everything had changed.

He had bumped into Jenny McCoy, quite by accident, and all the longing and passion of his youth had been reawakened. He realized how terribly much he had missed her, that he had never stopped loving her. Until that moment, he had believed that after twenty-five years he had all but forgotten her. God knows he had tried hard enough. And, in recent years, he'd almost been able to pretend that she had only been a dream. Almost . . . that is, until today.

He suddenly stood up, walked across the deep pile carpet, pressed a button, and watched as the doors to a mirrored bar slid back, revealing his white and strained face. Martin stared. At fifty-three, he'd considered himself still young. His belly was flat and firm, and until now he had accepted his thick grey hair as a mark of distinction. Now for the first time he saw himself as middle-aged – a man with the best already behind him.

From the moment he'd given up Jenny he had devoted himself to building the right kind of life. He had taken over his father's brokerage house, married the right woman, a girl he had been friends with since childhood, tried his best to bring up his two children with the right values. Yet two minutes after seeing Jenny again none of it made sense.

The fluorescent lights hardened the planes of his face, leaving dark hollows beneath his deep blue eyes. He wondered what Jenny had thought when she saw him today. The years had been so kind to her. She was still slender, with those incredible Irish amber eyes and hair the colour of warm molasses. She was more beautiful at forty-eight, if that was possible, than when he had first met her.

He dropped the ice cubes into the glass, filled it half full of scotch, then added soda. He took a long swallow, then walked back to the desk and sat down. Where the hell had the years gone? More important, how had he spent them?

'In a strange kind of capitulation, that's how,' he said aloud. 'An acceptance of the very privilege most people spend a lifetime trying to achieve.'

He had been born into one of San Francisco's wealthiest Jewish families. His wife, Sylvia, came from the same background. As far as marriages went, he had no reason to complain. Had there been compromises? Of course. But Sylvia had been a good wife, and he was more than aware of her virtues, even if he tended to handle his marriage by trying not to scrutinize it too closely. Today he knew that for all these years he'd been fooling himself. He had never forgotten Jenny.

Even this morning, driving to work, Jenny buried safely twenty-five years into his past, the memory of their affair had been lurking in the back of his mind, waiting to throw his life into turmoil once again.

Thursdays were Sylvia's days in town. She would leave the house in Woodside in time to meet Martin for lunch at the St Francis Hotel. Afterwards, she would spend the rest of the day shopping, often staying over at the apartment either to have dinner with friends or attend the theatre or opera.

As usual, Martin had met her at precisely noon for a light lunch; neither wanted a heavy midday meal. After all these years they could talk in an easy shorthand: about their house, the apartment they kept on Nob Hill, the children. At 1.30 they descended the broad stone steps of the St Francis, crossed Powell Street and walked past Union Square, where the children were assembling to sing Christmas carols. They stopped in front of I. Magnin's. Before hurrying in, Sylvia kissed him gently on the lips, then stepped back and said, 'Now, be nice to the Grants tonight, Martin.'

'I'm always nice.'

'No, you're not. I know you think Craig is a bore, but you

have to do this for my sake. Laura's indispensable to me. I need her for the upcoming Spring Ball . . . I really do. So be a darling – and don't argue politics, for heaven's sake!'

'I'll try my best.'

She smiled and said, 'Thanks. You know, Martin, you can be a complete charmer when you put your mind to it.'

He looked at her and smiled. 'Well, that's comforting to know. I'll see you back at the apartment.'

It was while he was waiting for the light to change that he saw Jenny walking past Gump's. For a moment he thought he was dreaming. His pulse raced and he stood frozen. Then, barely waiting for the traffic to stop, he ran across the street shouting her name.

She turned slowly, uncertain whether someone was really calling her. Then, all at once, they were face to face as the crowd flowed around them. Finally Jenny found her voice.

'I simply can't believe this.'

Martin shook his head yes. 'In one split second I might have missed you.'

'How did you know it was me with my back towards you?'

'I'd recognize that walk anywhere.'

'Even after all this time?'

'Yes, even after all this time. You haven't changed at all.'

She laughed. 'Of course I have. We've all changed. You look wonderful, Martin.'

'Really? Thank you . . . But life seems to have stood still for you.'

'Hardly. Are you happy, Martin?'

'Yes, I suppose. And what about you?'

'I'm just trying to keep adrift these days.'

'What are you doing in the city?'

Jenny hesitated a moment.

'I'm on my way to the Orient. The firm I'm with has a number of Japanese accounts.'

'Where are you staying?'

'At the Fairmont.'

'For how long?'

'Only until tomorrow. My plane leaves at seven in the evening.'

'Oh well . . . maybe we could have a drink in the afternoon sometime.'

'Are you sure that's a good idea?'

'I'm not sure if it's good or bad. I'd just like to see you.'

'That seems harmless enough.'

'What name shall I ask for?'

'McCoy, Jennifer McCoy. Same as when we met. It's been extraordinary, Martin, meeting so unexpectedly.'

He wanted to take her in his arms, hold her close, and this time never let her go. Instead he said, 'I'll call.'

Then she disappeared inside Shreve's. Martin didn't know how he made it back to his office. Yet suddenly he found himself standing in front of the massive oak doors, looking at the names of Roth, Seifer, Roth, Stern & Hines. He remembered how unsure of himself he'd felt that day his father had added the second Roth to the prestigious roster. He hadn't believed he was worthy of mention in the famous brokerage firm his great-grandfather had founded ninety years before.

It was strange about the accident of birth. If he had not been heir to the Roth firm, or if Jenny McCoy were not an Irish Catholic, how different their lives might have been. Seeing Jenny had threatened his resolve to carry on the traditions of his family. A small voice within him wanted to cry out: *You must forgive me, Papa. I know I disappointed you in many ways, but when it came to Jenny I did as you wished. I gave her up once but I can't do it again. Please forgive me but I feel I have a right now to reach out for the thing I need so much in my life. I don't want to hurt anybody, but something inside me can no longer be deprived.*

Abruptly shaking off the ghost of the past, Martin turned the knob on the door and walked down the hall towards his office. He was almost there when Charles Hines called to him through his open door, 'Come on in, Martin.'

Obediently he stood framed in the doorway.

'Jesus, Martin, I'm glad you got back, I need your advice

on what to do with this order of Normal Bells.' He waved a yellow memo in the air. 'It's imperative that we get into the market on Monday morning because . . . '

Martin knew he would never be able to muster a logical reply; he was too distracted. Cutting off Charles's explanation, he said, 'Okay, hand it to me and I'll take a look.'

Without glancing at the page he backed out of the office and continued on down to his own where his secretary, Nancy, was waiting. Nancy occupied a position of some importance since she had been with the firm even longer than Martin and knew his moods even better than Sylvia. The moment she saw his face she said, 'Is everything all right, Martin?'

But he just mumbled that he didn't wish to be disturbed and closed the door to his private office. He tried going over the portfolio on his desk but he could only think of Jenny. If he had been one minute earlier or later crossing Stockton Street, he would never have spotted her. It was as though fate wanted them to have a second chance.

He sat lost in the past, unaware of the passage of time. He was shocked when Nancy knocked on the door and he looked up to see that the desk clock said six.

'Is there anything I can do for you before I leave?' She stood in front of the desk and seemed reluctant to go, but it was Christmas Eve and she wanted to get home.

'Why are you still here?' he asked.

She smiled. 'Because I'm an old campaigner. And I had to finish up some loose ends. Merry Christmas.'

He got up and embraced her. 'You too, Nancy.'

After closing the door behind her Martin knew he should go, but he'd remained, sipping his drink. Now it was fully dark outside and he knew he'd be late. In a flurry of guilt, he got up, grabbed his raincoat, and walked out of the office.

It was 7.30 when he reached the apartment and walked to the bedroom, where Sylvia was applying makeup. 'For heaven's sake, Martin, you're late.'

'I know – I'm sorry.'

'Well, for heaven's sake, you could have called.'

'You're absolutely right. I'm so sorry.'

'Well, don't just stand there. You've got exactly twenty minutes to shave and dress. I've got your clothes laid out on the bed.'

Watching Martin sitting on the edge of the bed, her annoyance faded. He looked so tired. In a conciliatory voice she said, 'I'm going to fix a drink. Do you want one while you're dressing?'

'Please.' He needed a moment to pull himself together. To remind himself that this was Sylvia, whom he loved, and that Jenny was a dream he hadn't enjoyed for nearly a quarter of a century. He was finished in the bathroom and nearly dressed when Sylvia came back with his scotch. 'Here, darling,' she said, kissing him on the cheek. 'Sometimes I sound just like a nagging wife.'

'No, you don't. I was late and I'm sorry.'

'Well, now that makes two of us. I wasn't exactly charming. Okay, finish up and I'll call down for the car.'

Martin wasn't listening. He despised cocktail parties and tonight he sure as hell wasn't up to one, but he couldn't think of an excuse not to go, especially when he noticed that Sylvia was looking particularly radiant.

By the time they arrived at the penthouse atop Nob Hill, the party was in full swing. A number of guests were sitting on the stairs as Sylvia and Martin made their way to the second floor. The living room had been transformed into a winter wonderland. Trees in huge tubs from the Podesta Baldocchi florist were decorated with tiny Christmas lights. The room smelled of pine and expensive perfume. Martin found he could barely breathe. 'Darling,' said Laura, embracing Sylvia. 'I'm so glad you came! I was beginning to wonder . . . you're so late.'

Sylvia laughed. 'How could you have possibly missed us with this galaxy?'

'I'm terribly good at keeping track. And how are you, Martin?'

'Good. You look lovely,' Martin said, trying to escape

the cloud of gin and Joy.

'So nice of you to notice. Now go and have fun, both of you!'

Sylvia began to circulate, and Martin wandered about the room, idly listening to fragments of conversation. 'I think she looked perfectly *dreadful*. She has no right to wear a dress that tight . . . ' Martin moved on. 'You know they're having an affair . . . ' He plucked a scotch and soda off a waiter's tray, wandered over to a quiet corner. He was startled when Sylvia materialized at his elbow and said, 'A penny for your thoughts, Martin.'

'You'd get robbed, they weren't worth that.'

That strange feeling she'd had earlier persisted. 'Well, what are you doing here, standing by yourself?'

'Trying to avoid the stampede.'

Looking at her husband, Sylvia felt guilty. She knew that he hated big parties, but all her friends gave and went to them. She and Martin were like the couple in which the wife loved the seashore and he loved the mountains. Well, she wasn't going to think about that now. 'Maybe a little food will soothe whatever it is that ails you,' she said.

A wave of guilt washed over him, as though he'd already called Jenny. How did Sylvia know that *anything* ailed him?

Taking him by the hand, Sylvia led him to the buffet table.

It was overwhelming: a whole salmon glazed with mayonnaise and truffles; pâté in an aspic glaze; caviar and cucumber aspic; lobster cooked in brandy with toasted almonds. And at the other end of the table stood a ham en croute and a chafing dish filled with beef bourgignon.

'Isn't this the most sumptuous thing?' Sylvia said.

He looked at the enormous buffet. It was indeed incredible, but he seemed to have lost his appetite.

Sylvia handed him a plate and took one for herself. Tasting the lobster, she said, 'This is simply marvellous.' He remained silent. She watched as he stared blankly at the food.

'Aren't you going to eat, dear?'

She was suddenly afraid. Martin liked good food, and even though he was careful about his weight he never skipped a meal. Sensing her worry, Martin seemed to pull himself together. He ate a few bites and began moving through the crowd, saying hello to their friends. He even went over to Laura and Craig and smiled while Sylvia made plans for the Spring Ball.

It was after eleven when they finally got away and almost midnight before Martin turned off the bedroom light in their apartment. But even in the dark he could not escape his wife's growing concern.

Sylvia knew Martin hated being fussed over, but he had been acting oddly ever since he came home from work. Suddenly her pulse raced. Martin had been to the doctor a few days ago for his annual checkup, and maybe . . . maybe . . . God, she wasn't going to look for trouble. Yet three of their best friends had dropped dead from heart attacks in the last year or so. *That's enough, Sylvia.* The only way she'd find out would be to ask. 'Darling, are you feeling all right?'

'Yes, of course. Why do you ask?'

She shrugged. 'I don't know, Martin . . . ' She hesitated.

They lay silently for a few moments in their separate beds. Sylvia had never felt so lonely. Finally she said, 'You were so dreadfully quiet tonight, Martin. Are you worried about something?'

Martin's heart beat a little too rapidly. It was as though she were clairvoyant. He was worried, worried about hurting her.

'I wish you would talk to me, darling,' Sylvia persisted. 'I have the strangest feeling that you are facing some crisis.'

'No, of course not,' he answered quickly.

'Are you sure?'

'Yes . . . I'm sure.'

'Are you? Darling, if there is anything wrong, you know how much I care.'

'I know that, Sylvia,' he said contritely.

11

Again the thought struck her that Martin might be ill. She sighed and turned off the light. 'Well, sleep tight, Martin. I love you.'

Staring up at the ceiling with his hands behind his head, he thought, *Goddamn it – is a trick of timing, an accident, going to destroy our peace?* 'I love you too, Sylvia,' he said. And he did, but not quite in the way he would have wished.

Chapter Two

Sleep was impossible for Martin that night; he could not stop thinking about Jenny. Their affair had been doomed from the very beginning. She was a devout Roman Catholic; he was a Jew, and right after World War II that was not an easy bridge to cross. He had not been able to renounce his faith, even for her, for the bonds of family were too strong within him. And Hitler had made Judaism far more than a religion. According to the Nazis no Jew could escape his or her history.

Martin's great-grandfather had been among the multitude swept out of France in the early nineteenth century by a wave of anti-Semitism. Freed from the ghetto by Napoleon after the French Revolution, the Jews soon discovered that by the time of the Second Empire all they had won was a ghetto without walls; a Diaspora without dignity. They had hoped the Revolution had ensured their status as Frenchmen, but they were forbidden to own land, were barred from the universities, and were subjected to even more rigid regulations than before.

So the Jews of France joined that network of humanity pouring out of Russia, Poland, Germany and Hungary. And among the human tide was Ephraim Rothenberger.

America was the hope, the dream, the salvation they thirsted for. America was a word called *freedom*. But the price Ephraim paid to achieve that goal was years of pain and untold loneliness. As the oldest he was the son chosen to leave, and at twenty he said goodbye to everyone and everything that he loved and joined the legions who were making their way to the Promised Land.

The story of Ephraim's journey to America was never formally chronicled. Had he realized that his destiny would be to spawn a dynasty, he surely would have kept some form of journal. As it was, he tried to forget the terrible hardships and left much of the trip to his descendants' imaginations. But not even the most gifted imagination could evoke its real horrors.

When Ephraim left Paris, it was with the clothes on his back and a sack containing a few utensils, bread, potatoes, some cheese, and a small salami. Once outside of Paris, he took to the country roads, heading southward to Marseilles. The distance seemed so great that he refused to even contemplate it. Instead, he accepted each day as it came, trying only to survive. He rested only when he was too exhausted to go on and slept for a few hours each night in a hayloft, a meadow, in a grove of trees, wherever he happened to be. He kept alive by stealing a few eggs, which he cracked and swallowed whole. At first he almost gagged, but he forced himself to hold them down until the rumbling of his empty stomach subsided. When he came to a stream, he would bend down, cup his hand in the cold water, and drink until his stomach had the illusion of being full. Once he was lucky enough to spear a trout with his knife, though he had to eat it raw.

His source of strength was his belief that God was watching over him, for the destiny of his family had been vouchsafed into his keeping. Each day when he put on his phylacteries and chanted the ancient prayers, his faith was renewed. When he had the good fortune to ride on the back of a farmer's cart or get a lift downriver on a barge, he knew that it was because of God's blessing.

Two months later, he arrived in Marseilles. The soles of his shoes had worn out long ago, and he had wrapped his bleeding feet with pieces of thin, dirty blanket which he had torn in strips. He had earned and saved a few francs from jobs he'd done for farmers along the way, and with that he bought a pair of secondhand shoes and paid for a night's lodging. The luxury of sleeping on a straw mat, even in the company of ten others, was a joy he'd almost forgotten existed. That night he washed his clothes and laid them on the floor next to his mat to dry. Then he enjoyed his first bath in longer than he could remember.

When morning came, he went into the shipping office and waited his turn to be hired to work on one of the boats headed for the New World. His apprehensions grew when he saw the great number of men already in line. But Ephraim soon had more reason to believe he still enjoyed God's blessing: he was the last to be hired that day, and the next ship would not sail for over three weeks.

After the shoes were bought and the lodgings paid for, he had no more money, but he had a place on the ship and the opportunity to work during the crossing.

The worst was behind him, and he could almost taste the word freedom. The word seemed to trip from his tongue like honey. That afternoon, the freighter *La Liberté* lifted anchor and sailed.

Deep in the bowels of the ship, Ephraim shovelled coal into the furnace, whose appetite seemed insatiable. As soon as the monster was fed, he slammed the heavy iron door shut, but barely had time to wipe the sweat and soot from his forehead with his blackened arm before the fire again demanded his attention. Trembling with fatigue and holding on to the rail with his raw, blistered hands, he ascended the catwalk. Then, unsteadily, he inched his way along the narrow corridor until he reached his quarters. Too exhausted to wash or eat, he collapsed in his hammock and fell into a deep sleep.

For several days Ephraim did not see daylight. After passing the Straits of Gibraltar, the ship was gripped by a

14

terrible storm. Even when it lessened and Ephraim could go on deck and breathe the crisp salt air, he had little time or inclination to do so, for the old vessel still turned and twisted like a toy in the mighty Atlantic. To Ephraim, who had never been to sea, the ocean seemed angry and hostile even on fine days, when giant waves shot up like white fangs, then cascaded down in an icy torrent across the bow.

Belowdecks, hordes of immigrants were being tossed about in their cramped and fetid quarters. Some writhed in pain from hunger, holding their swollen bellies. Others, too weak even to cry out, lay oblivious to the misery around them. A few simply wished that death would overtake them, as was occasionally the case.

As happens with all things in life, there are beginnings and there are endings. Nearly six weeks after leaving Marseilles, *La Liberté* weighed anchor in New York harbour, where, as if to prolong the immigrants' misery, a torrential rain pounded against the portholes and the wind howled mournfully.

Weak and bedraggled women, men and children, families who until now had been faceless, began to emerge from belowdecks. Many wept with relief at their first sight of the New York skyline. Some, bewildered by the mere fact that they had survived, seemed unaware of the downpour. Others, too ill or weak to stand alone, clung to one another for support.

For a brief moment Ephraim looked at the crowd and was filled with compassion. Then he picked up his bag, swung it over his shoulder, and walked down the gangplank.

He went to the shipping office and waited in line for his pay, then watched grimly as a bursar counted out a dollar for each day they had been at sea. As he moved out of the line, he smiled sardonically; forty dollars for the agony he'd suffered. But then he thought to himself: *It took Moses forty years to get to the Promised Land, and I came in just forty days. Not that I'm comparing myself with Moses, God forbid.* With that happy reflection, he stuffed the money

15

into his pocket and walked out of the shipping office.

He was in New York. Even under the heavy clouds the city seemed to shimmer with promise. Ignoring the rain, he began to walk, trying to follow the directions one of the crew members had given him to the Lower East Side. An hour later he found a flophouse on the Bowery for twenty-five cents a night. Shedding his wet clothes, he collapsed onto an iron cot.

In the morning, when he opened his eyes to the bleak winter day, he felt exhausted. But at least his bed wasn't being tossed up and down by the storm. Maybe he should just rest . . . Then he looked around at the other men who filled the shabby, stifling room. For many, he suspected, that was how they spent their days. That depressing thought suddenly gave him the strength to get on with his new life. He rose, a little shakily, swung his bag over his shoulder, and looked around the dormitory. Although he had little in the way of worldly goods, Ephraim was a man who understood his own dignity – and he had not come this far to fail. Quickly he turned and ran down the steep flight of stairs to the street.

Shivering with cold, he stood huddled in the doorway, trying to get his bearings. Then, still uncertain of what direction he should take, he began to walk.

How far he had gone, he wasn't quite sure. He stopped to rest, watching his breath against the cold, sharp air. Until now he had been oblivious to his surroundings, but suddenly he saw the sign: COHEN'S KOSHER RESTAURANT.

A bell rang as he opened the door and rang again as he closed it. He stood alone among the vacant tables and chairs. There were no other customers.

Soon, a woman emerged from the back. Wiping her hands on her white apron, she told him to take any table. When their eyes met, he felt a lump in his throat; she looked like his mother.

'Nu. So what can I get you?' she asked in Yiddish.

Ephraim smiled back. 'A cup of coffee and a roll,

please,' he said, a little embarrassed by his accent.

'That's all you want?' she asked, looking at the handsome young stranger. A thousand young boys like this she had befriended throughout the years. It wasn't necessary to know from where they had come or how long they were staying. They were friendless and bewildered and Leah Cohen's heart went out to them. After all, she and Yankel knew what it was to be greenhorns.

She sighed as she went to get the order. Along with the coffee and roll, she brought him a piece of herring. 'I won't charge you,' she said quickly, forestalling his protest. 'Not this time. Eat and enjoy.'

Ephraim felt the tears sting his eyes. She did look like his mother. 'Thank you – you're very kind. But please, I want to pay.'

'Next time,' she answered as she sat down across from him at the table with a glass of tea. She placed a cube of sugar between her teeth in the Russian style and took a sip of the strong brew.

She watched him curiously. He had something that set him apart from the other immigrants she'd befriended over the years, a sense of purpose, destiny.

'Where did you come from?' she asked.

'From France. Paris.'

She shook her head in awe. Paris: the name had a magical ring here in the squalor of the Lower East Side. This young boychik was different. She and Yankel had fled the shtetl near Riga. She sighed, remembering how they had been spat upon, beaten, their synagogues and cemeteries desecrated. Even after all these years she could still hear the shouts of the drunken Cossacks. She was only thirteen when her family was annihilated. But Yankel had saved her. At sixteen he had become her protector, had rescued her from the ravaged shtetl, had buoyed her spirits through the long journey to the New World. How well she knew what this boy must be feeling; felt. 'So you're from Paris. And what is your name?'

'Ephraim Rothenberger.'

'Rothenberger?' she asked quizzically. 'You were born in France?'

'Yes – all of us. My mother and father, too.'

'But how is it you have a German name?'

'My grandfather left Bavaria and went to France, hoping that life would be better there. But he was wrong.'

'For us Jews, it's not really good anywhere.'

'You're right. But here I know we're going to survive, because America has a Constitution that says everybody is equal and has the right to life, liberty, and the pursuit of happiness.'

'Ho, ho, ho!' she said. 'We have a professor here! How do you know?'

'Because I found a book and I read about it. I love the history of this country. They had a real revolution to free the people. There are no Pales, no pogroms, nobody knocks down your door in the middle of the night. I can go anywhere I want – because I'm free.' And Ephraim truly believed that.

'Yes,' Leah said. 'This is a great country of freedom. But now you must consider the present. Where are you living?'

He told her about the Bowery: the squalor and how it had sickened him. 'Now I have to find a room and a job. Do you know of any place?'

'You came to the right person. Here, I'll write down the address of my husband's cousin. Her name is Malka Greenberg. Here, let me give you more coffee and I'll write down the street where she lives.'

After she handed him the slip of paper, he stood up and looked at her. He'd always remember today. 'Thank you, Mrs Cohen, for all your kindness. God is really so good to me.'

'What's to thank? Listen, when I came, it wouldn't have been so easy if it hadn't been for our people. The blessing is that we all stick together. Now, good luck! And you'll come back and see me, yes?'

Ephraim swallowed hard and nodded. 'Thank you,' he

said once again and heard the little bell ring twice as he opened the door, then closed it behind him.

He made his way carefully toward Canal Street with the aid of Leah's instructions.

Malka Greenberg had only one room in the attic. It was cold and rain came in between the eaves, but after the muddy roads of France and the ship, it seemed like a palace. At least he was alone.

As he stood warming his hands, he asked, 'If you have some newspaper, I can put it up to keep the wet out.'

'Of course.' Ephraim followed her down three flights of stairs and watched as she handed him copies of the Yiddish newspaper and an orange crate to stand on. That night the temperature dropped and the rain changed to snow. In the morning, Ephraim woke to find that the paper had fallen to the floor and was lying under a pile of dirty melting snow. He looked out the dormer window to the grey dawn, feeling the chill in the marrow of his bones. 'This, too, will pass,' he promised himself. He was in America now, and today would be the beginning of the rest of his life. He was going to find a job.

During the next few weeks, the verve and resoluteness that had fed him began to dissolve. He found only menial labour that paid almost nothing, and there was very little of that. How would he save sufficient money to bring his family to America?

As winter faded and spring came, the city slowly lost the glamour that had first impressed him. What he now saw was ugliness, squalor and decaying buildings. The streets were overcrowded; the people wan, harassed-looking and badly dressed.

Then, in the midst of the bleakness, an extraordinary thing happened. Above the usual tumult and shouting on Hester Street a new word rang out: *Gold! Gold! Gold!* In Yiddish newspapers, Ephraim read the accounts of the fantastic discoveries made in a distant place called California. He found himself being caught up in the fever. He had truly believed that all he had come to this new world for

19

was religious freedom and the right for his family to live in dignity. Any thought of riches had been far from his mind. Now he questioned his goals. Even in America could the poor live with dignity? Was there real freedom without wealth? Would a full stomach mean a shrivelled soul? For the first time Ephraim realized that it might be easier to achieve a great dream rather than a more modest one.

Once again he was confronted with a three-thousand-mile journey, and the fact that it was by land rather than sea made it no less dangerous. Those who returned from the West spoke about the terrible trip over the mountains, through the desert, and, worst of all, through the Indian territory. The reports came back that men, women and children had been scalped and tortured to death.

Still, Ephraim reasoned that if he had been able to reach New York alive, he could survive the journey to California. After considering the several routes to the gold fields, he chose to go by way of the Isthmus of Panama – this in spite of the warnings of those who said the heat, insects, diseases and incessant rains were beyond endurance. But he had a skill to sell – he could stoke coal – and this route seemed the fastest.

He found a job on the barque *John Benson*, headed for New Orleans, and as the weather warmed with each day's journey south, Ephraim's spirits rose.

Even though most of the crew drank, gambled and caroused as much as the passengers, and Ephraim frequently had to work double shifts, he never lost sight of his dream. The food was greasy and often included pork, which despite his hunger he would not eat. Instead, he filled up on lentils and beans and on his few hours off duty stood on deck trying to catch a glimpse of the changing shoreline.

New Orleans was colourful and exciting and Ephraim, enjoying the familiar French accents, would have liked to linger, but he was afraid to waste his carefully hoarded money, so he quickly found another steamer headed for the Isthmus.

This time the voyage was a nightmare: an endless pitching hell with giant waves crashing over the bow. One night a careless sailor was washed overboard to his death. Even if there had been palatable meals, Ephraim would have been unable to eat. As it was, he forced himself to chew just enough dry bread and heavily salted fish to keep himself alive. When he landed in the malarial Panamanian port called Chagres, he was a good fifteen pounds thinner and his clothes hung on him like a scarecrow. Yet when he stood on dry land again he thanked God with real gratitude for having let him survive and lost no time getting on with his journey to Panama City.

In Chagres, after waiting a week, he was able to hire a canoe from a local entrepreneur for $100 to take him partway up the Chagres River, where a riverboat would complete the journey to Panama City.

There was barely enough room in the canoe for Ephraim and the two native paddlers, so at his first stop he slept on shore, where mosquitoes ravished his flesh. A brief but fierce tropical rain fell during the night, soaking him through the thin blanket that covered him. The next morning he could barely stand up, and he had to force his exhausted body back to the canoe. The shallow river wound its way between muddy banks crawling with alligators. During the day, swarms of flies added to his misery, and at night he slept in the open, praying not to get sick.

When he reached the collection of huts where the river deepened and the riverboat waited, he heaved a sigh of relief. But the three-day trip, even with a hammock to sleep in, was far from pleasant. Fever swept the tiny craft, and Ephraim spent his days tending the sick and looking away when the stoker pitched the dead overboard. As they neared the Pacific the terrible heat diminished, and Ephraim, knowing he would have to work hard as soon as they landed, was able to save his strength for a short time. It had taken him a week and three times the amount of money he had anticipated spending to cover the sixty-odd miles between Chagres and Panama City.

Panama City, which pretty much resembled Chagres, was teeming with adventurers on their way to the gold fields. The overpriced food available in the marketplace was covered with flies or maggots; cholera and dysentery were rampant; and an epidemic of yellow fever had just broken out. The death wagons rattled back and forth along the garbage-strewn streets day and night.

The second night in the city Ephraim fell ill. He lay moaning and semiconscious on a sweat-soaked cot in one corner of a communal room he had rented for four dollars a night. Every breath he fought for burned his lungs. For nearly a week he was consumed with fever, deliriously imagining himself in that distant land which he once called home. At times he was certain he was back with his family, being called for by his mother and sister. Then one morning he opened his eyes and stared into the face of a total stranger.

'What place is this?' Ephraim whispered. And the man replied, 'This is Panama City, the hell of all hells, but you are alive.'

Ephraim stared at the man, finally found his voice, and asked, 'Who are you?'

'Patrick O'Shea. I'm from the old sod and probably as greedy as you.' His brogue was so thick Ephraim was barely able to understand him. But he did know Patrick was a friend.

'Why did you help me? I'm a Jew.'

'Because in Panama City there are no Jews, no Catholics – only mosquitoes who don't give a damn about faith. They would just as soon eat you as me.'

'How can I thank you for helping me?'

Patrick laughed. 'Maybe I'll convert you. Now, enough of all this nonsense.'

When Ephraim was finally able to get up, he and Patrick walked short distances each day. One of their walks took them to the far end of the burial grounds. New graves were everywhere one looked, raw mounds of earth unmarked by

22

stone or statue. Patrick was right – death was no respecter of religion.

After another week passed, Ephraim felt well enough to look for a ship to San Francisco. There were eight steamers making the trip back and forth, but the hordes of gold seekers were so plentiful it was over ten days before he could find a spot. This time, knowing he was too weak to work, Ephraim paid out almost the remainder of his money to go as a passenger. When he said goodbye to Patrick, who had found a job at one of the hotels and wanted to save more money before heading for California, Ephraim felt he was leaving the first real friend he'd made since France.

On November 26, 1849, after an uneventful passage, the brig *Golden Gate* dropped anchor in the San Francisco Bay. Standing on deck, Ephraim looked out into a dense, choking fog. After assembling his belongings, he walked gingerly down the rickety gangplank and stepped onto the shore of the promised Eldorado, only to sink to his knees in the icy mud. It had been raining for three weeks; today was the first day it had stopped. *That's a good omen*, he thought as he ploughed through the mire. He finally reached the top of a sand dune, from which he could see part of the city, though much of it was covered with mist. The docks that stretched from 'Montgomery Street' (a cow path) to the Bay were swarming with sailors and every sort of riffraff. Tents, shanties and corrugated-iron shacks were crowded together just beyond the wharfs. The beach was strewn with boxes, bales of cotton, barrels of sugar, and sacks of flour and cornmeal. When Ephraim tried to make his way to Stockton Street to find a place to sleep, he had to remove his shoes more than once in order to pour out the sand.

The energy of the city amazed him. Thousands of newcomers had arrived in recent months to seek their fortunes. San Francisco was a melting pot where the hardworking and the pious rubbed shoulders with prostitutes, cheap adventurers and criminals. Wherever he looked he saw hastily flung-up saloons, warehouses, hotels and stores.

The brothels and gambling dens seemed to be the most flourishing businesses. For a moment he stood listening to the ringing of carpenters' hammers to which the sound of tinny bar-room pianos seemed to provide an accompaniment. San Francisco was a city obsessed with quick wealth, with a morality that placed gold before God. But for Ephraim America's promise of freedom and opportunity had been kept.

The first thing he did was find a room, not much better than the garret he had left in New York. But here he could briefly savour the promise of the future. It was just a stopping-off place. He had barely enough money left to buy a grubstake, but he was willing to starve if it meant a chance to bring his family to the New World.

Three days later he joined the ragged, hopeful army of miners that left San Francisco and made its way to the rivers and fields where the first discovery of the golden metal had been made.

It was a time of frenzy, passion and intrigue. By day the miners panned for gold in the riverbeds and hacked away at the reluctant earth. At night they gambled, fought, and tried to cheat one another. It was a strange environment for a Jew from a shtetl. No one saw as he faithfully bound on his phylacteries each morning and each night. No one cared that he kept so much to himself. And then, one day, amidst shouts and jubilation, he struck gold.

He rushed back to San Francisco, registered the claim before it could be stolen from him, then stood in the assayer's office and watched as the precious metal was weighed. When the scales tipped, Ephraim was the possessor of one thousand dollars.

Sitting on the edge of his cot that night, Ephraim narrowed his eyes as he contemplated the coins in the palms of his calloused hands. There was money in gold, but the big claims had already been staked out. He had reached California late in the gold rush and he knew the earth would yield just so much. But perhaps the timing could be made to work to his advantage. Maybe success lay not in digging,

24

but in lending. After all, many of the great French–Jewish fortunes had been made in banking. Setting aside a small amount for himself, Ephraim financed two miners to a grubstake. He also had a document prepared which stipulated that, if there were any profits, he would receive half.

Ephraim's belief in himself was finally rewarded. The miners struck it rich and Ephraim doubled his money. The next time he financed four miners instead of two, and, within a year, Ephraim was an established banker. Small to be sure, but he had no doubts about the eventual growth of his establishment. After all, he was one of God's blessed.

Sitting behind his desk, dressed in a high, white, starched collar, a frock coat and fashionable curls, he looked every inch a Rothschild. Incongruous though he may have seemed in that primitive city of miners and pioneers, it was no less incongruous than the way he viewed himself. He enjoyed remembering the penniless boy who stood shivering on the Marseilles docks, his feet wrapped in rags. He could almost feel the wind pressing against his clothes, which were still damp from his attempts to wash them the previous night.

Now he had several suits and a woman to wash and iron them. But he never forgot who he was. Every morning and every night he went through the ritual of putting on his skullcap, tallis and phylacteries. As a mark of reverence, he placed one diminutive black box on the inner side of his left arm, just about the elbow, then coiled the thin leather strap around his forearm exactly seven times. It had been written that God made the world in seven days. Another black box was placed high up in the middle of his forehead, then he looped the thin strap around his head and knotted it. The two ends of the strap were joined over his shoulder and brought forward. Then he wound the strap from the armband three times around his little finger, which signified the Hebrew letter of *shin*. When all of this was done, Ephraim intoned the passages which were written on tiny parchments and placed inside the small boxes: *And thou shalt bind them for a sign upon thine hand, and they shall be for frontlets between thine eyes. And thou shalt write them upon the door posts of thy house and upon thy gates.* He swayed back and forth, chanting the singsong phrases as had his father before him. When he finished he was overcome with a feeling of peace and purpose. He had held fast to the beliefs to which he had been born. They were sustained all these years.

In that extraordinary moment of communion he found an added solace which nourished his soul. Soon he would be reunited with his family. His arms ached to embrace them and his heart overflowed with love. Nothing he had acquired would be meaningful until he was with them again.

But Ephraim's dreams were not to be fulfilled.

After almost one year of waiting, Ephraim received a letter from his oldest sister, Hannah. Tears rolled down his cheeks as he read . . .

My dearest brother Ephraim,

Knowing the great hardships you have had to endure makes this letter so very difficult for me to write. I wish I could have spared you this pain, but Momma and Poppa died this winter, less than one month apart. It was as if once she died he had no will to go on. Now they lie side by side buried in the French dirt. I weep because of that. Momma and Papa wanted to be buried in Palestine, high on the hills of Mount Olive, but God must have decided otherwise.

Now, dearest Ephraim, I beg you to try to understand and forgive us. The family that is left has no wish to go to America. Instead, it has been decided that we want to live out our lives in Jerusalem. In their last days on earth, this, not America, was your parents' dream.

Please, dearest Ephraim, know how much we love and miss you, but this is the way our lives were fated. Remember the love we share with you even at opposite ends of the world.

Take care, dear brother . . .

Ephraim could read no more.

He wailed as he tore the lapel of his jacket, rending it in

the traditional gesture of mourning. He then sat *shiva* for seven days, ignoring all his friends' and acquaintances' attempts to cheer him. In his bereavement, he was concerned that without his family, his accomplishments were meaningless. He had not left home and come to this alien place to become rich for his own sake. He had sustained the loneliness for only one reason: that one day he would be able to support his family in comfort and freedom. Well, now they had found their own freedom in the Holy Land and all his worldly success seemed futile.

With little but his business to occupy him, he worked tirelessly and his bank grew to be a serious force in the California financial world. But despite his increased success, Ephraim's spirits remained low until one summer day fate intervened in the person of Sarah Baum.

Sarah had journeyed West with her mother and father, three sisters and two brothers. Hearing that one of the San Francisco banks was run by a Jew, her father came in to apply for a loan. As soon as this transaction was concluded, Samuel Baum urged the young financier to visit their home for dinner. Ephraim, happy for some Jewish company in a city which contained few of his faith, accepted for the next day. And the minute he walked into their small boarding-house, his life changed forever. Sarah was a beautiful, blue-eyed blonde of sixteen, and as soon as Ephraim saw her he knew he had to have her for his wife. The years of loneliness seemed to disappear, and for the next few months he haunted the Baums' house until she said yes.

Their wedding day was an especially auspicious one. Ephraim had helped found the synagogue, and his was to be the first wedding since the modest building on Stockton Street had opened for services. The entire Jewish population of San Francisco seemed to have turned out for the ceremony.

As Ephraim waited under the *chuppa* for his bride, whatever loneliness he had endured was now forgotten as he saw Sarah walk slowly down the aisle with her parents on either side. When the tapered candles were lit, the Rabbi began the sacred ritual in Hebrew. Standing under the blue velvet canopy, they pledged their troth for everlasting devotion. The goblet was handed to the bride as she lifted her veil for the first time and drank from the cup offered by her husband-to-be. The goblet was handed back to Ephraim, whose hand shook as he too drank. The Rabbi pronounced them man and wife amidst happy shouts of *mazel tov*. After Ephraim had stomped on the wine goblet, he picked up Sarah's veil again. As tears gathered in the corners of his eyes, he kissed her with all the love he had stored up since his arrival in America. That was the beginning of their life together.

The years passed in peace and contentment. The Jewish community was a tightly knit one and marriage among these pioneers produced a staggering network of family connections. Although not restricted by the European boundaries of ghetto, they felt no need to go beyond the large family circle. They fraternized within the other communities by day, but their home lives remained aloof. At long last Jews had come into their own. In fact, they were usually welcomed by the rather snobbish pioneers of California society as highly valued citizens, and except for a few isolated cases, anti-Semitism was non-existent. The Jews were respected as a religious group who maintained their separate traditions.

As the gold rush died down in the 1850s, the European-bred Jews of San Francisco were particularly adept at making the transition from boomtown to sophisticated metropolis. In the years that followed, they elevated themselves from petty shopkeepers to department store magnates, from smalltime lenders to international bankers, from tentmakers to real estate developers and shipping tycoons.

The second generation moved into mansions on Pacific Heights and Nob Hill, and built summer estates in San Rafael, Woodside and Atherton. Wives and daughters were transformed into elegant ladies. Society gathered in their magnificent salons. Their generation established itself as standard-bearers for the city's cultural growth. The contributions they made to the arts were so enormous that San Francisco came to be considered a cultural rival of the great European capitals.

Chapter Three

Now the tyranny and injustices of Europe seemed very far away. Ephraim had become a part of the privileged upper class. His bank had expanded to such proportions that he controlled great parcels of land and underwrote much of the West Coast shipping industry. But the greatest reward of all had been watching his four sons and two daughters grow into fine adults.

He indulged his daughters shamefully. When they married, each was given a large house as a wedding gift. He endowed his younger sons with companies of their own and eventually gave control of his banking empire to his oldest, Simon. But though he counted his blessings, Ephraim knew that nothing in life was perfect. Somehow, with the ebb and flow of time, the family's structure seemed to have changed.

There was a watering-down of religious attitudes in the third generation and this pained Ephraim. Although they remained fervently Jewish, they tended to ignore the Sabbath and skip schul. Although they were among Temple Emanu-El's founding fathers, some families never went, even on the high holy days. And this pained Ephraim. Yet they supported the Temple and paid their dues. Birth, marriage and death required a rabbi.

In the twilight of his life, Ephraim thought about all he had gained and what he had really been able to give his children. He was a man of great self-introspection who tried never to hide from the truth, even when it was painful. How honest had he been when he questioned himself that day so long ago? He had been sure that it was possible to be both spiritual and rich. For him, that had been true. But he had been motivated by different dreams from his grandchildren. He had burned with a desire to provide for his mother and father, to free his sisters and brothers. And even though he had failed in that he rejoiced in the fact that he had been able to give his children an easier life. Yet now he wondered if its very ease had not diluted the religious tradition. It seemed that Jews clung tenaciously to their faith only when they were confined to the ghetto. It was there that they reached the zenith of learning, but once the yoke was broken, and Jews were permitted to live in peace and freedom, they soon became spiritually careless. Sometimes when he watched Simon's two children, a girl and a boy Simon had insisted on naming Ephraim despite the Jewish tradition against naming after the living, the old man wondered: would the new century mean an end to all the old values?

Then a miracle occurred. Simon's wife, already in her late thirties, unexpectedly became pregnant. Just before the turn of the century she had a little boy she insisted on naming Julian, after a hero she admired in a novel. The old Ephraim, now in his seventies, was fascinated with this child and Julian displayed an affection for Ephraim the other grandchildren had not. As the toddler grew into a solemn-eyed little boy, he would sit for hours listening to tales not just of the old man's adventures coming to San Francisco, but to the stories of the Old Testament as well. Sitting in the sun, on the porch of the grand estate, Ephraim would close his eyes and pray that Julian would remember these times and that unlike his older brother and sister would not forget the old ways. It was late on a long summer evening that he had a thought which comforted him during his final years.

Why did the Bible read, 'The God of Abraham, Isaac

and Jacob'? Why did it not simply say, 'the God of Abraham'? The more he reflected upon it, the more he felt it was so stated because God must have meant something different to each one of those generations. Abraham's struggle was not quite the same as his son Isaac's, nor was Jacob's quite the same as his father's. One's spiritual needs depended, it seemed, upon circumstances. And there was something else in which Ephraim could take great pride. He was giving his descendants more than riches. He was leaving them a legacy of freedom: freedom from fear, freedom from discrimination, freedom from tyranny. They could stand with their heads held high, and he thanked God for the great gift that was America.

Chapter Four

It was a time to remember: the year 1936, when three hundred guests had gathered to attend a yearly picnic at the Hillsborough estate of Ephraim's grandson, another Ephraim. The opulent surroundings were a far cry from the tent city where it had all begun. It was a day to rekindle old memories. Three generations were present, and the guests numbered the oldest and most distinguished of California's Jewish pioneers. Although the party was limited to direct descendants, and was an annual event, some were meeting for the first time.

The older guests spoke of the dreams that had motivated men like Ephraim; of the cherished legacies that had been handed down to them. They showed their children the daguerrotypes which were on display in the pavilion at the far end of the garden: dark, grainy images of unsmiling men and women in formal poses.

Among that assembly were Martin's mother and father. Julian Roth (the -enberger having been dropped by Julian's parents) had married Bess Unger, a cousin three times removed. They stood facing the image of Ephraim with a heavy heart. What would he have thought today had he known that his great-grandson, Martin, had been rejected by Yale? It was painful to contemplate in view of the fact that Ephraim thought that he had left discrimination behind in the old World. He had forgotten that much of the East struggled to duplicate European society right down to its faults. It was quite clear to Julian that Martin had been turned away only because Yale's 10 per cent Jewish quota had been filled.

For the first time the Roths realized that San Francisco was freer of prejudice than the rest of the country. Like many Western Jews, they had a very secular outlook. They gave large sums of money to non-Jewish causes, not because they felt Jewish ones were less worthy than others, but because they considered themselves part of a larger world where the needs of the underprivileged should not be categorized according to religion. For this very reason they were particularly shocked that Martin, a straight-A student, should be rejected. Martin had been in a state of shock when he handed the letter to his father.

' . . . It is with regret that, by the time your application was processed, our Freshman class had been filled.'

The next morning Julian was on the telephone with his attorney. 'Martin's going to Yale. Do you hear what I say?'

'You do remember, Julian? I told you about the quota.'

'I would have certainly not believed that it would apply to Martin. Not with his grades.'

'I don't want you to think that I'm underestimating Martin's abilities or his qualifications, but all students, Jew or gentile, have got to be damn good.'

'Well, I don't give a damn about that. Martin's going to Yale.'

Later, in their bedroom, Bess said to Julian, 'I still don't understand any of this, Julian. I find it impossible to believe that Yale could be anti-Semitic.'

'Not overtly. But they are all the same.'

'I had no idea that anything like this went on.'

'Oh, my dear – there is much worse than this happening. There are hotels in America with signs that say: NO JEWS, NO DOGS. There are business concerns that make no apologies for not hiring Jews.'

Bess shook her head. 'I just can't believe this. My God – where have we been?'

'Cloistered and insulated. Now, however, we have a choice. We can either fight or turn aside and have Martin apply to a school with lower standards or fewer Jewish applicants. I say we have to fight it.'

'I don't like the sound of that.' Bess had tears in her eyes. 'Maybe he'd be happier with his own kind. Maybe pushing in where we're not wanted is dangerous. Maybe it's even more dangerous if he *is* eventually accepted. I mean, we wouldn't want him to give up his Judaism.' She felt a cold premonition of disaster.

'You may be right,' Julian said. 'But with the slogans currently being shouted by the Nazis maybe we have to fight. We haven't seen that kind of anti-Semitism since the dark ages. Now if you'll excuse me, I'm going to speak to Martin.'

Julian found his son in his room, lying on the bed and staring up at the ceiling. 'I think we should talk.'

'There really isn't anything to talk about, Dad. They've turned me down.'

'We'll fight their decision!' Julian answered, smashing his fist into his palm. 'We have to stand up to tyranny no matter how subtle. If the world had done that when Hitler marched into the Rhineland, the Jews might be free in Germany today.'

But Martin was besieged with conflicting emotions. He'd never thought much about being a Jew; yet he'd never considered hiding his Jewishness either. But suddenly, for the first time, he was overcome with guilt. He really didn't want to spend four years in a place where he would at best

33

be tolerated. He saw no reason to apologize for being Jewish; if anything, he'd grown up proud of the fact. But he'd also grown up with a strong sense of justice. He believed in fighting for the underdog. It was just that he'd never seen himself in that role.

With a stiffening of resolve, he swung his legs off the bed and stood up to face his father.

'Okay, we'll fight,' he said. 'But it's a little like shadow-boxing. It's hard to know who's the enemy.'

'I'm sure he'll come forward,' said Julian with a dour smile. 'In any case we have until September – several months in our favour.'

But it didn't take that long. As in the great European universities that Yale emulated, money, big money, spoke in a loud, clear voice. Soon after Julian arranged to donate, anonymously, a new reading room in Sterling Memorial Library, Martin received a letter informing him of an unexpected vacancy and congratulating him on his acceptance.

As Julian swallowed the somewhat hollow victory, he tried to reassure himself that Ephraim would have been pleased. Yale was, after all, a long way from the Paris ghetto.

The first of August found Bess in a frenzy of excitement trying to get Martin ready for school. She sewed name tags just as she had when he had gone to summer camp. There was mending and sorting, and of course, shopping for a proper Yale wardrobe. She decided that they could buy raingear and a heavy wool overcoat when they got to New Haven. In addition, there was the purchase of Martin's car. He absolutely refused to take his yellow Buick convertible. He said he didn't think he'd need a car anyway, but if he was going to take one he insisted on trading in the Buick for a Ford. Bess was not entirely pleased with his demand, but still . . .

The day after Labour Day the three of them took the train to New York, where Julian picked out Martin's Ford. They spent a few days in the city shopping and seeing shows, then they drove up to New Haven to get Martin settled. It was the first time Bess had visited an Ivy League school and she was suitably impressed. With its Gothic buildings and landscaping, it seemed more like Oxford than an American college.

Martin went to the Bursar and was quickly assigned to a room on Old Campus, the freshman quad at the heart of Yale's campus. Bess was happy he was the first to arrive in his suite, which consisted of three bedrooms, one of which was a single, a bathroom, and a cosy living or study area. Bess insisted Martin take the single.

'You'll have lots of work. It will be quieter,' she insisted. 'You don't know the other boys. They may not be so interested in studying.'

Martin, who by now had done a little investigating of his own into Ivy League anti-Semitism, didn't argue. He might have suitemates who would not care to room with a Jew. But suspecting this and experiencing it were very different, Martin was to discover.

He helped his mother unpack and tried to reassure her he'd be fine. 'After all,' he said, 'I've been away to school. You'll see. This won't be very different. I'll bet you won't even miss me. You and Dad can plan a second honeymoon.'

Bess smiled, but once settled on the train back West she allowed herself to cry a little. She knew Yale would not be the same as high school. Menlo School for Boys had hardly required cutting the umbilical cord. It was thirty minutes away from Hillsborough, and Martin was home almost every weekend. But Yale was what Martin and Julian wanted, so she resolved to make the best of it. If she had had any idea of what Martin's first few days in that respected situation were to be, she might have jumped right out of the train and gone back to New Haven to protect him.

Martin's first suitemate, a tall, myopic blond, dressed in tweeds, whose bags contained enough booze for the whole dorm, glanced briefly at Martin's wavy black hair and olive skin and merely asked him if he'd like a drink.

'Not just yet,' Martin said. Although his parents served hard liquor at their parties, his family rarely drank more than a little wine.

'Right,' drawled the blond, who finally introduced himself as Lawrence Perry. 'Your kind frowns on the indulgence. Well, Yale should loosen you up,' he added tolerantly.

Martin retreated to his room. Lawrence was unlikely to become a friend, but he seemed harmless. His other suitemates were less innocuous. They arrived together with a welter of athletic equipment which amazed Martin, used though he was to team sports. Two were twins, Tim and Chris Sanders. The third, Mike, had roomed with them at Groton. The twins were from Newton, Massachusetts; Mike from Philadelphia's Main Line. They accepted Lawrence's offer of vodka and orange juice with alacrity, and once they saw Martin's awkward withdrawal, paid little attention. Only Chris asked as he mixed the drinks, 'Roth . . . Roth. That name German? We wouldn't want to room with a Nazi.'

'Hardly,' said Martin. Then, turning to face them all, he said bluntly, 'I'm Jewish.' No one answered and for a while Martin thought things must be okay. It was only when it was time for dinner that he knew that the Yale he had imagined existed only in his dreams. Lawrence pointed out that since classes hadn't begun, they didn't have to appear in the dining hall.

'Let's hit the Taft for steak and a beer.'

Martin started up to go with them when Tim said sharply, 'I doubt their beef's kosher. Isn't that the word? Anyway, I can't stop Yale from letting down their standards, but I can keep up my own.'

Lawrence started to protest, but three strong drinks did little to stiffen his backbone and he finally followed the three of them out of the room with an apologetic wave.

Martin sat stunned. He had always considered himself one of the privileged – and not just because his family had money. The Roths could hardly be called nouveau riche – Martin's roots went back three generations. They were as much a part of San Francisco society as the Cabots were of Boston. This was his first encounter with outright anti-Semitism.

He made his way uneasily down to the dining hall, deciding he just must have been exceedingly unlucky in his suitemates. But even though over the next week he ran into no other incidents outside his own rooms, he found he wasn't making friends. He wondered if he could be at fault. Perhaps his first experience in the dorm had made him too wary. But Martin had always been surrounded by friends – Jewish and gentile. He'd never thought about religion before. His father had told him he had to stand up for the Jews who were being persecuted in Germany, but Martin wasn't so happy to be fighting his own war during what should have been the happiest days of his life.

It didn't take long for him to realize that his suitemates were not so different from the rest of the men in his class. Over those first weeks, going to classes, the library, meals, he learned how small a 10 per cent quota really was. He noticed that many of the Jews hung out together – they were twice as smart as most of their classmates, but singularly aloof and hardworking.

It wasn't easy for Martin to find out who he was, not after believing for so long that he knew. But what hurt the most was the enormous endowment that his father had given to the university in order for him to be accepted.

Now that Martin had been made more aware of his Jewishness, he developed a devotion which drew him towards it. In the face of his roommates' rejection he felt a compulsion to proclaim his identity.

He began to understand the studious habits of his fellow Jews, and found himself spending longer and longer hours in the library. He tried to keep his parents from knowing he was unhappy, but from the noncommittal tone of his letters to Julian and his reluctance to discuss his life at Yale over the phone with Bess, he suspected they guessed.

The first break in his loneliness was none of his own doing. Suffering through a calculus class taught by a crusty old professor who seemed to delight in his students' misery, Martin caught sight of an animated young man two seats away who actually seemed to be enjoying the course. This bright-eyed enthusiast filed out of class with Martin. At the doorway the student turned to him, stuck out his hand, and said, 'Hi. I'm Dominic Gatti.'

After weeks of unabated solitude, this introduction seemed like a real gesture of friendship. Dominic was a far cry from the snobbish Mikes, Tims and Chrises who cold-shouldered him at every opportunity.

'I'm Martin Roth,' he replied eagerly, accepting Dominic's hand. 'So what do you think about this Professor Wheeler? Is he always that sarcastic? I live in fear and trembling he'll call on me.'

'Save fear and trembling for Lyons' Intro Philosophy,' Dominic said with a sly smile. 'But Wheeler is tough. He's a piranha. He'll gobble you up in one semester. If you don't make it, he doesn't fool around, I understand.'

'What do you mean, you understand?'

'Because Wheeler is notorious for extracting his pound of flesh.'

Never had a more astute statement been made, Martin found out in the weeks to come. For some reason, Professor Wheeler had singled him out among that vast ocean of faces, just why, Martin didn't know. Each time Martin raised his hand to a question he was sure he knew, the answer was barely out of his mouth before Wheeler had poked holes through every one of his arguments. Martin couldn't dismiss the thought that Wheeler's badgering was more personal than academic. *Goddamn*, he thought. *Am I becoming paranoid about my Jewishness*? As he and Dominic walked across campus, he tried to figure out a way to ask his friend what he thought without appearing ridiculous. It took him a week, but when he finally mentioned to Dominic that Wheeler might be anti-Semitic, the Italian just laughed and said, 'Don't take it personally. Wheeler's anti-everything. But especially anti-freshmen.'

As the days passed, Martin had to admit that Wheeler wasn't happy unless he flunked over half his class. Martin spent his nights cramming his head full of calculus, but the harder he tried the less he found he could concentrate. As midterms drew close, he became certain he was going to fail. He could barely listen to Wheeler's lecture.

'Now there are two fundamentals with which we must concern ourselves . . .'

That was the last of the lecture Martin heard. His mind drifted off. He was wondering why the hell he had wanted to come to Yale in the first place. He daydreamed about transferring to Stanford. He was happily imagining long, lazy days at the beach at Carmel when Dominic tapped him on the shoulder.

'Wrong class to sleep through,' he said. 'And anyway, it's over.'

Martin struggled to his feet.

'You may be right about his hating all freshmen, but I still feel as if there is a personal vendetta between the two of us, as if he's taking his own frustrations out on me.'

'I know what you mean,' Dominic said. 'He really does come down hard on you. But you have to understand that professors are not gods. Some are carried away with their own importance. Some bring their own paranoia to class. And some feed off the fears of their students. I don't know which category Wheeler falls into, but if you survive his class you'll have a great grounding in calculus because he really is a great teacher.'

Martin thought for a long moment. 'Maybe you're right, though I still get the feeling that Wheeler doesn't like me. Maybe if I could lick these damn differentials I wouldn't have to worry. But I just know I'm going to fail.'

Dominic saw the fear in Martin's eyes. 'You know what's happening to you, Martin? You have a malady common to almost all freshmen. It's the first time you've been pushed into a cold, hard world, where you don't get everything you want just by asking. You've allowed Wheeler to intimidate you so that you can't even think.'

'You're absolutely right,' Martin said. 'I'm trying so hard to prove that I can make it that I can't concentrate. Math was always my easiest subject, but this damn thing has got me licked.'

'It's rough. But look, let's take this page. There's a formula to it. Here, let me show you.' Dominic proceeded to show Martin how to work out the equations. It was all so basic that Martin almost laughed.

'Boy, it's so simple when you do it.'

'That's just my point,' Dominic said. 'Get Wheeler out of your head and you'll sail right through. Now let me show you again.' Dominic began with another problem.

It was beginning to sink in. 'You know, I think I'm beginning to get it,' Martin said.

'Great. Look, if you get into any trouble I'll be glad to help.'

'Gee, thanks a lot. I just might take you up on that offer. Can I have your phone number?'

Dominic was a local scholarship boy who lived off campus with his parents. He'd invited Martin over several times, but to date Martin hadn't come. Now he wrote Dominic's number carefully in his notebook.

'I'll try working some problems on my own, but if I get stuck I really will give you a call.'

Martin went back to his room. The suite was empty. He wondered if his roommates ever studied. He opened the math book and tried again. For a while he was able to answer some problems, but then he got stuck and his fear returned. It was relieved a little by a call from his parents, who were looking forward to the holidays and his visit home. They would never believe their brilliant son was in danger of failing.

Skipping dinner, he worked until seven-thirty, at which time he wanted to tear the book to pieces. Finally he picked it up and threw it against the wall. There was no doubt about it – he was going to flunk. He flung himself on the bed for a while and stared disconsolately at the ceiling. Then he remembered he had Dominic's number and decided to call.

'Hello?' the voice at the other end said.

'Is this the Gatti residence?'

'Yes.'

'I wonder if I could speak to Dominic, please.'

'I'll call him to the phone.'

Martin waited.

'Hello?'

For a moment Martin felt embarrassed. He wasn't used to asking for help.

'This is Martin Roth,' he said awkwardly.

'Yeah? What can I do for you?'

'Listen – you could do me a big favour. Could you explain once more how to do these equations? Wait a minute, I have the book right here.' Before Martin turned the page, Dominic said, 'Look, why don't you come over?'

'You mean it?'

'Sure. If you feel like it. It's a lot easier if we can sit down together.'

'I wouldn't be interrupting, would I?'

'No, not at all. Besides, it won't take more than half an hour. It's pretty simple when you catch on.'

Again, Martin had the feeling that he was imposing, but he was desperate. 'When can I come?'

'If you leave now you'll get here by eight-thirty.'

'You bet . . . and, Dominic, thanks a lot.'

'Nothing to it, friend.' Dominic gave him the address.

The Gattis lived in nearby Hamden in a two-storey brick house, one of many such dwellings along a narrow street. At one time the neighbourhood had been upper-middle class, but the population had shifted and Martin guessed that it was undoubtedly lower-middle income. It occurred to him that he'd never been in such a neighbourhood and he realized that in many ways he was as narrow and provincial as his roommates.

Finally he got out of the car, walked up the short flight of stairs, rang the bell and waited.

'Hi,' Dominic said as he stood framed in the doorway.

'Did you have a rough time finding the place?'

'No, it was much nearer than I realized.'

Dominic held open the door a little wider. 'Come on in.'

Standing in the dark hall, Martin observed the small living room with the overstuffed couch and two matching chairs. The rug was faded and worn. A grand piano took up most of one corner.

'My folks are in the sun room,' Dominic said, drawing Martin inside. 'Come on, I want you to meet them.'

Mr Gatti was stocky, of medium height, with a shock of white hair. He wore very thick lenses which somehow did not detract from his appearance. Mrs Gatti was a woman of almost her husband's size. Nonetheless, she appeared almost delicate. Her hands and feet were small and her fingers were elegantly tapered. Her violet-blue eyes seemed to look beyond Martin, giving the impression of studied aloofness.

'This is my mother,' Dominic said, interrupting Martin's thoughts. 'And this is Martin Roth, Mother.'

'It's a pleasure, Mrs Gatti,' Martin answered.

She merely nodded.

'And my father.'

Mr Gatti extended his hand. 'I'm glad to meet you,' he said and went back to reading his paper.

With those casual amenities out of the way, Dominic said, 'I think we ought to get cracking on the books.'

Martin followed Dominic up the dimly lit stairs to his room. It was sparsely furnished with a bed, dresser, and a long folding table which Dominic used as a desk. There was a wooden chair near the door, another by Dominic's bed, and a faded green mohair upholstered chair with a matching ottoman. On the wall was a picture of Jesus. The table was strewn with an assortment of books – economics, engineering, literature, and an assortment of other subjects.

'All right, let's get down to cases. Pull up a chair.'

After two hours, Martin began to see the clearing in the wilderness. He laughed. 'You thought it was going to take a half hour . . . I never thought I'd get it through my skull.

42

My God, Dominic, I don't know how I'm going to thank you.'

'Forget the thanks. Let me know if you have any more trouble.'

That night, for the first time in weeks, Martin's sleep was uninterrupted by nightmares of flunking. He was always going to hate calculus, but at least he understood enough now to feel that he had a reasonable chance of getting through. And Dominic's companionship made the prospect of four long years at Yale more endurable.

In the next weeks, Martin and Dominic saw each other in and out of class. Martin was developing an enormous affection for his newfound friend. His fascination with Dominic lay in the fact that their personalities were as different as their backgrounds.

Dominic was tough, proud, tenaciously independent, with a kind of street smartness that he had needed to survive. Under the façade of his wit was a cynicism born of the Depression.

He was nine the year his father lost his job. Dominic never forgot coming home from school and finding his father seated at the kitchen table, crying like a baby. It would have been better if he had screamed, or gotten drunk; but he was too broken. Later, Mr Gatti cursed the fates that had denied him an education.

Dominic never viewed his father as being uneducated. Quite the opposite. Antonio Gatti was a natural intellectual. Yet all his self-acquired knowledge was not enough to get him beyond being a shipping clerk. If life had been more equitable, there was no telling what Antonio Gatti might have achieved, but though in the years to come he was able to get jobs here and there, they never amounted to much.

Maria Gatti slowly sold her jewellery and the few other possessions she had brought to her marriage. As the Depression worsened and her husband remained unemployed, the tension in the house increased until she wished she could get a divorce. But that was impossible, since she

43

was a devout Catholic. Working ten hours a day in a factory making shoes for other women, she had plenty of time to think back over the past.

She'd married outside of her class. Because of that, she'd been ostracized by her family. Her mother had said that she would live to regret it, and she had. Now, looking back over the years, she wondered what the attraction had been. She had sacrificed herself, and in doing so, she destroyed her dreams of becoming a concert pianist. There was a strange irony to their lives. They were two very extraordinarily gifted people who were unable to exercise their talents.

It was Maria who had made Dominic realize that, without a college degree, he could never amount to anything. If his father had had that parchment, she said, he would never have been fired. If her bitterness blinded her to the fact that there were college professors standing in the breadlines, she had nonetheless imbued Dominic with an indomitable need to succeed. He vowed that what had happened to his father would never happen to him.

He was going to go to college and get a degree no matter what it took. When he was eleven, he worked for a bookie, mowed lawns, and delivered bootleg liquor to a whore-house. Later, he drove a truck and worked on the docks. He had hoarded everything he made. When he'd won a partial scholarship to Yale, he knew he had the world by a string. He tried to explain his confidence to Martin.

'I didn't have a doubt in the world that I was going to be able to compete . . . Don't look at me like that, Martin.' Dominic smiled and lit up a cigarette.

'Look like what?'

'Like you think I'm a cocky bastard.'

'If I gave you that impression, it was wrong. I think the look was one of admiration. You're just so sure of yourself. I wish that I were.'

'That's really funny, Martin. We always wish that we were someone else or somewhere else. Okay, Martin, you ready for this? The first day we really talked I was green with envy. You'd been to private school. You could afford to live in the dorms. Your parents were obviously well off. Well, now that we're friends I'm not so envious. I guess we all have our problems.'

'I guess that's right,' Martin said, thinking that one confidence inspired another. Hesitating a little, Martin described how he'd been affected by the 10 per cent quota.

Dominic laughed. 'Well, old buddy, you grew up believing that the world was round and then suddenly you discovered it was crooked. I don't know who's more privileged, you or me. At least I grew up knowing what it was all about; there were no surprises.'

Martin started to answer, then thought better of it.

As if reading his thoughts, Dominic asked, 'Do you think that sounds bitter?'

Martin shrugged.

'Well, maybe. But on the other hand, it's that bitterness that goads me on. Now to more frivolous things. I'd like to go to New York this weekend. Rubinstein's at Carnegie Hall Saturday. I've got a little dough stashed away – do you feel like going?'

Martin agreed. It would be good to get away from the pressures of school for a couple of days, and he knew his parents would be pleased if he heard the famous pianist. It was odd, Martin thought. He had always had every opportunity to attend concerts, opera and the theatre in California, but he and his friends had preferred just riding around, dancing, or simply hanging out with the gang. For Dominic, who had to scrimp to buy his tickets, a piano concert was a prize event.

On Saturday morning the boys got up at six and drove to New York in Martin's Ford coupé.

No sooner had they checked in to the YMCA than Dominic was ready for action. It was as though he were determined to conquer the city in twenty-four hours.

Martin found himself caught up in the excitement. They bought hot dogs from a street vendor on 49th and Madison, then hopped on a bus that dropped them near the Metropolitan Museum.

Martin followed Dominic up the wide staircase to the first landing. He'd visited the museum when he was thirteen, and his parents had taken him to New York for his bar mitzvah, but today with Dominic it was as though he were seeing everything for the first time. Until now he considered most art an excuse for his parents and their friends to get together and give parties. Now he saw that paintings themselves could inspire a real joy.

Later, as they walked downtown to the Automat, Martin was silent. Landscapes and portraits were unrolling again before his mind's eye. It was only when Dominic began showing him how to feed in nickels for their supper that he shook off his reverie and began laughing and joking again.

But if Rembrandt and Rubens had stimulated his senses, Rubinstein took away his breath. As they walked back to the Y, Martin said, 'Did you ever hear anything so great? Imagine Rubinstein being able to evoke all those feelings. Isn't it incredible what those ten fingers can do?'

Dominic thought of the piano in their dingy living room. He'd cut his eye teeth on Chopin. Dammit, his mother really could have become a concert pianist if life had been a little more charitable. He shoved the painful thought aside. 'I'm really glad you enjoyed it. Now I've got to get to bed if I want to make six o'clock mass.'

The next morning Dominic's alarm clock went off at 5.30. Watching him dress, Martin asked, 'How long does mass take?'

'An hour,' Dominic said, tying his shoes.

'Oh, then should I meet you here?'

'Anything you like. But it's a heck of a morning for walking. In fact, if you want, you can walk to St Patrick's Cathedral with me. But move it, move it!'

By the time they reached the magnificent church, they were winded. 'Okay,' Dominic said. 'How about meeting me here at seven-thirty?'

'It's a deal.' Martin watched as Dominic disappeared inside, then walked down Fifth Avenue and turned east on 42nd until he came to a coffee shop. As he sat at the counter he felt strangely envious of Dominic's easy relationship with his God. With all the Roths' insistence on tradition, religion seemed to be a very distant part of their lives. And suddenly Martin was consumed with curiosity about Catholicism. Judaism didn't exercise the same magnetic pull; at least not on the Jews Martin knew; and he experienced a peculiar sense of deprivation.

Quickly he paid for his coffee and left. When he got to the corner of 42nd and Fifth Avenue, he wondered what the hell he was going to do now. Without much thought he got on the bus which had stopped at the corner. It didn't really matter where it was going.

When Martin got off he found himself on the Lower East Side. In a state of shock he realized that the hordes of people crowding the streets were Jews, immigrants like his great-grandfather, Ephraim, whose birthday they celebrated each summer. As he walked past the dirty tenements, was jostled by the crowds around the pushcarts, and saw the pale-faced children, many of whom seemed like stunted adults, he felt a surge first of pity, then shame. An elevated train roared overhead and the very buildings appeared to sway. For a minute, Martin determined to catch the next bus uptown. Then something in the enthusiasm with which the women were outbidding each other for the vendors' goods, and the quick laughs of the children as they played around overflowing garbage cans, caught his attention. Although he was appalled by their living conditions, the inhabitants of Orchard Street did not seem defeated. Suddenly Martin understood the force which had sustained Ephraim on his journey West. Martin listened to the old men in skullcaps discussing the testaments, each one arguing the fine points of the Talmud and each thinking the other an idiot. They too seemed completely oblivious of their ugly surroundings. They were absorbed by their discussion, and more intensely alive than any of the rich old men who attended his temple in San Francisco. Martin was suddenly jealous of a heritage he felt he'd been denied. These were his people, and for all their poverty they seemed to embody the persistent strength that had ensured Jewish survival through centuries of persecution. These were the chosen people.

Suddenly, being Jewish without that spiritual force left Martin with a sense of being suspended in limbo. He again envied Dominic his simple faith.

Martin couldn't handle this new flood of emotion. He had to get away. As he hurried towards the bus, he almost stumbled over a little boy sitting on the kerb crying. The child looked so frail that Martin's heart went out to him. He sat down on the kerb alongside the child. 'What's wrong?'

The child looked wide-eyed at the stranger. 'I lost my ball.'

Taking out his handkerchief, Martin handed it to the child. 'Where did you lose it?'

'In the street. A guy picked it up and won't give it back.'

'How old are you?'

'Five.'

'Five? I thought you were at least six.'

'No, my brother Benny is six.'

'And what's your name?'

'Jeremy Cohen.'

'That's a nice name. How about an ice cream, Jeremy?'

The little boy shrugged his shoulders, 'Okay,' he answered, although he would have been happier to have been offered a new ball.

Martin took him by the hand and bought him a cone. Forgetting his loss for the moment, Jeremy smiled. Martin observed the child's tattered clothes and the hole in his left tennis shoe where his large toe stuck out. It was all an accident of birth, wasn't it? Like being born a Rockefeller, the Queen of England . . . or himself. Martin took a five-dollar bill from his wallet. As he handed it to the child he wondered if his gesture was born out of charity or guilt. Perhaps it was one and the same. He wasn't sure. 'I want you to buy a ball, Jeremy, and a pair of shoes. But put the money away until you get home to your mama.'

Jeremy was so intent on the five-dollar bill he didn't notice when Martin got up and walked to the bus.

Chapter Five

Martin's experience on the Lower East Side stayed with him for a long time. It left him with a greater drive to succeed. Professor Wheeler and his likes could no longer terrorize him. He had been born into privilege and given opportunities, and by God he was going to take advantage of them. There was no way he could fail. Perhaps a bit of Dominic's determination had rubbed off. But more important than his academic commitment was his decision to devote his free time to the Jewish Home for Children. Originally it was an orphanage, but now it had become a haven for the poor. The Home offered after-school classes, Hebrew instruction, and other activities for children whose mothers worked and who had nowhere to go except roam wild.

In the beginning the kids' resentment made it almost impossible for Martin to reach them. But his persistence won over first the teachers and then the children themselves. Their eventual admiration brought a joy to his life no monetary achievement could ever equal. The sound of their laughter as he coached their baseball team and their cheers the day he brought over the 'anonymously' donated uniforms he had purchased himself completely over-shadowed any lingering loneliness Martin felt at the dorm or in some of his classes.

Life had become a constantly changing kaleidoscope. Martin's experience working at the Home had been only one of the many things that had caused his transformation. Dominic had taught him a great deal about himself. He realized he'd been overprotected and overindulged. Perhaps it had not been a deliberate attempt on Dominic's part to open Martin's eyes to the real world, but deliberate or not, Dominic had. And in return he earned Martin's unconditional friendship. The confusion and uncertainty which Martin had brought to Yale seemed to have disappeared.

By the time Martin went home in June, he felt confident of who he was and what goals he wished to pursue. The problem was that his parents had sent away a boy and were not prepared to have him return a man.

Bess in particular was upset by the change. She couldn't lay a finger on it except to note that Martin was no longer amenable to her various social suggestions. If she had been willing to probe deeper, she might have recognized and even admired the extent of her son's maturity, but as it was she only saw that he rebelled against her arrangements for his summer, particularly as they involved Sylvia Lowenthal, the daughter of their long-time family friends.

Almost the moment Martin arrived home Bess began, 'Oh, Martin, darling, Mrs Lowenthal and I have so many wonderful plans for you this summer.'

'I'm not going to have much time, Mother. I want to spend the next few months working on my sociology project for next year. That's my only priority.'

'Well, dear, you can't just bury your head in books. Besides, you've done so well this year, why should you spend your summer – '

'Because I have a lot of catching up to do. I really wish you would check with me before you make any plans.'

Bess looked puzzled. 'Martin, dear, I have the distinct feeling we're arguing.'

'Look, I'm sorry if I gave you that impression. The point is I've already made other arrangements. I mean this weekend . . . '

'Well, that puts me in a bit of an awkward position, Martin.'

'Really? Why?'

'I asked Sylvia to keep Saturday night free so that you could escort her to the country club dance. I was sure you'd be delighted.'

He looked at his mother not knowing whether to laugh or scream. She knew that he'd be delighted? Imagine. 'Mother, I really just don't feel like going.'

Bess looked wounded. 'What am I going to say to the Lowenthals? This is just dreadful. I'm sure that Sylvia could have made other plans. Now you're standing her up.'

This time he did laugh. The whole thing was ridiculous. 'Since I didn't ask her, I can't stand her up. It's you who have the problem.'

She smiled. 'I suppose you're right. I guess I should have asked you first. But, darling, I truly thought you would *want* to take Sylvia. It's been three years since you've seen each other, with her being away at school in Switzerland. She's really grown quite lovely.' She paused for a long moment, giving Martin time to dwell upon that, then added, 'Do this for me, Martin.'

He looked at his mother and hesitated. She really looked so vulnerable and he did love her. Besides, it was such a small request. 'All right. But please do me a favour.'

'Of course, dear, anything.'

'From now on let me do the asking.'

'Yes, dear, of course.'

The country club hadn't changed in fifty years. Same red damask sofas and chairs. Maybe the draperies were more faded. Going away seemed to have made him notice all sorts of things he had previously ignored. Begrudgingly, though, he had to admit that, by God, Sylvia *had* changed. Without the braces, the horn-rimmed glasses, and the smell of horses which, he remembered, was an ever-present aroma since so much of her time had been spent riding, she was indeed lovely. And he might have been completely bowled over if she hadn't kept saying, 'You're stepping on my toes. Your feet were always much too big for you, Martin.'

At least she didn't say it was his head. 'I'm sorry. I'm really sorry, Sylvia.'

'And for heaven's sake, don't keep saying you're sorry. It's so irritating.'

'I'm sorry . . . I mean I'm sorry I said I was sorry. Would you rather not dance?'

'I think that's a very good idea.'

As they left the floor, he said, 'Can I get you something to drink?'

'Maybe a glass of champagne.'

On the fringes of the dance floor he stood and looked at her. 'Why are you so angry with me, Sylvia?'

'Well, I'm not going to tell you here with the whole club staring. The whole thing is just so irritating.'

'What are you talking about?'

'I just told you, Martin. I'm not going to discuss it now, here.'

'All right. Let me get the champagne and we'll take it out on the terrace.'

As they sat on a stone bench sipping champagne in the moonlight, Martin watched Sylvia out of the corners of his eyes. Putting down the glass he said, 'All right, Sylvia, what's the problem?'

'The problem, Martin, is that our mothers have combined forces and decided you and I should be thrown together this summer. I resent it. I don't like feeling like a business merger.'

'I know, Sylvia, and I apologize.'

'Well, thank you. That's very comforting. But I have a more serious problem.'

'Anything I can help you with?' Martin asked, ready now to acknowledge her as the close friend she'd been before going to Switzerland.

'I don't know.'

'It sounds serious.'

'It is. I'm in love.'

Martin wasn't sure why he minded. But he did. He had a

sudden memory of the day his mother caught them playing doctor. 'Why should being in love present a problem?'

'Because he comes from a long line of middle-class dentists. Need I say more? My father hit the ceiling when he found out his name was Maury Orloff. That was when the inquisition started.'

'Where did you meet him?'

'At the Rosen Delicatessen on Third Avenue.'

Even for somebody as emancipated as Martin, he was rather taken aback. 'Really? That's a strange place to meet.'

'Now don't be stuffy, Martin. People meet all sorts of ways. They don't all grow up sharing the same treehouse.'

'I'm sorry if I sounded stuffy.'

She smiled. 'There you go again. Anyway, when I tell you about Maury it won't sound all that dreadful. When Karen and I came back from Switzerland, we stayed at my Aunt Blanche's apartment in New York . . . can I have a cigarette?'

Martin reached for one inside the pocket of his dinner jacket, lit hers, then one for himself. Sylvia inhaled and then continued. 'Well, Karen and I decided to shop by ourselves one day. And here we were laden with a bunch of goodies from Bloomingdale's when we realized we hadn't eaten lunch. We stopped at Rosen's and were going to our table when all of a sudden a package fell out of my hand and landed on his head.'

Martin laughed. 'His head? That's quite a feat.'

'Well, the tables were so damned close I had to raise my arms to slither through. I'm not apologizing, Martin, but I did say I was sorry.'

He laughed. 'You better watch out or you'll get into the habit.'

She wrinkled her nose at him. 'Well, he stood up abruptly, but then when he looked at me he didn't seem one bit angry.'

'Well, I can understand that. You've really changed.'

'To what?'

'From a gangling, argumentative brat to a beautiful woman.'

She laughed. 'Gee, that's the nicest thing you've ever said to me, Martin. Well, anyway, I kept apologizing. He insisted it wasn't necessary and if I wanted to redeem myself, I'd join him for lunch.'

'Oh, I see. Well, obviously you did, but after all he was a stranger.'

'I know. But what else could I do? Well, anyway, while I was munching my corned beef sandwich I decided he was damned attractive. And then I said to myself, this has to be more than a coincidence. Why else would I have dropped that box at that particular moment on the head of someone who was both Jewish and handsome. Do you believe in fate?'

Martin thought about it for a long moment. 'I'm not really sure. Do you?'

'I don't have a doubt. By the time we finished, I was terribly smitten with him and when he asked me if he could see me again I didn't hesitate, though my hand shook as I wrote my name and number on a matchbox cover. Are you sure I'm not boring you?'

'I'm sure. Go on.'

'Well, when I got back to Aunt Blanche's, I found he'd called. I called back and made a date for dinner that night. We went to a marvellous little Italian restaurant in the Fifties and, well, Martin, what can I say?'

'What did your aunt say about all this?'

'I didn't tell her about it . . . I mean, about how we'd met. She'd have been appalled. After one phone call to California I would have been shipped out on the first train. Oh, what else could I do, Martin? I lied and said he was from Princeton.'

'Well, you're resourceful, Sylvia. I'll say that.'

She looked at him strangely. 'What kind of thing is that to say to me?'

'No, I really meant it in the most complimentary way.'

She hesitated for a moment. 'Thank you . . . I think. Well, anyway, after the pasta and that first glass of red wine, I knew Maury Orloff was for me.'

While Sylvia took a sip of champagne, Martin asked, 'Do people fall in love just like that?'

'That's what the songs say.'

'Maybe, but don't two people have to get to know one another better?'

'Not when the chemistry is right, Martin. People can know one another all their lives and never fall in love. Look at you and me.'

'Well, that's a little different. It would be like incest.'

Sylvia took another sip of champagne. 'If I tell you a secret, promise not to laugh?'

'Scout's honour.'

'I was wildly, madly in love with you.'

'You were?' he answered, secretly pleased. 'I didn't know.'

'Of course you didn't. When you're thirteen and terrified that the object of your affection is going to find out, you act in a lot of strange ways.'

'I would have never guessed you felt that way about me.'

'Well, I did. But that was ages ago.'

Martin wasn't all that pleased at the way she relegated her affection for him to the past, but he smiled and asked, 'Where do you go from here?'

'Either the family accepts him or else.'

'You mean it's that serious?'

'It's that serious,' she said, suddenly on the verge of tears.

If there was one thing that Martin couldn't abide, it was a woman crying. For an unfathomable reason he felt responsible no matter what the cause of her tears. Worse than responsible, he felt guilty. Handing her his handkerchief, he said, 'Please don't cry, Sylvia. I hate to see you unhappy.'

She looked up as a tear spilled down her cheek. 'Do you really?'

'Well, of course I do, for God's sake!'

She blew her nose and said, 'I suppose I'm just sort of confused. It seems so difficult to break Mother out of her mould. Our parents are so rigid. My God, their ideas are almost archaic about our marrying our own kind. You know, Martin, we're not exactly the Rothschilds.'

'Still, even though we don't always agree with them, we have to try to look at it from their point of view.'

Sylvia looked irritated. 'Gosh, I thought you were on my side, Martin.'

'I am.'

'Then why are you taking their side?'

'I'm not. I just think it's important to see their point of view – to try and understand them.'

Sylvia laughed, not happily. 'You sound like a parent yourself. They're the ones who should be understanding. This is not the dark ages.'

'You still have to listen. Families are terribly important. They may be a little out of touch, but the point is that they're trying to perpetuate a tradition . . . Sylvia, promise you won't be upset at this.'

'I can't promise . . . but at least I'll listen.'

He smiled. 'Good. Now let's take it from your point of view. I suppose it's possible to fall in love with someone the first time you meet. But it's also possible that his attraction is simply because he is different.'

'Now wait a minute, Martin. Don't you think I know when I'm in love?'

'Well, you just said you were a little confused.'

'Not about him, about them, their attitudes, their intolerance. They haven't even met him, Martin, and they already assume that he's not good enough for me. I'm not a child. I'm eighteen and I haven't been as sheltered as you think. What I mean is, going to girls' school you learn a lot. Now don't get the wrong idea; I'm still a virgin. But don't tell me I don't know my own mind.' Once again she was on the verge of tears.

'All right, I'm sorry I upset you. I guess I just didn't put it right. What I'm trying to say is, before you start knocking down walls, be sure, absolutely sure, that he's the man you want to marry. I think you have to get to know him better.'

Sylvia sighed. 'Gee, we seem to be saying "sorry" a lot tonight. But I am. I didn't mean to fly off the handle.'

He smiled at her.

After a long silence, Sylvia said, 'Maybe you're right. You know what I'm going to do, Martin? I've decided I'm going to live with Aunt Blanche for a while. Really get to know Maury better. And if I find that he's right for me, I'll fight like hell.'

'That's fair. But while you're fighting, Sylvia, keep the door open so that you can always come home with or without your dentist.'

She shook her head. 'You know, I really love you, Martin. You're such a good friend.'

'That's what it's all about.'

A week later, Martin was with Sylvia's parents, seeing her off at the train station. They looked at each other as two friends do who share a very important secret. Then she mounted the steps to her compartment. Inside, she pulled up the shade and waved until the train pulled out of sight.

For all the sage advice he had given Sylvia, Martin found it difficult maintaining good relations with his own parents. As the three of them sat having dinner that evening, Martin tried to be tolerant of his father's attitudes, but found he couldn't as his father began complaining about some of the new members being admitted to the country club.

'Today it seems it's only money that counts,' Julian was saying. 'There's an entirely new element taking over. They've got this Harry Shorn on the Greens Committee who wants to straighten out the eighteenth hole.'

'Why would he want to do that?'

'It's probably a little too complicated for him. It's the prettiest and most challenging drive of any course in the country and he can't seem to leave it alone. In my day he would have never gotten through the front door. Well, I guess everything is changing.' Julian was warming to his theme. 'The whole country's going to hell. I never thought I'd live to see the day when the government could pry into my private business affairs. Roosevelt won't be happy until he sees the country go communist. And God knows he's not doing anything to help the Jews. I tell you, Bess, it's as though the old order of things is dying. Nobody gives a damn about perpetuating tradition any more.'

The conversation had gotten far afield from Harry Shorn. In Julian's mind Harry Shorn and Roosevelt became synonymous. Both represented a threat to the world as he knew it.

Martin thought for a moment before saying anything. He'd met Shorn at the country club and to all outward appearances he seemed a suitable member. 'Don't you think that changes are good sometimes, Dad? I talked to Harry the other night and he seemed like he'd fit anywhere.'

'Strip Harry Shorn of the tailormade suit and you have a man with no breeding. He's ostentatious and obnoxious.'

'I didn't get that feeling, Dad.'

'Well, you haven't had to put up with some of the obscene jokes he tells at lunch. He simply doesn't belong.'

Martin was convinced that his father was more upset about Harry Shorn breaking down the barriers of their closed society than the fact that he wanted the eighteenth hole changed. 'Dad, I hope you'll forgive me, but I think you're confusing the issues. I don't know how the government got involved with Harry Shorn, but the truth is the world can't stand still. And I think that progress is good.'

Julian exploded. 'Progress you call it? Well, you can't have a future unless you preserve the past.'

Watching his father's hand tremble with anger as he picked up his wineglass, Martin was afraid it was bad for Julian's health to get so worked up. Martin's point no longer seemed so important. 'I suppose you're right, Dad.'

Ignoring his son, Julian said, 'What do you think about it

all, Bess? You haven't said much.'

His mother looked at Martin angrily, as though she had not heard his capitulation. She'd never heard him stand up to his father before and it troubled her. Maybe it was called growing up, but she didn't much care for it. Turning to Julian, she said, 'You can learn a great deal from listening, but you're absolutely right, my dear. I believe the world is moving in the wrong direction.'

That night was only the first of many such conversations. Although Martin tried not to argue, he found it impossible to remain silent when Bess or particularly Julian voiced their frequently reactionary opinions. As the summer drew to a close, Martin found himself unexpectedly eager to go back to school. Dominic's scholarship had been expanded to cover living expenses and he and Martin were sharing a room in Martin's college, Jonathan Edwards. This fact had triggered a particularly angry fight between Julian and Martin, who couldn't understand why his father would rather he room with an anti-Semitic Brahman than a studious Catholic.

Both parents and son stepped back a bit from their positions the week before Martin left and all three tried to enjoy their last days together. They were careful to avoid politics or the approaching war in Europe, though Hitler was one subject they were in agreement on.

When Martin finally boarded the train East, he looked with love at his parents standing on the platform. He wished he could in some way protect them from a rapidly changing world.

It was well into the following spring that he received a letter which made him decide maybe the older generation needed less protection than he'd suspected. One day in late May of his sophomore year, he returned to class to find an envelope with Sylvia's San Francisco address on the back. He was surprised to see she'd left Aunt Blanche's and began reading the letter as he walked up the stairs to his room.

Dear Martin:

Before I say anything I want to thank you for the profound pearls of wisdom that you gave me eight months ago. The echo of those words has come back to haunt me, I must say. I suppose because no one wants to admit that they have made a great error in judgement. Yet my impetuosity almost resulted in total disaster. I don't quite know how I can tell you all the things that have happened in one letter, so please bear with me.

I did believe in the beginning that I was madly in love with Maury. He was so terribly exciting, like forbidden fruit. I confess, the first night I went out with him I fantasized about becoming his wife. Maybe I'd been seeing too many movies, but I really did believe Maury looked like Robert Taylor.

Well, we saw each other secretly for the first few months and both Maury and I agreed that we'd say nothing to our parents until we found we couldn't live without each other. It wasn't long before I began to feel that way. I was really in love. That was when I told Aunt Blanche that the family would either accept Maury or else. They knew if they persisted in rejecting him, it would only result in my wanting to marry him more. They were a lot smarter than I gave them credit for.

Now that we were no longer two against the world, we discovered we had vast differences of opinion. Till then I knew nothing about his family. We were no sooner engaged than his mother insisted I keep a kosher house. Need I say more? I would never marry outside our faith, but how would I ever be able to adjust to orthodoxy? Good Lord, I don't know *anything* about Judaism. Well, one word led to another and we began finding fault with one another. I with his religious fervour and he with my lack of it. At first there were mild spats, but then he began to criticize me – calling me a Jewish princess. He said I gave the impression that I was above his family. The truth, I realize now, was that we came from two different worlds. I could no more fit into his than he could mine.

Anyway, Martin, I've come home a little wiser than I was before. I've grown up a lot since then and I know one thing. Breaking off a love affair whether it's good or bad is always painful. I'm not going to say forever, but it will be a long time before I fall in love again.

Martin, darling, this letter is so long I will sign off here.

Please write and let me know how you are, though I admit your mother keeps us informed. Well, dear friend, I'm sure that we will look back upon our callow youth and reflect upon it in years to come.

With deep affection,
Sylvia

Chapter Six

Two years had passed since Sylvia had exhorted Martin to reflect upon his callow youth, and now he was graduating from Yale. Martin's parents had driven up from New York, bringing Sylvia, who had come East on a shopping trip. Martin found himself less angry with his father in recent months. The deteriorating situation in Europe gave them a broader base on which to agree. And since Sylvia's confession about Maury, she and Martin had seemed to pick up the carefree friendship they had enjoyed as kids.

After the ceremony Martin began pushing through the crowds. Parents were taking pictures, sweethearts were kissing, and kids were running around trying to attract their older brothers' attention. Finally he saw Sylvia waving.

He ran to meet her and took her in his arms. 'Martin . . . Oh, Martin,' she said breathlessly. 'I'm so proud of you!' Kissing her, he was unaware that his family was watching with approval. Martin, still carried away by the excitement of the day, hugged his mother, also unaware that she had laid a much more serious interpretation to Sylvia's kiss. She hoped that, in Sylvia, Martin had found a woman who cherished him as much as she did.

Bess's eyes filled. This was her son, her only child, in cap and gown. 'Oh, darling,' she said, 'you've made us so very proud.' Something in his mother's voice made Martin remember all the years of devotion she had lavished upon him as a child. Today all the resentments of his youth had abated. They had been growing pains at worst, and now he could say with a grateful heart, 'Thank you, Mom. I hope I'll always justify that feeling.'

Julian put an arm around his son's shoulders. 'I doubt if there is a father here today who is more proud and happy than I. I thank God you're my son. Congratulations.'

'Thank you, Dad,' Martin answered softly.

As his father turned away, Martin felt enormous guilt for all the hard words he had exchanged with Julian over the past four years. He vowed to be more understanding in the future.

Dominic and his family came over, and the Roths went out of their way to be pleasant. It was as if they too were trying to turn over a new leaf. Dominic had taken a job with an advertising agency on Madison Avenue, and Martin's desk waited for him at his father's brokerage firm. An additional Roth had been added that week to Roth and Seifer, Brokers.

The two friends said goodbye and the next morning Martin was on his way back West. He had some doubts about joining the family business, but this time he decided to at least give his parents' way a fair trial. He was determined, however, to succeed in his own right. The first day he'd gone to the office, his father's partner had said, 'You have a brilliant future ahead of you, Martin. Welcome aboard.'

In the first six months Martin justified their confidence. He had acquired McMillian Steel Company as an account. Even more impressive was the fact that Martin had taken them away from the prestigious brokerage firm of Townsend Wittier. As of that moment Martin began to feel his potential impact on the business world.

It was only a week later that he announced to his parents that he had taken an apartment in San Francisco.

Martin was grown up now, but that seemed a difficult fact for Bess to comprehend. It certainly wasn't his desire to hurt her. She would just have to understand. She would also have to stop deluding herself that Martin was in love with Sylvia. She had romanticized their friendship to the brink of marriage.

Once faced with Martin's new apartment, she capitulated gracefully and for a time seemed to divert her energies away from playing Cupid into decorating the perfect bachelor abode. When she'd finished, the apartment was a showplace. The walls of the living room were deep blue. An extraordinary array of modern art hung over the leather sofa, and an enormous glass and brass coffee table sat on a plush carpet the colour of autumn leaves. There were two large chairs in plaid corduroy on either side of the fireplace, and bookshelves with a built-in bar on the remaining wall. The dining room was as impeccably furnished as the rest of the apartment, but the most splendid sight of all was beyond the perimeters of the penthouse walls: the spectacular view of the Golden Gate Bridge extending across the Bay.

Bess was more than rewarded by the look on Martin's face. 'It's simply beautiful, Mother. You're an artistic genius,' he said, smiling. How could he ever be upset with her?

'I'd rather be a magician,' she said. 'If I were, then you'd be getting –'

'Don't say it, Mother. What is your obsession anyway? I'm only twenty-two. Give me a chance to enjoy myself.'

'I understand. But you must admit that Sylvia is so right for you, Martin. You have so much in common and I know you care a great deal about her. And she about you.'

'Yes I do, but I don't want to think about anybody right now.'

'Well, you can't blame me for hoping. What are your plans for tonight?'

Martin smiled. 'I have a date.'

'Really? Is she anybody we know?'

'No. As a matter of fact, Mother, she's a voluptuous blonde model.'

'A what?'

'A model.'

'Oh, dear me! Well, don't get too involved, Martin.'

Again he smiled. 'I'll try not to.'

Since it was Carey's sensuality he was taken with rather than her intellect, it was easy for Martin not to become involved. She was a purring kitten who generally fled his thoughts the moment she was out of sight. But this Sunday morning when he woke up and smelled her lingering scent he could not help remembering the night before. He could almost hear the echo of his voice.

'Champagne?'

'Love it.'

He had poured the champagne into the glass, watched as the bubbles danced, then walked out onto the balcony. For a while they watched the moon. Then, after taking the glass from her hand and placing it on the wrought-iron table, he had taken her in his arms, kissing her gently at first, then with more urgency. Once he sensed her response, he picked her up in his arms and carried her to the bedroom. He set her down in the darkened room and stood for a moment with his hands cupping her face. She was incredibly beautiful. His desire for her heightened as he traced the outline of her nose, eyes, forehead, until his fingers found the first button of the chiffon bodice. He kissed her while his hands slowly inched downward until the front of her dress was open. He slid it from her shoulders until it fell to the floor. He unfastened the lace bra and slipped it off. He stroked her rounded breasts and brushed her nipples first with his fingers and then with his lips and tongue. She gasped at the sensation and from there it was like a kaleidoscope of motion.

When he had finished undressing her he lay facing her, caressing every contour of her body. Without words he guided her hand down to his groin and placed his hand over hers for a moment, moving it slowly up and down until she felt him harden. His tongue played over her lips, probed to meet hers. The taste of her was like honey. He heard the sigh of her breathing, the soft moan as his fingers teased down the front of her body and between her legs. Then he moved on top of her and slowly began to put himself inside, pushing deeper and deeper still. She arched her back to receive him as he thrust faster and faster until the explosion inside him erupted.

When it was over, he lay quiet still on top of her. His breathing still heavy, he whispered, 'Sweet Carey. Lovely, sweet Carey . . .'

He rolled over onto his back. For some reason Carey realized that the magic had gone. Martin dozed off and was in a deep slumber in less than five minutes. An annoyed Carey got out of bed and went to the bathroom feeling more than disgruntled. Martin had surely given her the impression that he was really interested in her. After she dressed, she appraised herself. She was every inch a lady, and no one was going to demean her. Taking out her lipstick, she scribbled on the bathroom mirror, 'Thanks for *nothing*.' For a moment Carey stood there, wanting to say something more vicious, but she couldn't think of anything. On her way out she slammed the door but Martin just rolled over in his sleep.

The next morning it wasn't difficult to understand why she had left. Falling asleep the way he had must have made her feel used. But dammit, she didn't realize how exhausting she was. Well, he'd call and apologize later. He got out of bed and went to the bathroom. The first thing he saw was what she'd written on the mirror. It made him think of the first girl he'd ever slept with.

It had been at a Vassar sorority party. He'd danced with this one girl, lithe and intense, for most of the evening. And when they weren't together, wherever he looked she was there staring at him. Later she took him by the hand and led him to her parked car. 'Let's get away from this, it's so boring . . .'

He couldn't remember what he'd said – probably nothing. They had driven to a quiet street off-campus, stopped the car, and switched off the lights. Before Martin knew it his zipper was down, he was pulled on top of her, and she was kissing his penis. Within seconds he had come and the girl was furious. 'Get out of my car, you yid. You little pipsqueak. Giving me the idea you knew what it was all about . . . Get out!' She opened the door, pushed him out, and drove away, leaving him standing in the street.

He'd come a long way since then as a Casanova. Girls adored him, and he knew that even though Carey had been angry all he had to do was call to get her back. Still, his mother was right about one thing. Perhaps Sylvia wasn't the girl, but he would like to be in love with someone about whom he really cared.

Martin showered and went into the kitchen. He opened the refrigerator, took out the orange juice, poured himself a glass, and while he drank it, popped the bread into the toaster, then went to the front door and retrieved the *Sunday Examiner*. He poured himself a cup of coffee, went back into the living room, and settled himself on the couch, but the toast remained uneaten, the coffee untouched once he saw the headlines: PEARL HARBOR BOMBED!

For a moment Martin thought it had to be a hoax, some stupid, asinine joke. Quickly he got up and turned on the radio. 'Pearl Harbor was bombed this morning in a sneak attack by the Japanese. It occurred while all of – ' He quickly switched to another station: ' . . . there's much confusion here in Hawaii that something the magnitude – '

Martin sat in a state of shock. He shook his head, unable to comprehend it all. Hawaii belonged to the United States, and that meant they were at war. At least it meant that Roosevelt would have to go to the aid of the European Jews. He and his father had remained in agreement on that one issue. America could not turn her back forever on the rumours coming out of Poland and Germany. Now they would have no choice.

The ringing phone startled him. Picking it up, he heard

his father's voice. 'I don't believe this, Martin! Those damn Japs were in Washington only this week talking peace.'

Martin found his voice. 'Well, at least it looks as if we're going to get a chance to lick the Nazis.'

Julian swallowed. At twenty-two, Martin would be one of the first to be drafted; or, knowing Martin, be one of the first to enlist. 'I think you'd better come home, Martin. Your mother's quite distraught.'

'Of course, Dad.'

That night Martin couldn't sleep. Every district in the city was setting up a draft board, and Martin watched as an enlistment office prepared to open across the street. By early morning dozens of volunteers were lined up before its doors. Martin knew before the day was out he would join their numbers. His parents would have to understand. In any case it would only be a matter of months before he was called up. He had joined ROTC his last two years of college and would be going in as an officer, a fact he hoped would prove some consolation to his mother.

Martin shivered as he crossed the street to the draft office. He wouldn't be human if he didn't have fears of dying, fears he could not even articulate. Yet when he stood outside the draft office after having been inducted, he felt a strange sense of relief.

The next few days passed in a state of unreality: it was business as usual. Martin went to the office every morning until the time came for him to be inducted as a first lieutenant. It was time to tell his parents.

He would never forget the look of anguish in his mother's eyes as he stood before her dressed in his uniform. She could not control her emotions. She cursed the war and finally burst into tears saying, 'You needn't have volunteered. Couldn't you have waited to be called? Maybe your father could have arranged something.'

Martin paused, hearing the echoes from his childhood about honour. Without it a man had nothing. But he realized that he was her son and honour had nothing to do with it. 'I don't think you would have really wanted me to do that, Mother. I did what I had to do.'

As the tears rolled down her cheeks she said, 'You're right, Martin. You're right. I apologize. It's just that – ' But she couldn't finish.

The days flowed on with fearful anticipation while Martin waited for his orders. Finally the waiting ended as Martin read: 'Assigned to report to Fort Ord on December 27, 1941.' There'd be six weeks of basic training; beyond that he didn't know exactly where he would be shipped.

One of the most heavenly spots on earth is the Monterey Peninsula, but Martin was oblivious to the scenery as the army bus sped along the highway towards Fort Ord. He saw neither the windswept pines nor the formidable sea crashing against the enormous boulders. He could not erase the picture of his mother's anguished face, his father's look of despair. The only bright spot in the party was Sylvia's cheerful smile and her promise to look after his parents.

When Martin lay on his bunk bed that night he thought about Sylvia. She'd been so comforting these past weeks and he felt closer to her than at any other time in his life. Maybe he should marry her after all. She belonged to his world. That is, if there was a world to come back to.

The thought of having a child suddenly became very important to him. To think of dying without leaving a part of himself behind seemed more than Martin could face. But then, just as quickly, he realized how selfish the thought had been. He didn't love Sylvia, not in the way she deserved. If he married her, it would be for all the wrong reasons.

As the days passed the gruelling pace of basic gave him little time to think. At night when he fell into his bunk he was asleep the second his head touched the pillow. In any case, he reasoned, thoughts of Sylvia were academic. In a few short weeks he'd be heading overseas.

But fate had a different plan. When the six weeks were over, Martin was informed that he was being held at Ord to train new recruits. He was frustrated, but like a good lieutenant he kept his objections to himself.

For three months he commuted to San Francisco each weekend. But as the weeks passed, the partings became so painful to his parents, he almost hesitated to go home. Finally Martin got his wish. One Wednesday morning he received orders for Fort Dix. From there he would be assigned to somewhere in England or Scotland, probably to prepare for the invasion of Europe.

Wanting to make his last weekend as happy as she could, Bess tried to set aside her own grief. There wasn't a favourite dish of Martin's that she didn't prepare. There wasn't a friend he enjoyed whom she didn't invite over. Much as she tried not to, she couldn't keep from following him from room to room, hovering over him as though he were a small boy.

Another time Martin would have resented her, but her attempted valour was too touching. It left him with an emotion so strong it was almost physical. If Martin had had any questions about his life, they had never concerned his having been loved. Until he was five his mother had been his whole world. He remembered when she'd come to his bedroom to say goodnight, dressed for the opera or a party. He knew he'd carry that picture with him always.

Bess tried hard to let Martin enjoy the weekend. The night before his departure she invited only Sylvia and her parents for dinner. Everyone did their best to be cheerful, but it was with a sense of relief that after coffee Martin was able to draw Sylvia out on the terrace.

In their absence, Mr Lowenthal said softly, 'I guess we're in for a long siege. Terrible, simply terrible . . . it's worse than the one we fought in.'

Julian got up, took a cigar from the humidor, clipped off the end, and lit it. Watching the thick smoke spiral up, he said, 'Dear God, I beg you. Please bring Martin back to us whole.'

At that moment Bess looked across the room and saw Julian standing there with his eyes closed. She got up slowly and went to his side. 'Martin is going to be all right. So are we, dear,' she said, though she herself wasn't sure she believed it. Still, if they were going to survive they had to support each other.

Julian took Bess's hand in his and whispered, 'Oh, my dear, whatever would I do without you?'

'I'm not going to let you find out.'

Standing on the terrace overlooking the rose garden, Sylvia said, 'Thank God some things never change. It's so beautiful here even during the winter.'

'I never appreciated it as much as I have in the last few days.'

'Would you like to take a stroll?' she said, taking his arm.

They walked up the slight incline to where the cypress trees circled the lush green lawn. He could almost hear the sounds of his childhood. He remembered the day his Aunt Matty had been married on this spot. How old was he then? About eight maybe? He'd dropped the rings.

Smiling, he led Sylvia on past the greenhouse, across the broadstone patio and into the pavilion. It was filled with the fragrance of gardenias.

He remembered playing here with Sylvia. Suddenly he heard her soft weeping and took her in his arms. 'You mustn't do that, Sylvia, dear. I can't stand hearing you cry.'

'I love you, Martin,' she sobbed. 'I can't help it but I do. I always have and I would never have told you if it weren't for you going away. I have never loved anybody but you, Martin, never.'

Holding her close to him, he said, 'You mustn't say these things, Sylvia. It's just the war. You don't really mean them.'

'No, you're wrong. It's the war that's made it possible for me to tell you how I feel.'

She kissed him with all her pent-up passion.

'Sylvia, please, you mustn't do this. It's wrong.'

'Wrong? Can't you love me just a little, Martin?'

'But I do, Sylvia. I *do* love you.'

'Then why don't you make love to me, Martin?'

70

'Because . . . ' But before he could finish she kissed him with such passion that he found himself drowning in desire. He could not stop himself as she sank to the floor, pulling him down to her. It was like falling through a bottomless sea. Wave upon wave of passion consumed him. But when it was over and they began straightening their clothes he was consumed with guilt.

'I shouldn't have let myself get that carried away,' he said, trying to avoid her eyes.

'Please don't say that, Martin. Please. I love you. I want you to carry the memory of this night with you. But I want you to remember it with joy.'

'I will, Sylvia. Forever. But, dear, I don't want you to be hurt because of this.'

'You could never hurt me, Martin. Never.'

Chapter Seven

Monday morning arrived with relentless punctuality. This time Bess and Julian accompanied Martin. At the last minute Sylvia drove up in her convertible and was welcomed into the Roths' limousine. When they reached the station she stood back a little so as not to intrude on Martin's goodbye to his parents. Bess was oblivious to everything but her son's face. She didn't see the other soldiers, the other agonized families who, like herself, felt a sense of privacy as they said those painful last goodbyes.

Martin looked at his watch. It was time to board. Suddenly he felt his mother in his arms; she seemed so frail and vulnerable. He'd never remembered her as being this small. He knew how much she was suffering. Then Julian embraced him, wanting to protect him yet knowing that the boy's assured safety was the one thing he could not buy.

Finally, Sylvia stood before Martin. It was time for their goodbye. 'Take care of yourself, Martin,' she said.

He nodded. 'I will. Thank you for helping my parents.'

She nodded. He kissed her with affection and boarded the train, where he found a seat by the window. He saw Sylvia and his parents trying to wave bravely. Then the train moved out.

The Roths stood for a long moment amidst the swirling crowds, staring into the distance as they watched the train disappear. They seemed old today as they clung to each other in their grief. Sylvia hoped she could help fill the void Martin's going had created, but she doubted it. He was, after all, flesh of their flesh; their only son. She wiped her own tears away and gently said, 'I think it's time to go home now.'

During the drive back to Woodside, Sylvia sat lost in thought. The events of the past week had been more than sobering and Sylvia decided she had to be honest, at least with herself. She had daydreamed about Martin for years, but now she had to face the truth: she'd never had the slightest intention of marrying Maury. She understood that now.

'Be sure, Sylvia,' Martin had cautioned. 'Go slowly, maybe this is only a rebellion.'

Wise Martin, that's really what it had been. Not only against her own narrow little world, but against Martin. She thought that she could make him jealous, perhaps force him to rescue her. But that had been foolish. She knew Martin didn't love her. Of his deep affection she was more than certain, remembering how gently he had taken her last night. Perhaps in a relationship one person always loved more than the other. If there was a commitment to be made, she made it to herself. Martin was going to love her. They were right for each other, meant for each other. When he came home, she'd make him realize that. They were both cut from the same piece of cloth, understood each other's worlds, spoke the same language as she and

Maury never had. She trembled at the thought that to spite Martin she could have destroyed her life. She'd been tempted to explore her sexuality, but even at the height of her desire for Maury, she had held back. Martin had stood in the way even then.

It had taken something as catastrophic as the war for her to throw herself at Martin's feet. But pride be damned. At least Martin knew how she felt. Sylvia was so lost in thought that she didn't notice the car had stopped until Edward, the chauffeur, reached in to help her out.

As soon as they reached the house Julian said, 'My dear, if you don't mind, I'll skip lunch. I have a headache and I think I'll lie down.'

'Of course,' Bess said. 'I'll have a tray sent up to you, darling.'

The women watched as he slowly ascended the stairs. When they heard the door shut behind him, Bess sighed and said, 'Dear me. You must be famished.'

'Not especially. But I think you should have something, Aunt Bess.'

Bess looked at the girl she had known since birth, wishing that Sylvia were the daughter that she had never had. But then Sylvia had never been all that close to her own mother. Whenever she had a problem, it was Bess to whom she turned. Perhaps the tie between them was stronger even than blood.

Sylvia settled herself into the down pillows of the chair and looked about the familiar room. Thank God nothing seemed to have changed. She remembered the time Martin was twelve and had fallen off the library stairs reaching for a book. She had run to him and tried to help him up, but he couldn't move.

'Gosh, Sylvia, wait a minute. I think I broke my ankle.'

'Oh, you couldn't have.'

'Don't argue with me, Sylvia. I think it's broken.'

'How can you tell?'

' 'Cause it throbs like hell.'

'You better not let your mother hear you say hell.'

'Sylvia, do me a favour. Go home.'

'After I've helped you up.'

Between Sylvia and the arm of the chair, Martin got up, hobbled out of the room and up the stairs. He sat gingerly on the bed, swung his leg over and then lay down. The pain was excruciating and his ankle was the size of a grapefruit.

'Holy cow. I really think I've broken it, Sylvia.'

'Okay, don't move. I'll go down and get Anna.'

She slid down the banister and ran to the kitchen to tell Anna, the Roths' housekeeper. 'Anna, Martin broke his leg,' she said breathlessly.

'Now where does it hurt?' Anna said when she reached his bedroom.

'It's my ankle. I think it's broken.'

'I'm sure it's no such thing,' she said, much like Sylvia.

'Because it hurts like hell.'

Anna's eyebrows knitted together.

'What did you say, young man?'

'I said it hurts so much.'

'Well, I hope that's what you said.' But Anna was concerned, particularly since the Roths were away. 'Now don't move, Martin. This may hurt for a moment, but let me put one of these pillows under your leg.'

He let out a yell as she lifted his foot.

'Now, Sylvia. You'll have to step out for a while,' Anna said.

'Why?' Sylvia asked in mild defiance.

'I'm going to try and get off Martin's pants and make him comfortable.'

'But why can't I stay? I've seen him lots without his pants.'

'Have you really, young lady? Well, there's much to tell when Mr and Mrs Roth come home. Now leave the room immediately.'

Sylvia glared at Anna and reluctantly obeyed. For the next week she sat in Martin's room, since he was confined to bed with a compound fracture.

Her memory of those innocent days was interrupted by

Bess asking, 'Would you like a little sherry?'

'That would be nice.'

They sipped in silence. After a while Bess said, 'Remarkable how resilient we are. I never would have thought I'd be this calm. The one I'm worried about is Julian.

'There's a strange thing about marriage, Sylvia. Even after all these years there are moments that cannot be shared. I suppose they belong between man and his God.' Bess looked at Sylvia's concerned face and added, 'My dear, you will never know how grateful I am to you for being here at this moment. You are such a comfort.'

'This is where I want to be, where I'm happiest. If you don't mind, I've decided I'm going to be your houseguest for a while.'

'Mind? Oh, my dearest girl, I'm overjoyed. But as close as your mother and I are, I wouldn't want your mother to feel that I was alienating you.'

Sylvia smiled. 'She already knows that and she won't feel jealous.'

That night Sylvia sat down at the desk and wrote Martin a letter. Not a love letter, really, but one of nostalgia in the hope that memories of their happy childhood would give him something to hold on to, to support him during the terrible weeks and months ahead.

Chapter Eight

Long before Martin received the letter he was on ship bound for Italy. Nothing in his life had prepared him for the horrors of years to come. Nothing would ever erase the sounds and sights of the brutality and carnage. He saw the unburied dead rotting by the roadside, old people and children starving, girls barely in their teens who knew just enough English to say, 'Okay, GI Joe. You give me chocolate, I give you good time.'

In a back street of Palermo, after the Italian army had retreated, Martin watched as a drunken paratrooper and an emaciated thirteen-year-old girl climbed the rickety stairs to her bedroom while her little brothers fought each other for scraps of food in the garbage cans outside.

But nothing he saw in defeated Italy equalled Germany after VE Day.

Hitler had told the world exactly what he intended to do when he'd written *Mein Kampf*, but no one had believed he would carry out his final solution. Even the first stories that filtered back after the destruction of the Third Reich seemed too terrible to be true.

For centuries European governments had stood by while Jews were persecuted, but never had the civilized world been faced by murder on such a scale. Six million Jews. Six million innocent lives. The Allies rushed in to cover the shame of the denial. And no one felt more outrage than Martin Roth. Captain Martin Roth, assigned to locate and reunite survivors of Dachau, Auschwitz, Bergen-Belsen – names that would make their instigators pariahs until the end of time.

Sitting in his makeshift office amidst the bomb craters of Berlin, trying to pair off names and sort the legacy of the dead, Martin thought at moments that he would die of grief and shame. How could he not have known as early as 1940? Every Jew in the world should have made it his or her business to have realized what was going on. Every family smugly writing checks to Zionist groups, to their local temple, should have raised a cry to heaven. But they had sat back and allowed genocide to be perpetrated on a scale never before seen.

Never again would Martin take his Judaism for granted. The lessons he had learned were bitter, but at last he knew who he was, what he was. And for the first time in his entire life he felt like a Jew.

When he was finally ordered back to the States, he wasn't sure he wanted to go. His work was not finished and he tried to extend his tour to help the refugees. But his commanding officer took one look at Martin's ravaged face and sent him home. As his troop ship pulled into New York harbour, he took out his mother's last letter. 'Thank God you're whole and will be coming home to us soon . . .'

But that wasn't quite what was going to happen. Martin wasn't going *home* right away. And although it might not have shown, he wasn't *exactly whole*. If there were lines on his face, they were a mere reflection of the scars on his soul.

As soon as he finished the paperwork at Fort Dix and was once again a civilian, he decided to take a room at the Gotham Hotel in Manhattan while he tried to sort out his life.

After the bellboy put his gear in the closet, Martin sat on the edge of the bed, staring at the silent black phone on the nightstand. He had gone over the dialogue many times. How best to tell his parents he wasn't coming home – for a while? It was going to be difficult, but the war had taught him the importance of living his own life. His parents would have to manage a little longer without him. But when he had placed the call and heard his mother's voice, he was tempted to take the first train West.

He heard himself saying, 'Yes. Well, Mother, I'm going to stay in New York for just a little while and –'

'And what, Martin? I mean for how long?' she said, unable to disguise the painful disappointment in her voice.

He swallowed hard and heard the echo of his deception as he said, 'Maybe a week or so. I really hadn't thought about it, Mother. Since I'm here in New York, I'd like to see Dominic.'

The tears rolled down her cheeks. She would never have believed that Martin could be so insensitive. Home should have been the only place on earth where he wanted to be. But it seemed he preferred to reach out to Dominic instead of to them, and that was something she could not understand. Drying her tears, she steadied her voice and said,

'I'm sure you know what is best for you, Martin. And I think you should do what pleases you. I'm disappointed, of course.'

'I'm terribly sorry about all of this, but please try to understand – I need this time alone.'

She didn't understand at all. He wasn't going to be alone, he was going to be with Dominic. 'Of course I understand. Take care, Martin . . . and, dear, we love you.'

'And I love you. May I speak to Dad?'

'He's not here at the moment.'

'Oh? Well, give him my love. I'll call you tomorrow, I'm staying at the Gotham.' He gave her the number, hung up, and placed two other calls: one to the bell captain to have a bottle of scotch and a bucket of ice sent up to his room, the other to Dominic.

The next day at 11.30 Martin joined the throngs of pedestrians on the streets as he made his way uptown to Dominic's office. The crowds and the heavy flow of traffic overwhelmed him. He wasn't used to such enormous structures of concrete, steel and glass that jutted upward, like modern towers of Babel obliterating the sky.

In spite of the crush he managed to find Dominic's office. When he entered the building, he stopped at the cigarette counter to buy a package of Camels, and saw that his hand was trembling ever so slightly. He wasn't sure why. Maybe it had something to do with the guilt he felt about not going home. Maybe it was because he was having a tough time getting back into the world. Maybe it was because he had just passed a soldier who had lost both legs. For one terrible moment he was back in Europe, bending over some poor German bastard in a burned-over field outside of Rome. The kid must have been all of sixteen. A typical Aryan, hair the colour of corn, eyes blue and open in death. Martin had stood in horrified fascination as blood spewed out of the boy's mouth. For that moment Martin saw not a Nazi, but a human being lying on that blood-soaked earth.

The memory dissipated once the match burned down to Martin's fingers. He cursed under his breath and walked over to the elevator. He watched the dial as it paused at each floor coming down. Then the doors opened and he walked in. Suddenly all he saw was hands reaching out to push the buttons for the floors they desired. He started to reach for number 36, but it was already red. As he waited among the press of bodies, he felt a rush of claustrophobia. Since he had seen the pictures of the Jews they had packed, without food or water, into cattle cars, small spaces made him anxious. He was relieved when they reached his floor.

As he walked over to the receptionist he experienced a moment of panic. Dominic had been 4F. He hadn't experienced the war. Dominic . . . *Jesus Christ, what the hell were they going to talk about?* It was a million years since they'd said goodbye on graduation day.

Dominic had written to Martin about his experience with the draft board. After going through all the indignities of his physical, standing nude, legs spread, while being none-too-gently examined for haemorrhoids, the doctor found he had a heart murmur. Once he stopped reeling with happy delirium, he rushed to his own doctor, only to be told that the murmur was purely functional. He had every expectation of a long and healthy life. He had used the war years to build the successful advertising agency that Martin was now visiting.

'Martin,' said Dominic when his secretary brought Martin into his office. 'It's so Goddamn great to see you.'

They went out for a quick lunch, but neither man was able to say much about what he was thinking. That would have to wait for later. As they finished coffee Dominic said, 'We haven't even scratched the surface. Four years is a lot to catch up on. What are your plans for tonight?'

'I don't have any.'

'You do now. I'm taking you to dinner.'

They went to the Yale Club on Vanderbilt Avenue, just across from Grand Central. As Martin sipped the chablis, his mind kept drifting in a dozen different directions. He thought of college, of home, of Sylvia. He wondered how he would deal with her when he saw her. He was grateful when Dominic called his attention to the menu. 'Well, what do you feel like ordering?'

'I don't know. Why don't you choose. It all looks good.'

While Dominic placed the order, Martin glanced from table to table. He heard snips and bits of conversation. It all seemed like business as usual. Dammit, why couldn't he feel at ease? He wasn't the only one here tonight who had returned from the war.

'Like old times, huh, Martin?'

He looked at Dominic blankly. 'Sorry, Dominic. What were you saying?'

'You're really out of it tonight, old buddy. I was saying it was a little like being back at Yale. Like old times.'

'Nothing will ever be like old times. We were so naive. We really thought we had the world by a string.'

'Boy, it really got to you, didn't it? I've felt it since we met.'

'Well, dammit, Dominic. You can't go through four years of hell and act like it was a John Wayne movie.'

Dominic picked up his wineglass. 'It really must have been tough,' he said with an unprecedented amount of guilt.

Martin nodded. 'You might say that.'

Dominic lit a cigarette, looked at Martin, and said, 'You know, old buddy, you're evoking all kinds of memories tonight.'

'Really? Such as . . . ?'

'Such as I used to walk down Madison Avenue during the war and see everyone in uniform. They looked handsome with those shiny brass buttons. But I've got to tell you, old pal, I was damned happy that I was in civvies. You can call me anything you damned well please, but I celebrated the night I learned I was 4F. You know what I did? I called a model, who unlike most is really stacked, brought five bottles of the best champagne I could buy, went to her apartment, got plastered, and screwed her until dawn's early light. You have no idea how patriotic I felt the next day.'

Martin felt a flash of anger remembering the landing in Sicily, the fear that made his stomach hurt as he splashed from the landing craft to the beach, the icy water soaking him to the armpits. He had fallen on a boulder as he scrambled across the exposed sand and nearly knocked himself out. Somehow the pain had distracted him momentarily from the thought of mutilation or death . . .

'So you really had a ball during the war?' Martin said with ill-concealed bitterness.

Dominic knew he had sounded more glib than he felt. Much of the time he'd been embarrassed not to be in uniform, but he didn't know how to admit this to Martin. Instead he just said, 'It wasn't all that great, and I missed my friends. I thought about you a lot, buddy.'

Dominic began to cut his steak. They ate in silence for a few minutes. Then Dominic seemed to shrug off the feelings of discomfort that the talk of the war engendered. 'Look, Martin, I didn't plan to stay at home. But since the Lord saw fit to spare me, I made the best of the time that I had. I've established a thriving agency and it's only the beginning. What I'd really like is to have you join me. I know you were never that happy at your father's brokerage firm. But all that financial savvy would come in handy at the agency. I need you, Martin. You have an incredible understanding of business. And an ability to make things work. I'm good with the ideas, and the clients love me, but I'd make a lot more money if the agency were properly run. Give it a try, Martin. Come in with me.'

Martin played with the crumbs on the table. Finally he said, 'Thanks for the offer. Let me think it over.'

'You can't say yes because you're worried about upsetting your parents. You've slogged your way across Europe, but you never cut the umbilical cord. You've got to try making it on your own sometime, old buddy.'

Martin remembered his earlier debate with himself, his obligation to his parents and his desire to stay East and choose his own career. The more he thought about it, the more he saw that his whole life had been spent fulfilling obligations to his family, his religion, his country. But then he thought of the future. If he had sons wouldn't he want them to carry on the legacy Ephraim had fought so valiantly to bequeath?

Martin looked across the table at his friend. 'Most of what you say is right, Dom. But I think it's more involved. My great-grandfather fled the ghettos of Europe so his descendants could live in freedom. If he had stayed in France my parents and I might well have been shipped to one of the camps. I saw some of the survivors. Their faces will haunt me till I die. It's not just my parents I feel I can't let down. It's all those tortured men and women. Butchered by the Nazis. Right now it would be very hard for me to turn my back on my great-grandfather's legacy. Can you understand that?'

Remembering his own parents' tales of hardships suffered during the First World War, and the economic breakdown that followed, and their hopes for a better life in America, Dominic could not brush Martin's argument aside. 'Well, sure I can understand,' he said. 'I'm not going to say that what the Italians endured was as horrendous as the Holocaust, but dead is dead, and Italian mothers shed their tears.'

They both were silent. Finally Dominic said, 'I suppose this means you're going home.'

Martin nodded. 'Yes. I really don't have any choice. We owe them something, Dominic. We really do.' He paused for a long moment and thought about the house and the gardens bathing in the golden summer light. He could see himself silhouetted against the sky, that blue, languid California sky, as he dived off the board. 'And,' he added with a laugh born out of love and nostalgia, 'I can think of worse fates.'

In spite of his disappointment at not having persuaded his friend to stay, Dominic nodded. 'Touché.'

Chapter Nine

The first face Martin saw as he walked across the airfield was Sylvia's. She ran to him, her hair flying in the wind as she threw herself into his arms. She'd waited for this moment for so long. The pain of those four years was erased as she felt his arms around her. 'Oh, darling, Martin,' she said, kissing him. 'Dearest Martin. Thank God you're home.'

He was too filled with emotion to speak. Instead he took her hand and silently let her walk him back to Bess and Julian. As he held his mother close, he knew how hard the years had been on her and that he had done the right thing coming home.

'God must have heard my prayers,' she said. 'You're home. I can't believe it, but you're home.' She took his face in her hands and kissed him tenderly. Then she held him at arms' length. Smiling through her tears she said, 'I'm afraid you've lost weight.'

'Oh, stop fussing over him,' Julian said. 'Welcome home, dear boy.'

Martin embraced his father, saying, 'This is the only place in the world I want to be. I know that now.'

They walked out of the airport into the warm September afternoon. Martin looked up into the California sun and thanked God that he had had the sense to recognize his birthright. When he looked down he saw Edward bringing the silver-grey Rolls-Royce to a halt in front of them. The chauffeur got out and opened the back door. 'We've missed you, Martin. Welcome home.' Edward had been with the family since Martin had been very young. He remembered it was Edward who had taken him to the circus every year.

When they reached the Woodside Estate, Martin could scarcely believe he was there. He went from room to room with a strange sense of disbelief. It was as though he was seeing the house for the first time. The paintings seemed more brilliant, the flowers more beautiful. Martin walked upstairs to his room and closed the door. He looked at the snapshots still pinned to the bulletin board, the pictures of himself as a small boy. There was one of him standing at the rail of the *Matsonia* with his mother and father in the background. He remembered that day so well. It was the ship's maiden voyage to Honolulu. As he reached the edge of the bay that opened into the Pacific, Martin saw the horizon. He felt as if they were going to fall off the edge. He had been frightened until his mother spotted his pale face and reassured him that the world was round. His eyes wandered to the other pictures of happy events, picnics, tennis games, shots of himself and Sylvia. Suddenly he experienced a moment of fear. *That* Martin no longer existed. He had endured too much; the scars of his experience were deep.

He went to the bathroom, turned on the shower as hot as he could stand, and let the water pelt his body. Then he turned on the cold until he shivered. Getting out, he stared at the full-length mirror as he towelled himself vigorously. *My God, it's like looking into the eyes of a stranger*, he thought. Perhaps it was the surroundings of home that made him realize how much he had changed. He dressed hurriedly and made his way back downstairs to dinner.

He was glad that his mother had not made his homecoming a gala affair, inviting only Sylvia and her mother and father. As he looked around the table in the oak-panelled dining room, he realized that here nothing had changed. Conversation still revolved around politics — would Eisenhower try for the Republican ticket? — and the usual local gossip. Dinner, too, was the same formal affair. As he sat observing, Martin felt strangely alien.

As he lifted his napkin from his lap, Martin felt Sylvia's hand on his. He was chilled with guilt at her touch. He didn't love her in that way and he had no idea how he was going to be able to break away from her without hurting her. How could he do that to someone as tender and decent as Sylvia? And how could he not if only for her own sake? If only he hadn't gotten carried away that last night home.

If Sylvia was disappointed in his reaction to seeing her, she kept her thoughts to herself. She knew she had been too demonstrative when she'd welcomed him today. But how else could she have acted? She'd lived for that moment for four years.

When dinner was over, Martin and Sylvia walked out to the terrace and stood looking out at the gardens. Silently she turned and regarded his face. She was troubled by the haunted look in his eyes. She knew that he'd been through hell. If only he would allow her to reach out to him, to hold him. Finally she asked, 'What are you thinking about?'

Martin sighed. 'The past. We've changed, haven't we?'

'Yes.'

'Sylvia, I don't want to hurt you and yet I don't know how else to say this . . . '

'Just be honest, Martin.'

'Yes, but the truth can be cruel.'

'So can deception. Martin, I'm going to make this easy for you. I know you love me, but you're not in love with me, and that makes the difference between friends and lovers. I have no regrets about that night. Please believe me. If I had it to do over again, I would.' During the past four years she'd scarcely thought about anything except how she would make Martin fall in love with her. She had spent her days and nights fantasizing, but tonight she realized that to have Martin without his love was not worth it.

She knew Martin's vulnerability: his sense of loyalty and honour. She knew that if she pursued him now she could goad him into marriage. But she also knew that if she did she would ultimately lose even his friendship and she'd be left with nothing. 'Do you have a cigarette?' she said at last, deciding to let go gracefully.

He lit one for her, then one for himself.

'My parents didn't mention it at dinner, but I'll be going abroad. I'm tired of filling my time with silly charity work. There's a Jewish orphanage in London where they have brought many of the camp survivors. I've taken a job there.'

Martin knew he was responsible for this choice of self-imposed exile, yet he felt helpless to do anything about it. If he asked her to stay, what could he give her? 'When did you make up your mind about this, Sylvia?'

'Some time ago when I was waiting for the war to be over,' she listened to herself lie. She'd only made up her mind that moment, although she had known about the organization for several months.

The look in her eyes touched him so deeply that all the logic was replaced with pity. He reached out to her. 'Stay, Sylvia. Don't go.'

'For what?'

'I've just come home, Sylvia. Maybe after I've had a chance to reorganize my life, you and I can . . . '

'Work something out? Don't be silly, Martin.'

'Well, what you're doing may not work either . . . because it's for all the wrong reasons.'

'And you, dear Martin, want me to stay for all the wrong reasons. You think that maybe if you feel guilty enough it'll give you the courage to ask me to marry you. Well, that would be terrible, Martin. I love you too much for that.'

Martin took her hand and said, 'You're too special not to find someone who will really adore you.'

Tears flooded her eyes. 'Thank you very much for being that concerned about my future.' She turned, but Martin grabbed her arm.

'Sylvia, don't be upset. It's just such a difficult time . . . please, let's try.'

Her first impulse was to run, but she wanted Martin so badly, wanted to believe he needed her. Softly, she said, 'Are you sure, Martin?'

'I'm sure.'

She looked at him and then ever so slowly reached up,

put her arms around him, and kissed him.

Martin responded. He hadn't kissed a woman in a long time.

'I want you, Martin,' she whispered.

'Please . . . let's wait.'

Bess looked up as they entered the drawing room. 'Did you have a nice walk?'

'Lovely, simply lovely,' Sylvia answered.

Then Bess turned to Martin. 'You looked tired.'

'I am. I hope you'll forgive me if I go to bed.'

'Of course, darling.'

That night neither Martin nor Sylvia slept much. Lying in his old room, Martin tossed and turned until almost dawn. He simply couldn't make sense of his life. He wondered what had forced him to ask Sylvia to stay. Why did he feel such great guilt where she was concerned? Forget that he had slept with her once. This was the twentieth century. Lots of girls had lost their virginity during the war. No, the real guilt, the real feelings he sustained for Sylvia stemmed from a much earlier time, from their shared childhood. It was as if she too were part of Ephraim's legacy. He asked her to stay, quite simply, because he felt an obligation to protect her. He suddenly realized that Sylvia mattered to him more than anyone else. He began to wonder where affection for her ended and love began. Entwined with those thoughts was the love he felt for his mother. If he married Sylvia, his mother's joy would be supreme. Sylvia's devotion to her during his absence had been stressed by both his parents. Of course, he felt grateful, but gratitude after all wasn't love . . . or was it? Too weary to sort out these thoughts, he finally fell asleep.

Sylvia lay in her bed with thoughts much the same as Martin's. Martin could have let her go without so much as a word, but he had asked her to stay. Wasn't that a commitment? She knew that he loved her in his fashion, and suddenly the realization came to her that if she loved him, she had to make him aware that she was a grown woman and not the frenzied girl he'd left four years before.

Trembling, she slipped out of bed and put on her peignoir. Quietly opening her door, she padded softly down the hall to Martin's room. She opened his door and locked it behind her.

Martin bolted up in bed and called out, 'Who is it?'

'Shhh . . . . it's only me, darling.' Quickly she was in his arms, holding him, caressing him, pouring out her need and love for him.

But something in her ardour overwhelmed him. Without thinking he got out of bed, went into the bathroom, and looked at himself in the mirror. The man who stared back might have been a hundred years old. He knew that he had to go back to her. That he had wounded her cruelly.

Summoning the courage, he walked back and sat on the edge of the bed. Taking her hand, he said gently, 'I'm sorry. This has nothing to do with you. Coming home today was more than I was prepared for.'

The anger Sylvia felt was for herself. She had pushed Martin when he asked her to wait. Why hadn't she listened? 'I understand, Martin. Believe me, I understand. Can you forgive me?'

He was grateful the room was in darkness so she couldn't see his face. 'I'm not good for you, Sylvia. Something terrible happened to me in Germany and I haven't been able to come to terms with it.'

She started to cry. 'And I caused you to be more unsure of yourself than you were before. I really understand, Martin, and I'm sorry.'

'I'm not deserving of anyone like you.'

Sylvia got up, kissed him tenderly and, without a word, left the room.

In the morning, Bess was bewildered. 'I can't make any sense out of this at all,' she said as they sat at the breakfast table. 'Here, Martin, read Sylvia's note.'

He knew what was in it before she even handed it to him. Sylvia was leaving. It was her only salvation and Martin had never felt more self-hatred than he did at that moment.

*

Over the next few months Martin tried his best to readjust to civilian life. He went back to work at the brokerage firm and put in long hours, frequently coming home well after dinner. He found it too painful to face his mother across the table. She couldn't understand why he had let Sylvia leave after she had waited for him so patiently through the long war years. Martin couldn't explain any more than he could explain his occasional need for a night with one of the newly liberated girls he met. They had jobs, they had apartments, and many were happy to invite Martin to stay over. Good God, he deserved a little fun. But his mother's reproachful face tortured him.

Finally he decided that even though it would hurt his parents he had to get his own place in the city. He was right to have returned to San Francisco, to his family, and family business, but he never should have returned to the family home. He had made the break once and now would have to do it again. As gently as he could he told his mother he'd taken a furnished apartment at the end of Lombard Street on Russian Hill. It was in the Italian neighbourhood called North Beach, and Bess most vehemently disapproved, not because of the ethnic mix – the area bordered on Chinatown – but because it was incomprehensible that Martin could settle for something so outlandishly Bohemian.

As far as she was concerned, it made no sense even though Martin hadn't lived at home before Pearl Harbor. It was as though his years away had made his mother's possessiveness wax instead of wane; she almost cried when she saw 'that dreadful little cell' he had taken while they still owned the palatial apartment on Nob Hill. 'It's yours, Martin. Why don't you use that?' she said.

'Because it's not mine.'

'What do you mean by that? Of course it's yours.'

'Not really, Mother. It belongs to you and Dad.'

Bess was dumbfounded. 'You must forgive me, Martin, but whatever your father and I have is yours. Can't you understand that? I wouldn't think I'd have to explain. This whole thing is ludicrous.'

But it wasn't ludicrous from Martin's point of view. His parents' wealth made him uncomfortable. He could not forget the thousands of homeless still roaming Europe or forced to live in displaced persons camps. He couldn't reconcile their meagre circumstances with his own lavish ones. It was impossible for Martin to explain to his parents, but their lifestyle was too much for him. Martin could only say he needed his own place and Bess stopped arguing after he moved the last of his things from Woodside.

Martin hoped moving would help him pick up the pieces of his life, but he discovered that all he had changed was his address. He still worked for his father and in his mind was accepted by Julian only because he was his father's son. He had not earned his place in the world. He was a parasite, really. Everything had been handed to him on a silver platter. Unlike Dominic, he had never had a chance to find out what he could do on his own.

He lost the ability to evaluate his contributions realistically. Anyone else would have had to put in twenty years to achieve his salary. As the weeks passed, Martin became obsessed with his own unworthiness. The pressures became so great that he simply had to reach out.

Impulsively, he picked up the phone one day and called Dominic.

'What did I do to deserve this call?' Dominic asked.

'Well, I'm having some problems.'

'Really? I'd never have guessed from your letters.'

'I suppose I was trying to convince myself all I needed was time. That's why I didn't mention anything.'

'Okay. Well, what *is* wrong?'

Martin lit a cigarette. 'I don't know where to begin, so much has happened.'

'The beginning's always a good place.'

'This could take a long time . . . ' Martin said, trying to figure out exactly when things had started to go wrong.

'It's your dime. I've got all afternoon.'

'Thanks. Remember the night we sat at the Yale Club?'

'Right.'

'Well, I'm more confused about things now than I was then.'

'In what way?'

'Well, I feel like an automaton.'

'That doesn't tell me much. Is it possible you're fooling yourself, refusing to look at the problem and face it?'

There was a long silence. 'You're right. But I can't seem to articulate it. I keep swaying back and forth between obligations, love and loyalty. That's what makes all this so tough. I just can't seem to find the answers.'

'Okay, sort out the pieces. I mean, what's happened since?'

'Well, I think when I first got home I just needed to crawl back into the womb. I was glad to be living with my parents, working for my father. But for the last few months I seem to be getting more and more depressed.'

'I can hear that . . . go on.'

'Well, I sit in my huge plush office going through the motions, but nothing makes any sense. What I'm saying is, I never built any of it. It's all been handed to me. Do you see what I mean?'

'Up to a point, yes. Except, when Papa's a great success, he usually wants to pass that success on to his son.'

'I know. That's exactly the point. I don't feel comfortable with the idea. I don't really know what the hell I'm trying to say. Jesus, maybe I need a psychiatrist.'

'No, you don't, old buddy. Your feelings are understandable after what you've been through.'

'But for Christ's sake, I'm not the only one who went through it!'

'Well, in a sense everyone went through the war alone. Maybe I can verbalize it for you, Martin.'

'I wish to God someone could.'

'You're a man in search of his soul. You feel guilty because of all those starving kids you saw and their memory makes you ashamed you were privileged.'

'You're absolutely right. That's what I can't come to terms with.'

'Well, take my word for it. There are always going to be those who have and those who don't, and you're not responsible for the whole world. Everyone has to find their own salvation, and so do you.'

'And how do I do that?'

'You're not going to come to terms with your life in San Francisco, that's for sure.'

'Well, I know. But it gets down to owing once again, doesn't it?'

'I'm not insensitive to that, Martin, and I admire your loyalty. But you owe yourself too. Why don't you come to New York?'

Martin knew that he wanted to say yes, but how could he tell his father he was leaving? Everything Dominic said was right. 'I'll have to think about it,' Martin said at last.

'Don't take too long, old buddy. Those who procrastinate very often wake up in the morning to find themselves sullen old men. Disillusioned and disenchanted. Give yourself a break.'

'Yeah . . . well . . . how do I tell my father?'

'Just tell him, Martin. Nobody owns you. Just don't get bogged down with a lot of Jewish guilt. I was impressed with what you told me about your great-grandfather, but you have to remember that he went out on his own. Maybe that's what he was fighting for, to give you that right.'

Martin knew the rationale was not quite accurate. Ephraim's father had not built a dynasty for him to inherit. Still, it was nice of Dominic to try to give Martin the courage he needed to confront his father. 'Look, Dom,' he said, 'you're a good friend. I'll call you back in a couple of days. And thanks . . . '

'Don't mention it, old buddy. Now, are there any other problems we can solve tonight?'

There was a long pause. Then Martin told Dominic about Sylvia. He had never meant to hurt her, but now he elt he could never make up for the pain he'd caused her.

'Yes, but you didn't do anything,' Dominic said. 'It was unfortunate, the whole set of circumstances, but so far as you're concerned, Sylvia was hurt as much by the war as by you. Keep remembering that and one of these days you'll find a girl to really love. Now, don't forget, my offer still holds. I really need you in my business, Martin. And remember, people are more resilient than you think. Your father will get over it.'

Martin wasn't quite so sure as he held the silent receiver in his sweating palm. Finally, he replaced it on the cradle, got up and poured himself a stiff drink. Cutting the cord was never easy, but Jesus, he had to straighten out his life. He tried remembering that the next day when he drove down to Woodside to see his father.

Julian sat in the large wing chair, watching the flames dance in the fireplace, trying to understand what Martin was saying. He'd been unaware that his son was so unhappy. He had thought that Martin's adjustment after coming home had been more than admirable. Now he was upset he had been so insensitive to his son's needs. He got up and walked to the French doors and looked out on the garden. 'Life is really very confusing,' he said, his back towards Martin. 'It never works out the way one expects. You think you're building something you can hand down to your children and then you realize the things you built mean nothing to them.' Julian turned around and looked at his son. 'I suppose this is what they're calling the generation gap.' He sighed deeply. 'So be it. Your mother will be very disappointed about this, just as I am, but if this is what you think will fulfil your life, I'll not stand in the way.'

For a moment Martin almost gave in. He wanted to say, *Forgive me. I'm sorry I've hurt you and I'm not leaving.* But a voice within him warned, *You'll regret this for the rest of your life if you don't make the choice now.*

'Dad, I know how hurt you are and there's nothing I can say that will make you feel different. But I wish you'd understand. What you've built means a lot to me – more than you know. But I've got to build something myself. And I need time to find out who I am, not just what I've inherited.'

Julian sighed. 'I hope you find out, Martin, for your sake.'

Julian drew Martin to him, wishing he could turn back the clock to a time when Martin was a small child. He took the handkerchief from his back pocket and blew his nose. 'Well, I think we should go in and join your mother for dinner.'

This parting was almost more difficult than when he'd gone to war. Bess and Julian were unprepared for this, and Martin still felt as though he was abandoning them. He begged them not to come to the airport and, picking up his suitcases, followed Edward out to the car.

Looking back, seeing them standing forlornly on the front steps, he could only say, 'I'll call as soon as I get to New York.'

Chapter Ten

Martin soon settled into his life in New York. He found a small apartment and was fast absorbed in the hectic pace at the agency. He forgot much of the guilt he felt leaving his parents. He called them every week, but his thoughts and energy were caught up in the challenges of his new position.

Dominic had given Martin a free rein, and within a month he had secured the Aqua Baby Soap account, a subsidiary of Acme Chemical Company. It was a bonanza for a small agency and the coup gave Martin far more satisfaction than when he had brought McMillian Steel Company into the brokerage.

That evening Dominic and Martin celebrated. After popping a bottle of champagne, Dominic said, 'Cheers to you, old buddy. With my creativity and your business ability, we'll give the big boys on Madison Avenue a run for their money.'

Within six months, Martin's contributions were more than gratifying. He felt he was at last carrying his own weight and, better yet, he was beginning to like himself again. By the end of each day he found he was too tired to dwell upon the fact that his parents considered him a prodigal son.

In the evenings, when he returned to his apartment, he could relax in peace. There were no questions and no friends or relations on weekends; no one to make demands. He was his own man, independent to come and go as he pleased.

As his eyes wandered about the shabby little place, he thought of his mother. If she had disapproved of the apartment in San Francisco, she would have been horrified by this. But he didn't have to explain his choice of residence to anybody. Actually that wasn't quite true. Lately Dominic had begun to organize Martin's life outside office hours.

Dominic loved to have a good time. There wasn't an invitation he didn't accept. He had a bevy of girlfriends, but Martin's desire for women was much the same as when he returned from the war. A quick night out from time to time was all he wanted.

From Dominic's point of view, that wasn't enough for his friend. He believed Martin's spartan life was unhealthy. 'I'm going to a party Saturday night,' he said to Martin one Friday. 'You're invited, too, and this time your answer's going to be yes.'

'I really don't feel like it, Dom.'

'Did you ever think of going into a monastery?' Dominic laughed.

'What kind of a crack is that?'

'No booze. No broads. It's not normal.'

'Look, back off, Dominic. I have my share of broads.'

'When?'

'We don't live together. I don't tell you everything. I got out of my playpen when I left home.'

Dominic laughed and continued badgering. 'Listen, this is me you're talking to, old buddy. Remember when we used to go on the town in New Haven? Well, I haven't seen that glint in your eye for a long time.'

'Lay off, will you? I don't feel like lusting any more. I also got rid of my acne.'

'What is that supposed to mean?'

'I haven't met anybody I want to have an affair with.'

'Who's talking about an affair? Now, about Saturday night?'

'Okay, in self-defence, I'll go.'

'Great. You've got a date, Marty, old boy.'

Dominic knew from the smile on Martin's face that he had shaken him up. Well, a little baiting goes a long way.

When Martin walked into the party, it seemed as if half of Manhattan was gathered in the apartment. He looked around for Dominic, but there was no sign of him. People stood in small groups talking. He wandered through the rooms with a glass of champagne, hearing bits of conversation.

' . . . The best buy on the market is American . . . Did you hear the one about . . . And Becky said to Abie, besides, every time I do it, I get a headache.' Martin was bored. Who cared whether Becky had a headache before, during or after?

If Martin had found Dom he would have given him a piece of his mind. Here he was standing alone, not knowing a soul. He was ready to leave when Dominic finally made his way over to him. He was about to say, *Next time, don't do me any favours, butt out of my social life*, when he got a good look at the girl Dom had in tow. She was a knockout. Damned if she wasn't the most beautiful woman he'd ever seen. Dom had good taste, Martin grudgingly conceded, as Dominic said, 'Martin, I want you to meet Jennifer McCoy.

Jenny, this is Martin Roth. Now may you live happily ever after.'

Martin knew Dom had set him up. Jennifer McCoy was supposed to rescue Martin from a life of celibacy. How dare his *old buddy* think he couldn't get someone on his own? But with a girl who looked like Jenny, who would object? He was struck with an overwhelming desire. His sudden physical reaction to her was shocking, and a little frightening. His feelings intensified as he observed her more closely. Her hair was a rich, deep brown with golden glints, like sun on autumn leaves. She wore it brushed back like a lion's wild mane, unlike the sleek pageboys. Her wide-set eyes were amber with green flecks that sparkled like the facets of a gem. The delicate peach tones of her skin gave her face a subtle glow. She was dressed in a creamy beige two-piece silk dress, with a small turquoise-and-diamond brooch pinned near her shoulder. Her perfume was so discreet he could not identify it, but it conjured up delicious images. Her rouged lips parted as she smiled and said, 'Dominic likes to own his friends' lives.'

Martin smiled back. 'Yes, but that's part of his charm.'

Jenny's laugh was low and sensuous. 'I hope you won't think I'm too bold,' he found himself saying, 'but if you're free for the rest of the evening, how would you like to go someplace a little quieter?'

'I will think you're bold, but I am free.'

Any resentment he might have felt towards Dominic was overcome by fascination for Jenny. 'I'd love to be able to have a conversation with you without having to shout.'

'What?' she laughed. 'I can't hear you.'

'I said . . . how would you like to leave?'

'You don't waste any time, do you, Mr Roth?'

She wove through the crowd to retrieve her coat. Martin looked around, but couldn't find Dominic. Giving up the idea of saying goodnight, he led Jenny downstairs to the street.

'Why do people give parties like that?' Martin said as they stood on the kerb waiting for a taxi.

'Loneliness, I suppose.'

Martin looked at her from the corner of his eye. He knew Jenny McCoy was bright, but the depth of that simple statement impressed him.

'Now, where would you like to go?'

'If you're concerned about loss of hearing, there's a place on Fifty-sixth off Third that has candlelight, wine and soft music.'

Martin smiled. 'You're on.'

Sophie's Place was exactly what Jenny had promised. She looked enchanting in the candlelight as he observed her from across the table. The wine was mellow and the music soft.

As they danced to the sounds of 'Tenderly', he remembered when he had asked Sylvia, 'Does love really happen that quickly?' He knew he wasn't in love with Jenny yet, but the way he felt for her, so strangely and suddenly, was something he had never felt for any other woman.

When the music stopped, he led her back to the table, wondering why Dominic had been so generous, 'How long have you known Dom?'

'Well . . . ' she began. Jenny had graduated from Hunter College during the war. She had submitted her résumé to most of the advertising firms on Madison Avenue. What impressed her about the Dominic Gatti Agency was its energy and swift growth. It seemed a woman might actually make a career there. She had done very well and was happy, but when the Elmo Cosmetic Company offered her a top PR post, she couldn't resist the opportunity or the money. Dominic had been sorry to lose her but had not tried to stand in her way. The cosmetics industry was a place women could flourish. She hadn't heard from Dom, she told Martin, until last week. 'I don't know whether to tell you this or not,' she said.

'You can tell me anything.'

'I almost didn't go to the party tonight.'

'That's funny, neither did I.'

'Really, how did Dom coerce *you*?'

'He thought I was leading a monastic life.'

'Were you?'

'Well, according to Dom's standards, if you don't go to four parties a night, you're not having any fun.'

'That's our friend. He just told me I had to meet you. Need I say more?'

'No, but I'm certainly grateful for his concern.'

'Maybe you won't be so grateful after you get to know me.'

'I'll take that chance. How about tomorrow night?'

'I'm sorry, but I have to be in Chicago on business.'

He was disappointed. 'When will you be back?'

'Not till next Friday.'

'Does your firm send you away often?'

'When they're promoting a new line, yes.'

'Well, I guess I'll have to settle for that. Do you feel like dancing?'

Once again he was holding her in his arms, and they danced until the piano player went home.

When he brought her to the door of her apartment, they looked at each other for a long moment. He wondered if he should kiss her. She handed him the key and he opened the door. 'It's been a lovely evening, Martin,' she said.

'For me, too.'

As he started to walk towards the elevator she called out, 'Martin, I believe you have my key.'

He looked down at his palm, then burst out laughing as he handed it back to her. 'I don't know if this is according to Hoyle, but would it be rushing things, Miss McCoy, if I kissed you goodnight?'

'Yes, yes, it would be. Why not give it a whirl anyway.'

He took her in his arms and kissed her gently. 'Jenny,' he said, 'don't go to Chicago tomorrow.'

'You're not only rushing things, you're interfering with my livelihood. I have to be at Marshall Fields at eight o'clock Monday morning, but I'll be back Friday.'

He looked at her, then brushed the curls back off her face. 'Call me, will you?'

'I can't promise . . . If I have time, I will.'

'Make time. In fact, I'll pick you up at La Guardia.'

'Well, that's a deal. I'll call.'

After he had gone, she shut the door and leaned against it. *I think I like you a whole lot, Martin Roth. And I'd like to know more about what goes on inside your head.* The fascination for Jenny was not only that she'd found Martin very attractive, but that he was a Jew. He represented something forbidden. Growing up in Biloxi, Louisiana, she hadn't seen a Jew until she went to Hunter. Then she found them exotic and exciting. Until now she hadn't dated one, but Martin Roth heightened her senses. She went to bed wondering what it would be like to make love to him.

Monday morning Dominic stopped by Martin's office. 'Well, how did it go, old buddy?' Dominic said.

'What go?'

'Your date with the Queen of Sheba – with Jenny, of course.'

'Just as you planned. You're always on target, Dominic.'

'I take it you like her.'

Martin nodded. 'She's a very nice girl.'

'That's the best you can say? She's fabulous and you know it.'

'If you think she's that great, how come you were so generous?'

'Well, truth to tell, old buddy, I tried. But I couldn't score with that lady. How'd you make out?'

'Let me tell you something, Dom – you're beginning to sound like a yenta.'

'Sticks and stones . . . what did you think of her?'

'I'll let you know if I see her again.'

'I'm really shocked. I thought by now I would have heard the sound of the mating call. Okay, old buddy, you don't want to talk about it, we won't. Just tell me one thing. Did she turn you on?'

Martin stood for a long moment looking at Dominic and then smiled. 'Jenny McCoy would turn on the Sphinx.'

'Well, thank God. There's still hope for you, Martin, boy. I was beginning to worry.'

In the week to come, Martin found his thoughts kept turning to Jenny. Like a schoolboy with his first crush, he lay in bed at night fantasizing what she would feel like. The days dragged interminably and it was sheer agony when Friday came and she hadn't called. Every time the phone rang he lunged for it. By four o'clock he'd almost given up hope. Then, finally, the phone rang. It was Jenny. Controlling a sudden inclination to stammer, he said, 'How did your promotion go?'

'Wonderful.'

'That's good. What time does your plane arrive?'

'Well, my flight's been grounded. I should be in, give or take a few minutes, around seven-thirty.'

'I'll be there.'

Envisioning those long legs and the perfect body, he felt a stirring in his groin and realized it would be a while before he could get up. That hadn't happened to him since high school, but damn, it was a great feeling.

He arrived at the airport half an hour early and was frantic with expectation when he saw her coming down the ramp with her long elegant stride. His eyes took in the tawny mane of hair, the deep amber eyes. Composing himself as best he could, he said casually, 'Welcome home. Where would you like to go to dinner?'

'Surprise me.'

But she wasn't at all surprised when they went back to the same little restaurant they'd gone to the night of the party.

As she sat across the table looking at Martin over the rim of her wineglass, she admitted to herself how much she had missed him. Martin had not been the only one plagued by fantasies. Jenny had fallen asleep and woken up each day she was in Chicago thinking about him. She knew she was going to have an affair with him. Had he pressed, she'd have let him carry her off to her bedroom that first night; nothing would have prevented her from losing her virginity. Yet, till now, her discipline had less to do with her strict Catholic upbringing than the fact that she hadn't met anybody who had aroused her to the point where she felt it was worth risking purgatory. Now, dammit, the one man she wanted to give herself to had to be a Jew. Mother Superior obviously would have instructed Jenny McCoy to exorcise Martin Roth from her thoughts. And even Jenny was afraid Martin was wrong for her, but looking at him, she suddenly didn't care.

Jenny felt a sense of unreality. His nearness, the sound of his husky voice, sent soft flutters through her.

'What would you like to eat?' Martin asked, bringing her back down to earth.

'What? Oh . . . I . . . why don't you order for both of us.'

He gave the order to the Italian waiter in what was apparently flawless Italian.

She was impressed. 'I didn't understand a word, but I know your Italian must be impeccable. How did you learn that?'

'A little something I picked up when I was touring the war zones of Palermo.' Martin laughed. 'The army paid for that vacation as well as the lessons in Italian.'

There was something sobering in his voice that made Jenny uncomfortable.

Then he smiled and they both began talking at once. Jenny knew she was acting like a sixteen-year-old on her first date. She kept picturing him in her arms, in her bed. His Italian had impressed her. It had taken four years after leaving Biloxi for her to learn to speak English correctly. Now she felt intimidated by his sophistication. She sat with a fixed smile, answering his questions about Chicago with one-word answers. What a departure from the self-assured Jenny of a week ago. Tonight she was subdued, and just seeing Martin made her feel unsure. She was going to try like hell not to let him know it, but she knew she wasn't in his league. He had class written all over him and she still thought of herself as poor white trash. But she'd made a

102

life, she reminded herself. Working since she was twelve at the local soda fountain, ushering at the Bijou Theatre, and at fourteen moving into Cora Belle Collingworth's anteroom so she could be at her beck and call and wash her fanny during all those years of her supposed illness. Illness – she was a drunk, that's all, and Jenny thought back to the times Cora Belle had the screaming meemees and slapped her around until she was black and blue. She'd come a long way since then, but that's what she'd had to go through to earn the money that got her through Hunter College. Well, Jenny said to herself, she might not have been so classy then, but no one would know it now.

Remembering her long struggle restored her self-esteem, and by the time the waiter brought dinner, she had recovered her spirits and her voice.

'Has New York always been home for you?' she asked.

'No. San Francisco. And you?'

That was always a delicate question for Jenny. 'Biloxi – Louisiana as opposed to Mississippi.'

'Oh? For some reason you don't seem like someone from the South. You have no accent for one thing. But even aside from that, I don't see you as a Southern belle.'

'Really? And what is a Southern belle supposed to be like?'

'I don't know. Pampered, spoiled?'

'You think that's only a Southern trait? Truth is, Mr Roth, there's a little Scarlett in every lady.' Jenny laughed, but Martin realized that there was a great deal more to Jenny than appeared on the surface.

To break the mood he asked her to dance. After they sat down again, Martin kept staring at her. In spite of her sophisticated manner, there was an air of vulnerability about Jenny. And although nothing about her seemed contrived, Martin sensed something studied about her poise. 'Jenny, tell me about yourself,' he asked.

'What would you like to hear?' she said, looking totally enchanting in the candlelight.

'I'd like to know about your childhood.'

She looked at him for a long moment. 'Well,' Jenny said, starting slowly, 'it's not a very original or very pretty story.'

'I'd still like to know, that is if you want –'

'To tell? I suppose I don't mind. Well, talk about living on the other side of the tracks, the McCoys certainly did. When I was a little girl, I used to sit on the park bench in the town square and watch the elegant ladies coming out of the Bonton Department Store. Well, I thought they were elegant at the time. Anyway, they used to carry all kinds of packages out to the black chauffeurs, and at Christmas, I used to dream about all the things I wanted. I'm sure it was then that I made up my mind that I was going to be rich and I was going to be a lady. You sure you want to hear all this, Martin?'

'Please, I want to know more.'

'All right. Maybe my ambition was greater than that of most kids my age. Even then I knew that life was what you made of it. No matter what the cost, you had to salvage yourself. I suppose that's what I did.' Suddenly she stopped. 'Why am I telling you all this?'

'Because you know I'm interested in you. Please go on.'

'Okay. Well, my mother drank too much because she couldn't accept herself or life. She died five years ago, not from cirrhosis of the liver as the death certificate stated, but by committing suicide day by day until she finally drowned herself in the bottle.' Jenny hesitated. 'Do you have a cigarette?'

He lit one for her.

'My father ran away from my mother when I was five. Strange thing is, I never really hated him. Don't ask me why. I just felt that he was going to come back. I dreamed about it, really. Well, anyway, I saved money from the time I was able to earn. I'd always known that I was going to New York, and I had a teacher in the eighth grade who became my mentor. She told me I could do anything I wanted with an education. She was the one who really inspired me. Well, when my mother died, the bank sold the small house we lived in and put the money in trust. Then I took it out and went to college in New York. So now you know the happy saga of Jenny McCoy.' She looked at Martin as though studying him.

It was the honesty in her eyes that impressed him most. It took real courage to talk about her past, and what he felt now for Jenny was more than just physical attraction. He wanted to protect her, to make up for her past.

'Well, you know about Jenny McCoy. What about Martin Roth?' she said.

Since he didn't want to discuss the war, his relationship with Sylvia, the areas of disagreement with his mother and father, it left him with little to talk about except his happy days at Yale with Dominic.

When he'd finished, Jenny suspected there was much he was leaving out. 'So why did you leave your father's firm?' she said.

'I wanted to make it on my own. Find out who I was.'

'And what have you found so far?'

'That I'm happy to be here at this moment with you . . . Now how would you like to take a walk?'

'I'd like that.'

The night was clear and cool and they walked without speaking. It seemed to Jenny that more words would be superfluous after all they'd said tonight. It wasn't until they reached 73rd and Lexington that Martin broke the silence. 'I live in that building,' he said.

She made no comment and they kept walking. From time to time they stopped to look at the displays in store windows, but much too soon she found herself in front of her own building.

For an awkward moment she stood silently looking at him. She wanted Martin and knew she was going to have an affair with him, but she wasn't ready quite yet. She was saved from finding an excuse not to invite him up when he asked, 'Are you busy tomorrow night?'

Knowing that magic moment was yet to come, she answered with a strange sense of relief, 'No, I'm not busy.' Then she found herself being drawn into his arms and gently kissed.

'This has been the best evening I've had in a long time.'

'Thank you, Martin, it was for me too.'

'Sleep tight,' he said. Then he kissed her again and walked off.

Upstairs, she closed the door to her apartment and, without turning on the lights, walked into her bedroom and inexplicably began to cry. She knew she wouldn't be able to hold out much longer, but the thought of the confessional on Sunday terrified her.

After an almost sleepless night, Jenny was awakened from a light doze by the phone. As soon as she heard Martin's voice, her fears fled.

'I just wanted to say hello,' he said.

'Hello.'

'What would you like to do tonight?'

Go to the moon with you, she thought, but said only, 'Whatever you feel like.'

I'd like to take you to bed. 'Do you like Mamma Leone's?'

I could skip dinner. 'That sounds wonderful.'

'Great. I'll pick you up at eight.'

By eight o'clock, Jenny was a nervous wreck. In the last hour she had changed five times and was still not sure she was wearing the right thing, because she wasn't entirely sure what Martin liked, what kind of woman pleased him. For some reason she could not fathom, she settled for a demure lilac chiffon that enhanced the delicate colouring of her skin and made her amber eyes glow. She was studying herself in the mirror when the bell rang.

Afraid to ask him in, she grabbed her purse and wrap, opened the door, stepped into the hall. He kissed her without restraint.

'You look enchanting,' Martin said.

Jenny smiled. 'You certainly know the right thing to say to a lady.'

He took her by the arm and before she knew it they were sitting side by side in the taxi.

At Mamma Leone's the maître d' showed them to a quiet table. Their enormous meal went almost untouched. Course after course went back after just a few bites. Jenny knew Martin was as impatient as she was for them to be alone. Neither of them ordered dessert. Jenny felt as if she were poised at the top of a roller coaster.

Outside in the cab Martin said, 'There's a place on Ninety-fourth that plays marvellous music. Would you like to go?'

'If you like,' Jenny said, looking down.

Martin hesitated. 'Well, actually I'd prefer my place.'

'So would I,' Jenny said honestly. She was happy that Martin hadn't suggested her apartment, since her landlady acted like a warden: no men, no booze, no loud noises, no animals, no fun.

As they entered Martin's building, Jenny was conscious only of the pressure of his warm hand on hers. She didn't notice the doorman or the click of their footsteps across the marble hall. She moved as if in a dream.

When they got upstairs she snapped back to reality and looked around her. Martin's apartment surprised her. The room was in total disarray. There were newspapers strewn around the floor, a stale cup of coffee and a bagel sitting on the coffee table, ashtrays full of butts. Living with a drunken mother who had no sense of order, Jenny had grown up with an abhorrence of clutter. For a swift moment she was annoyed that he hadn't bothered to tidy up, knowing he was going to bring her home, but then she decided he was just hopelessly messy.

Martin went to the refrigerator, took out a bottle of champagne, and brought it back with two glasses. He pried the cork off gently, but the fluid still spurted up like a geyser. Quickly he filled her glass. She watched as the bubbles danced, then looked up at him. Taking the glass from her, he placed it on the table and took her in his arms. He kissed her gently, then with more urgency. She thought that if this was a dream, she didn't want to wake up. When he sensed her response, he leaned over and turned off the lamp and in the darkened room he stood for a moment with his hands cupping her face. Then he took her into his arms and kissed her passionately.

Without speaking he unbuttoned the back of her dress and slowly removed her clothing. Jenny heard herself gasp as he picked her up and laid her on the couch. Soon he was beside her, holding her, caressing her, exploring her body as gently as possible. Lying beneath him, feeling him inside her, the pain soon became a joy. And for him, it was a moment of surprising sweetness, different from any other he'd known . . .

For a long time afterwards he continued to hold her. No one had ever evoked the passion and the fire that Jenny ignited. For the first time since the war he felt whole again.

'Oh, Jenny,' he whispered, 'you're simply wonderful.'

And she felt wonderful. But she knew the next day was Sunday and she would have to face her priest. Without a word she slipped out of bed and started to dress.

Martin was totally taken off balance. 'Hey, what do you think you're doing?'

Without looking at him she answered, 'My landlady will notice if I don't go home.'

'Please don't go.' Even as he spoke, he was surprised by his words. He'd never asked a girl to stay. But then he'd never met anyone who affected him like Jenny McCoy. He only knew that he wanted her to be with him in a way he had never wanted another human being. 'Please stay, Jenny.'

She picked up her satin slip and put it on. Martin watched her in the light from the table lamp. She seemed so small and fragile. 'I can't stay, Martin.'

Martin got out of bed, walked over to her, and tried to take her in his arms, but Jenny backed away. 'What's wrong, Jenny?'

'I feel terrible. I guess I'm ashamed. I must have made a fool out of myself.'

He took her gently by the arms. 'You have nothing to be ashamed of.'

'Yes, I do. A lady doesn't act the way I have tonight.

Where I come from, they'd call me a bitch in heat.'

'For God's sake, don't say that, Jenny! Don't do this to yourself. Wanting to share with someone isn't wrong. It's the most natural thing in the world. Don't cheapen what happened between us.'

Jenny's problem was that she didn't see the act of love as a beautiful and wonderful thing. She had been conditioned to think that any woman who gave herself to a man outside of marriage was a slut. For the moment she couldn't face her sense of guilt, and Martin's very presence deepened her remorse. With no further explanation, she finished dressing.

'I wish you wouldn't feel this way. I wish there was something I could say that would tell you how wonderful I think you are.'

Jenny scarcely heard as she watched Martin dress.

It was three in the morning when Martin told the cab to pull up in front of the brownstone where she lived. When she saw that Martin was about to get out with her she said, 'Thank you, Martin, but I prefer to go in alone.'

'Of course. I understand,' he said, kissing her. 'I'll call tomorrow.'

She merely nodded and ran inside. She felt a wave of loneliness sweep over her as she started up the stairs. To her horror she met her neighbour, who was taking his dog out for a walk. He looked at her as though he could see the colour of her underwear. Her face turned crimson when he said, 'Hello there. How did Cinderella make out at the ball tonight?'

She mumbled something under her breath and fumbled for her keys in her purse. Once inside she leaned against the door and angrily wiped away her tears. She ripped off her dress and sat on the edge of the bed, blowing her nose and wiping her eyes. *Oh God, how can I go to mass this morning*?

She went to the bathroom and let the water run in the tub. She lathered herself with a lavender-scented soap, then lay back and thought back over the evening. A million contradicting emotions cluttered her mind. In spite of herself, she was suddenly frightened Martin wouldn't call her again, especially after the way she'd acted.

Jenny got out of the tub and dried herself with a towel. Then she put on her nightgown and got into bed. Soon her eyes closed and she fell asleep. Two hours later she woke with a start, terrified she might have slept through early mass.

Quickly, she jumped out of bed, ran to the bathroom, brushed her teeth, slipped into a sweater and a wool skirt, and hurried down the hall.

She was breathless by the time she ran up the steps of St Patrick's Cathedral. She went through agony realizing she couldn't stand in the line waiting for communion. Even if she had gone to confession, she wouldn't have been able to participate; her sin had occurred after twelve that night. Kneeling, she watched the priest as he took the wafer and placed it on the tongue of the first parishioner. She was filled with her own need for redemption.

Stealthily she walked down the aisle and out of the cathedral. Sighing, she walked along the street until she found a coffee shop a few blocks away where she ordered tea and toast. She tried reading the Sunday paper but found that she could not concentrate. Martin Roth filled her thoughts. Purgatory and salvation seemed to weigh in the balance as she visualized him lying in his bed, his thick black hair in disarray, his blue eyes shut in sleep. In her fantasy she saw him getting out of bed, showering, having coffee. She pictured him deciding to go out, leaving the apartment. Leaving the bed unmade, coffee cup unwashed.

Why couldn't she stop thinking about him? There would be another penance to pay at confession when she would have to admit that she was still filled with lust and passion.

She got up, leaving much of the toast and tea untouched, paid the check, and walked for hours before returning to her apartment.

Sitting on the edge of the bed, she stared out the window.

110

God, how lonely Sundays were, particularly this Sunday. Martin had aroused feelings that she had never known. If this wasn't love, she wondered what the pain of the real thing would be like. How could anyone stand it? Damn him. He had penetrated all the protective walls she'd erected since coming to New York.

Desperate to speak to someone, she tried several of her girlfriends, but they were out. She even called Dominic but again there was no answer. Close to tears, she realized that Martin hadn't even tried to call. Except for the morning she had been home all day. Jenny felt abandoned, used. How was she going to face the rest of this evening alone? She sighed deeply and decided that even sitting in a darkened movie theatre would be better. Slowly, she got up, took her purse, and locked the door behind her.

The moment Martin got to his apartment he put down his golf clubs and phoned Jenny. The line was busy. He kept trying every few minutes, but whoever she was talking to was certainly long-winded. When he finally rang through, Jenny was only a few feet down the hall, but by the time she reached her apartment and grabbed up the receiver, the caller had hung up. *It had to be Martin, it simply had to be.* Sitting on the edge of the bed, she debated whether or not to call him. At the very same moment, Martin was thinking: *Damn, first it's busy, then no answer. She must have gone out for the evening.* Well, he was going to do the same thing.

By the time Jenny summoned up the courage to call his number, he was in the elevator. *It must not have been him after all*, she decided.

Monday night Martin worked in his office until eleven o'clock, sending out for sandwiches and coffee. By the time he came up for air, he realized it was too late to call Jenny.

On Tuesday he called Elmo Cosmetics only to be told that she had gone to upstate New York and that they didn't think she'd be back until late. Martin called her every half hour from six to nine-thirty, but got no answer. *Dammit, she must have gone out on the town again*, he thought sullenly. *She seems to live a very social life.*

Jenny arrived home at nine-forty – just ten minutes after Martin had hung up for the last time.

That night she slept badly. Why hadn't he called? *Face it, Jenny, you were a one-night stand.* She was hurt, but she vowed not to call him under any circumstances. She'd made a fool of herself once, that was enough. More than enough. Oh, if only she had clung to the teachings of the Church, she would still have her virginity and her pride. Well, if she ever went beyond a casual date with another man, she would make him suffer as she was doing now.

On Wednesday Martin was out of town negotiating a new account, and he became so involved with the client, he didn't get home till midnight. *Dammit, too late.* He set his alarm for six. He was going to reach Jenny if it killed him. At six-fifteen, Jenny picked up the ringing phone. 'Hello?'

Trying to keep his voice even, he said, 'Hello is *right* . . . do you know I've been trying to get you since Sunday night?'

Jenny's hand began to shake. All those dreadful things she had thought. 'I'm so sorry – but did you call my office?'

'Yes, I did.'

'I didn't get any messages.'

'I didn't leave any since every time I called you at home you never answered. I just thought maybe you'd be too busy to return my calls.'

'Oh, Martin, I wasn't all that busy. In fact, I wasn't busy at all. If only you had left a message.'

Martin was about to tell her how jealous he'd been. 'I guess it *was* pretty foolish not to leave a message,' he said. 'Are we still friends?'

She laughed nervously. 'Still friends.'

'In that case, I'd like to take you to dinner tonight.'

'I'd love that, too, but it will have to be a short evening.'

'Why?'

'I have to go to Albany to work with a department store buyer.'

'I'll pick you up at seven-thirty.'

'Can we make it six?'

'Sure.'

Jenny smiled as she hung up the phone.

At dinner they talked about the office, the weather, the food. It was as if they each felt too vulnerable to explore their real feelings. When they finished coffee Jenny looked at her watch and said apologetically, 'I hate to end the evening, but it's almost nine.'

'Can't we even go out for a walk?' he said, annoyed.

'Well, I did say it was going to be an early evening. I really have to work on my presentation.'

'Oh, sure. Well, what are you doing Saturday night?'

She hesitated. 'I'll be in Bar Harbor this weekend.'

'Bar Harbor! That's a summer resort. What would they do with make-up there?'

She smiled. 'Buy it. That's just the market we want to go after.'

He couldn't believe what she was saying. Maybe God was punishing him for having lied to his mother when she asked if he was involved with anyone. Or maybe he was taking too much for granted, expecting her to be at his beck and call. 'Do you really have to go? I mean, this weekend?' he asked, trying to keep the hurt out of his voice.

'Of course I do, Martin. It's my job. And my career is as important to me as yours is to you.'

'So when did you say you were leaving?'

'I'm taking the six-thirty flight tomorrow.'

He sighed. 'Oh . . . well, I'll drive you to the airport.'

'You're very sweet.'

'That's me. Used to be an Eagle Scout, youngest in the troop, and if you ever stay around long enough I'll show you my good-conduct medals.'

Jenny heard the pique in his voice, but she didn't know what to do. The next day she worked longer than expected with a cosmetic buyer from Macy's, and by the time the session was over she was a complete wreck. When she looked at her watch she was terrified that Martin would have gotten impatient and given up waiting for her.

She got to the street just in time to see Martin driving off. He must have been around the block a dozen times, since it was the height of the rush hour and no parking was permitted. Anxiously glancing at her watch, she prayed that he hadn't given up and gone home. After what seemed an eternity she recognized his car inching back down the block. When he reached the kerb in front of her she hastily opened the door and slid in.

'Now you know why I take taxis instead of my car,' he said, impatiently grabbing the suitcase and throwing it on the back seat.

'I'm awfully sorry, Martin, but I couldn't get away from the buyer. And I couldn't get a message to you.'

'It's *okay*,' he said, but his tone implied it was not and they fell into an uncomfortable silence.

The traffic going out of Manhattan moved at a crawl and as Jenny looked at the clock on the dashboard she asked, 'Do you think we'll make it?'

'Who knows?' he said tightly. 'It probably takes less time to fly to Bar Harbor than to get to the airport this time of day.'

Jenny was getting more nervous in silent frustration at the slow-moving cars and trucks. When at last they arrived at LaGuardia they drove around and around the parking lots until they finally found a spot. Carrying Jenny's suitcase, Martin took her by the arm and the two ran through the crowded terminal, arriving at United's waiting area just in time to watch Jenny's plane taking off.

She looked at Martin on the verge of tears. Martin had never been able to stand seeing a woman cry. He felt so sorry for her. She seemed incapable of using tears as a ploy; she was exactly what she appeared to be: a lovely young woman whose tough childhood had tended to harden her. 'Let's see if we can get a later flight,' he said.

114

'This is the last one.'

'We'll try another airline.'

'Same thing. Bar Harbor, Maine, isn't the crossroads of the world. I don't know what to do,' she said, almost beside herself. 'My job is so important to me, Martin.'

'Look, you can make a phone call tomorrow morning and explain. This is an act of God, Jenny.' He spoke with quiet concern, but in truth he was not disappointed by the turn of events.

'Well, Martin, maybe I can get a flight for tomorrow morning.'

'Okay, Jenny. Let's try.' But once again his spirits were lifted. He knew the gods were on his side when the airline clerk said, 'There are no flights to Bar Harbor till Monday.'

On the way back to Manhattan, Martin had one hand on the steering wheel and the other on Jenny's knee. He drove into his garage and asked, 'Do you feel hungry?'

'Not really.'

'Well, what do you feel like?'

Confused, she said to herself. *As if events were conspiring to send me back into Martin's bed.*

'What do you feel like doing?' Martin asked again.

'Well, I think I'd like to go back to my place, get rid of my suitcase, and freshen up a bit.'

'Why bother? My apartment is across the street. You can wash up there and then we can decide.'

He took her hand and guided her across the street and up to his apartment. She sat on the couch exhausted, and let her eyes wander around the room. She looked at the pictures of Martin's mother and father in their large silver frames. Jenny wondered what it must have been like to be born into a family like that – to have lived in the apparent style that they did. She glanced at the picture of Martin as a little boy standing with his parents in the gardens of a luxurious Riviera hotel. Then she took in the disordered apartment. Well, it was understandable. He must have been used to maids picking up after him.

'What would you like?' Martin asked, interrupting her thoughts. 'I have champagne on ice.'

To get me high enough to go to bed with you, she thought cynically. 'I think I'd like sherry if you have it.'

He poured a sherry for her and a scotch and soda for himself.

As she sat listening to the soft music on his phonograph she began to relax. Martin handed her the sherry, then sat down next to her and raised his drink in a silent toast. She sipped slowly and sighed. 'You know, the nicest thing about this place is your view.'

'I know. I love it this time of day,' he said looking out at the fading sunset.

As though speaking to herself, she said, 'When I lived at home I never ever noticed a sunset . . . ' She took a sip of sherry. 'But this really is beautiful.'

'So are you.'

'Am I really?'

'Why, do you have any doubts?'

Jenny reddened and turned away. 'I don't think of myself that way. I don't think I'm pretty at all, despite what people tell me. It's all very confusing.'

'In what way?'

'Well, sometimes I feel like a store mannequin, not a person.'

He never would have guessed the insecurity that lay behind Jenny's charm and beauty. Under her sophisticated façade lay the Jenny who had arrived in New York from a broken home in Biloxi. Poor Jenny. He hoped he would always be able to protect her. Then he caught himself. He could never have a permanent relationship. She was Catholic. She came from a different world and anyway, he had just met her.

He got up abruptly and switched the soft music to something more discordant. As he sat down again he said, 'You must be starving.'

'I'm not, but I'm sure you are.'

'A little. Where would you like to go?'

116

'You decide. But if you don't mind, I'd like to wash up first.'

'Sure.' Martin sat in the living room. The light was fading and Martin watched, tired of the view. He felt comfortable here. In fact, Jenny was shaking up his very orderly life. He shrugged off an uneasy premonition and reached in the closet for a clean shirt, tossed it on the chair, and stripped off the old one. The door to the bathroom was open and he could see Jenny combing her magnificent head of hair.

Overwhelmed with desire, he took her in his arms. They emerged from the bathroom and he kissed her without restraint. Their lips and tongues met in breathless longing. He undressed her quickly with an impatient eagerness. Then they were lying together, their bodies clinging, and suddenly everything was forgotten except for the building hunger of their lovemaking. The climax left them mutually breathless. Martin had never been caught up so completely in the act of love. And the difference was Jenny. Reluctantly he rolled onto his back, then drew her to him and put his arms around her.

'I know it's selfish of me,' he said, 'but I'm happy, damned happy, that you missed the plane.'

'I'm not – not about that. I'll die if they don't put in that line.'

They lay in silence. Martin trailed his hand along the curves of her body. 'How would you like Chinese food?'

She smiled. 'That would be marvellous.'

'There's a terrific Chinese restaurant that delivers.' He reached over, took the phone book. 'Here it is,' he said. 'Do you like almond duck?'

'Yes, sure, but order what you like. I'm no expert.'

'You trust me?' he asked. They both knew he was speaking about more than Chinese food.

'Well, I trust you, Martin, but I'm not sure I trust myself. You know what I'm doing is terribly wrong, don't you?'

'No, I don't know anything of the kind, Jenny.' He hadn't spent four years with Dominic not to understand Catholic guilt. 'Would you feel quite this wicked and guilty if I weren't a Jew?'

'Yes, yes, of course I would.' But Jenny knew she wasn't telling the whole truth. If Martin had been Catholic they could at least be planning marriage. As it was, she would probably never be able to expiate her sin.

She turned to Martin, whose words seemed to confirm her fears. 'I don't want to feel guilty.'

'Look, Jenny, we're just two human beings who love each other. But we've both been through a lot and we've each just begun to find ourselves. I don't know what the future will bring. I can't make promises, but if every time you see me I make you feel as if you're headed straight for hell, maybe we should break this off now.' Martin walked stiffly to the window and stood with his back to Jenny, who was overcome with tears.

Suddenly her love for him became so all-encompassing that she didn't care about anything else. Not the priests, not her mother's warnings, not even the Church itself.

'Martin, would you like me to stay?' she asked.

He thought for a long moment, then turned and looked at her. Of course he wanted her to stay. He didn't quite know what he felt for her, but he wanted her to stay. 'Only if you want to, Jenny,' he said.

'Yes, I want to.'

'You're sure?'

'I'm sure. But may I ask you one question, Martin? How do you feel about my being a Catholic?'

'I feel that you're a desirable woman,' he said. He had told her she could walk away, but he hadn't told her that if she stayed he would marry her. 'If you feel, in all honesty, that we can be friends as well as lovers, and just try to take what the other has to give, I think we could make it, Jenny. Is that possible for you?'

The more she thought about it the more she believed that Martin's feelings were deeper for her than he realized. It wasn't the things he'd said, but the things he had left unsaid. If he had wanted to, he could have sent her away. Maybe if she stayed he would accept her beliefs. Certainly he seemed less of a Jew than she was a Catholic. She was the one who felt the conflict. Like most women, Jenny was convinced love could conquer all.

She looked across the room at Martin and said, 'Do you think you could get my suitcase?'

He hesitated only for a moment. 'Sure. I'll have one of the doormen come up and get the car keys.'

While they waited, Martin put on his robe. When he heard the doorbell ring, he opened and handed the doorman his keys with the instructions. Then he went into the kitchen for the champagne. 'What shall we drink to, beautiful Jenny?'

'To friends?'

'Yes, and lovers too.'

The next two days were filled with small pleasures. Jenny and Martin did all the ordinary things people do on weekends in the city, but just being together made everything exciting. They bicycled through Central Park, stopping for hot dogs and ice cream cones. They rolled on the grass like two silly children. They strolled through the Museum of Modern Art, wandered down Fifth Avenue to the Public Library, and raced each other up the steps, collapsing at the top, arms around each other, laughing and kissing at the same time. They walked down the crooked streets of Greenwich Village. The whole city seemed to take on a new dimension.

On Saturday evening they shopped at an Italian grocery and Jenny cooked. Then they went to bed and Jenny shut out all thoughts of confession and sin. On Sunday she fixed breakfast while Martin showered. Setting the breakfast tray on the coffee table, she called to him, 'Come and get it while it's hot.'

He poked his head out of the bathroom and grinned through the lather on his face. 'It will always be hot,' he assured her.

She laughed. 'The scrambled eggs, you idiot.'

When he returned from the bathroom, he slid into the

bed, pulling the sheet up to his naked waist, and Jenny placed the tray over his knees. Patting her side of the bed, he said, 'Boy, to look at you one wouldn't believe you could boil water.'

'It just goes to show you can never judge a cook by its cover.'

'Well, you're a genius. That pasta last night was fantastic. No kidding, a work of art.'

'I have many hidden talents.'

'It's okay to keep them hidden, but not from me.' He reached over to draw off her robe and she settled next to him, knowing that when it was over it would be too late for her to go to mass. Afterwards he put the tray on the floor and they read the Sunday *Times*. *It seems so natural, as if we were married*, Jenny thought, and suddenly she wanted to marry Martin more than anything in the world. She knew the relationship was getting stronger, and she knew instinctively that he was more involved than he had planned. The physical part was fantastic – feeling his lean, taut body next to hers was ecstasy, but there was so much more to the relationship than that.

Even now, as they lay in each other's arms with the *Times* strewn on the floor and the sheets rumpled at the bottom of the bed, she wanted to know more about his childhood. She listened as he told her about growing up with a wonderful but overly protective mother. She thought about the irony of it all. Martin's mother being overly protective and hers not giving a damn.

'Martin,' she said, 'remember the first night we met? I would never have thought then that I would have fallen in love with you. But I have.'

She waited for his answer. As he looked at her and brushed her hair back against the pillow, fanning it about her head, he smiled with pleasure at the sight of her. That was his answer, and right now it was enough for her.

After Martin drove her back to her apartment that evening, she stood in the centre of her room, feeling suddenly sad and alone. Lovers, she reminded herself,

120

didn't live together like married people. But, dammit, it wasn't going to be this way forever. Martin was going to marry her. She knew it. He simply had to. She took her mauve silk robe out of her suitcase and hung it in the closet. She wondered what Martin was doing at that moment. It was only nine-thirty. Impulsively she picked up the phone but immediately put it down again. Instead, she got into the shower and washed her hair, scrubbing her scalp until it hurt.

Chapter Eleven

On Monday night Martin called, asked her how her day had gone. He didn't mention the weekend. It was almost as though he'd forgotten those two wonderful days. If he'd just said, 'I haven't been able to get you out of my mind.' But he didn't. *Take what you can, Jenny*, she reminded herself. *You've been doing that all your life.*

Tuesday she had dinner with him, and lunch on Wednesday and dinner at his apartment on Thursday. Then Friday Martin drove her to the airport for her rescheduled meeting in Bar Harbor.

As the plane taxied down the runway for takeoff Jenny wondered how Martin would spend his time without her. Would he miss her? Would he take anyone else out? If Jenny could have read Martin's thoughts, she would have laughed at her own anxious ones.

Martin watched as Jenny boarded the plane and then waited for the takeoff. Only when the plane had streaked into the sky did he turn and slowly walk to his car. He missed her already, **more than** he wanted to. In fact, more than he'd ever missed **anyone**. Back in his apartment, he sat staring out into the dark.

You can't pretend any longer, he thought. *Face it. Jenny's gotten under your skin and you know now it's much more than infatuation. You've fallen in love with her. Now where do you go from here? You can't possibly take her home to meet your family. Nothing makes one goddamn bit of sense, because you can't have her and have your family too.*

He reached for the phone and called Dominic.

'It's me, Dom. Jesus, I'm glad you're home.'

'What's up, old buddy?'

'Are you doing anything now?'

'What did you have in mind? A gin game, billiards, a broad?'

'I've really got to talk to you, Dom.'

'Okay, give me an hour. Meet me at eight-thirty at Harry's Bar.'

By the time Dominic arrived, around nine-thirty, Martin had already gotten down to some very serious drinking.

'What the hell took you so long?' he asked as Dominic slid into the booth.

'Well, I had a few little loose ends to tidy up. Don't get nervous, everything will be all right. Okay, old buddy, I'm buying.' Looking at the waiter he said; 'Irish whiskey and a scotch and soda.'

As the two men picked up their glasses, Dominic asked, 'Okay?'

'I've got a problem.'

In spite of the pain in Martin's eyes, Dominic tried to keep it light. 'If it's about Jenny, she's only going to be gone for the weekend.'

Martin took a long swallow of scotch. 'That's not my problem.'

'What then?'

'I'm in love with Jenny.'

Dominic nodded. 'That is a problem.'

'I don't know what to do about it, Dom. When I thought it was only physical, it was okay, but I know it's much more than that. And the trouble is she loves me too. I don't want to hurt her and yet I can't ever marry her. What should I do, Dominic?'

This time Dominic looked upset. He felt responsible for having brought them together. 'It's never easy when you love someone, but it's just as easy to drown in three feet of water as it is in ten. Break it off now. Jesus, I'm really sorry about this, Martin.'

'So am I, because, dammit, I can't tell you how much knowing her has meant to me. I just don't know how to tell her.'

It was after one when Martin got home. He woke the next morning with a hangover, but spent the day visiting the places they had seen the weekend before. Finally he gave up and went home. He picked up Chinese food on the way, but remembering the dinner he and Jenny had shared, found he had no appetite. He took the cartons out to the incinerator and threw them down the chute, went back into the living room, and poured himself a stiff drink. God-dammit, it was going to be tough to let Jenny go. He tossed back the drink and poured another. Well, booze helped. Didn't have to think, didn't have to feel. With a half-empty bottle at his side, he passed out on the living room sofa.

He didn't awaken until early Sunday afternoon. His head felt like a balloon, and every muscle in his body ached. He'd never really gotten drunk before.

When he looked at himself in the bathroom mirror, he saw he looked as bad as he felt. *I'd better pull myself together*, he thought, opening the medicine chest and reaching for a bottle of eyedrops. He had to drive out to the airport and pick Jenny up at six-thirty.

He made himself a mug of coffee, brought it into the living room, and sat down. The room was a mess. There was a large, wet stain on the rug where his glass had fallen. It must have dropped out of his hand when he passed out. The ashtray was overflowing with cigarette butts. A wonder he hadn't set the place on fire. Well, one shouldn't smoke when one's drunk and one mustn't fall in love with a girl who isn't the right religion.

As he drove to the airport he rehearsed ways of telling her they should break up. But the very thought almost destroyed him. Maybe they could stay together for a while. He would take care of her, give her everything she needed, look after her in every way but one. According to her religion he would endanger her immortal soul, because he could not offer her marriage. No, it was impossible. Better that they end it before they were more deeply hurt. One day he would eventually marry and have children and so would Jenny. Yet, when he saw her walking down the steps from the plane, he wondered how he would summon the courage to tell her. Losing Jenny would break his heart.

As they drove into the city, Jenny sensed something was wrong, terribly wrong, but she was afraid to ask questions. As soon as they reached his apartment Martin went to the refrigerator and took out a bottle of champagne. When he came back to the living room, he found Jenny emptying the ashtrays. She smiled at him. 'The one virtue you don't have, Martin, is neatness.'

He looked at her. 'I know. But it's only one of my minor vices.'

The sound of his voice was strangely foreboding. Picking up the newspapers, she said quietly, I think I will have some champagne.' He handed her the glass and sat across from her. 'Did you miss me, Martin?' she asked.

'Terribly. I never felt anything like it before.'

For a moment she was confused. 'And yet you didn't seem very happy to see me. What's bothering you, Martin?'

He looked at her, hating himself for what he was about to say. 'Jenny, I don't quite know how to put this, and God only knows I don't want to hurt you. I was wrong when I said I thought things would work out. I've fallen in love with you and that's what makes the difference. I want to marry you and I can't. The end of our story was written three thousand years ago in Jerusalem. I'm a Jew and nothing will ever change that. I can't change my religion or give up my family. If we stay together you'll learn to hate me.'

Jenny sat in a state of shock. When she left on Friday, Martin had given no indication that he was going to break off with her. 'I don't understand any of this,' Jenny wept. 'What happened between the time I left and now?'

'I found myself missing you far too much. I realize how involved we've become. Believe me, this may seem cruel, but one day you'll –'

'Thank you?' she cried. 'You're a hypocrite, Martin. It was fine when I told you I loved you even though it was a sin according to my God. But when you realized you had the same feelings for me, you weren't so eager to have that loving relationship. What you're really saying is that as long as you didn't love me, you didn't mind sleeping with me. I hate you!' she screamed. Jenny grabbed her coat and ran out of the apartment.

Her words left Martin frozen. By the time he pulled himself together and went to the elevator, Jenny was gone. He hoped he'd find her waiting for a taxi, but when he opened the door, she was nowhere in sight. He ran a few blocks and then hailed a cab. It was almost ten o'clock by the time he arrived at Jenny's apartment. He ran up the stairs and rang the bell. When there was no answer, he knocked and spoke through the closed door. 'Jenny, please open up. Please, I have to talk to you.' She didn't answer, but after he shouted a few more times the landlady came out of her apartment and protested. 'You can't come barging in here banging on doors. Who do you think you are?'

Martin interrupted her. 'I don't think Miss McCoy's well. Would you be kind enough to open the door?' The landlady refused until Martin took ten dollars from his wallet. Then she reconsidered. She went in with Martin and waited, but it took very little time to realize Jenny hadn't been home. Beside himself with worry, he went home and began telephoning her apartment every ten minutes. By three o'clock in the morning, still with no answer, he was frantic.

She probably wanted to avoid him, knowing he might follow her home. But where else could she have gone? If she had called Dominic she would have discovered that he was away until the next day. Could she have gone to a hotel? Fearfully he looked through the directory and called the most likely possibilities. The answers at the Plaza, the St Regis and the Waldorf were all the same. No Jennifer McCoy registered. He could have tried more, but what was the use? New York had a million hotels. He sat on the bed and dropped his head into his hands. Why had he ever thought it would be easier breaking up with Jenny now than later? He couldn't stop worrying. It was freezing cold outside. Maybe she was hurt.

There were only two places left to call: the police or the hospitals. When he was told no Jenny McCoy had been found, he became even more frightened. Savagely, he grabbed the phone and called Jenny's landlady. When she told him Jenny still hadn't returned, he grabbed his coat and ran from the room.

After leaving Martin, Jenny had run for blocks on the icy pavement, oblivious to the blinding tears and the cold that penetrated her coat and her thin pumps. The night air was bitterly cold, but she hardly noticed. She only wanted to run – away from the apartment, Martin, and her emotions. Finally, exhausted, she huddled in a doorway, leaning against the wall, fighting for breath. Then she slid down and sat on the damp concrete.

Now there were no more tears, only the numbing realization that it was over. She had blinded herself with the hope that one day he would want her so badly that he would give up his religion, a faith that seemed to serve no spiritual purpose in his life. He said he rarely went to temple and was surprised when she said she attended church every week. Yet she was prepared to risk excommunication to be with Martin. Her religion meant so much to her, but she was willing to leave the Church if only they could marry. It was, she felt, the only way she could justify her affair with Martin. But in her heart hadn't she always known it would end this way? In fact, she was more to blame than he. Wanting him so much, she had refused to face reality.

Closing her eyes, she tried to shut out the world. The cold had made her drowsy. Sleep. Maybe she could sleep forever.

She had no idea how much time had passed when she was wakened by a pair of hungry dogs trying to nuzzle past her to some garbage cans. Unsteadily, she got up and walked along the empty streets, barely able to lift her arm to flag a taxi. She remembered little of the ride home or how she got up to her room.

She crawled under the covers, shivering with cold. She could not get warm. In a little while she lost consciousness.

Hours later, when Jenny opened her eyes, everything was white – was she still indoors? She had no idea where she was, and didn't care. All she wanted to do was go back to sleep.

She heard a voice – her father's, no, her father had abandoned her . . . as Martin had. The voice persisted; it couldn't be Martin. He existed now only in her memory. She closed out his image and fell into deep sleep.

Martin walked back to the hospital waiting room where he and Dominic had spent most of the last two days. Looking at his ravaged face, Dominic wished he knew how to help his friend. But he hadn't been able to reach Martin, not since Martin had burst into his apartment early Monday morning, beside himself with fear and grief.

For the first time since their days at Yale, Dominic's sense of protectiveness was aroused as his friend described his wretched quarrel with Jenny. Despite all the material things Martin's parents had showered on him, they had left him singularly ill-equipped to handle the ugliness of everyday living.

'Let me fix you some hot coffee,' was all Dominic said.

As Martin accepted the cup his hand shook. 'What do

you think happened to her?'

'I wish to God I knew. I feel so damn helpless,' Martin said. 'I walked the streets knowing I'd never find her. Finally I called the Police. I don't know what to do now.'

'Well, we'll keep trying. We'll call Mrs Bloomer every hour.'

Martin wasn't listening. He stared up at the ceiling. 'I'm a fool. She's the best thing that's ever happened to me and I sent her away.'

'Well, at least now you recognize the depth of your feelings. That should mean something.'

'How can it when for all I know I may never see her again?'

They sat in silence. Dominic occasionally tried to get his friend to eat, but without success. Every hour one of them would dial Jenny's landlady but there was no answer.

Dominic took the day off from work and told Martin to do the same. Finally, at four-thirty in the afternoon, Mrs Bloomer said she'd heard Jenny come in.

When they reached her room they found her unconscious. Martin sat on the edge of the bed and held her cold hands while Dominic called an ambulance.

In the two days that followed, Martin had refused to leave the hospital. Jenny didn't regain consciousness until Wednesday. She was out of the oxygen tent and her vital signs had improved.

When a nurse came to the waiting room to tell Martin the good news, he insisted Dominic be the first to see her.

'Tell her I'm sorry. Beg her to see me,' Martin said, urging his friend out the door.

'Thank you for coming. How did you know where I was?' Jenny asked when she saw Dominic's face.

'Because I'm a super sleuth. Why are you thanking me? That's what friends are for.'

With tears in her eyes, she said, 'I love you, Dominic.'

'And I love you, baby. The doctor says you're coming along great. Be as good as new in a few days,' Dominic hoped he sounded more convincing than he felt.

'How long have I been here?'

'Three days.'

'I guess I just fell apart. When Martin . . . when Martin said . . . Oh, Dominic, I guess I'm not very good at facing life. Do you think I'll ever grow up?'

'Of course you will. But now let me do the talking. You haven't lost Martin. He was the one who found you. He rode in the ambulance with you and hasn't left the hospital since. Look, you know I'm the world's greatest cynic, but Martin is head over heels in love with you.'

She looked at him for a long moment. 'When you love someone, you don't try and send them away. Even for their own good.'

'Jenny, if you could have seen him Monday morning when he came to my apartment. He was out of his mind with grief. He knows he's hurt you. But he's desperate to see you. Can I tell him to come in?'

Jenny wondered if she should risk it. In his fashion maybe Martin did love her. Maybe she had expected too much.

'Jenny, he's waiting outside,' Dominic continued. 'What should I tell him?'

'Before I answer that, let me ask you something. Do you think he will ever be able to give up his religion and marry me?'

Dominic thought carefully. 'Time is a wonderful thing. Maybe if you both just let things evolve there will be a happy ending. Take that chance, Jenny. Martin loves you. Now what shall I tell him?'

'To come in.'

When Martin sat by her bed, she was as shocked by his appearance as he had been by hers. There was no question about his suffering. He was gaunt and haggard.

Looking at her, Martin blamed himself. *I brought her to this*, he thought. There were dark circles under her eyes, and her once shiny hair hung dull and limp. For a few minutes he was unable to speak.

Finally, he said huskily, 'I love you, Jenny. I'm sorry it took this to make me realize, but I do love you. Do you think we could – '

'Start again? I don't think so, Martin. Because there just isn't any place for our love to go. I can't just move in with you. It's a sin . . . ' Her voice trailed off.

'God, Jenny. I know I've hurt you, but just give me the chance to *show* you.'

She was so tired, so weary. 'We'll talk about it when I'm well. When we both feel less emotional. It's been a bad time.'

He got up and kissed her. 'I love you, Jenny. I've never said that to anyone before except you. At least know that. I love you. Just give me some hope that you'll – '

'Not today.'

He walked out of the room to find Dominic. 'I don't think she's ever going to forgive me.'

'Did she say so?'

'No, but she didn't say she would.'

'Look – Jenny's been hurt and she's very frightened. If you really want her, you're going to have to fight for her.'

'How do I do that?'

'By making up your mind that you can't have the best of all possible worlds. You're going to have to make compromises, old buddy. That's what life's all about. You can't please her and your parents.'

'You mean I should just go ahead and marry her?'

'That's right. It's the only fair thing to do.'

Martin swallowed hard. 'Jesus, there has never been any intermarriage in my family. This would kill my folks.'

'Don't be silly, Martin. I doubt if your mother or father would be that affected. They'd be unhappy for a while – they were unhappy you came to New York, but they got over it – and knowing that you love Jenny, they would accept her in time. Martin, we talked about this once before. The decision is yours.'

'You're right,' Martin said. 'And I wouldn't have to

convert – just promise that if we have kids, they'd be raised Catholic.'

But as he walked down the hospital corridor with Dominic he had an uneasy sense that nothing would be as easy as it sounded.

Chapter Twelve

Each day found Jenny just a little stronger. Martin visited her frequently, often twice a day. He filled her room with flowers and had special food sent. Every day he bought her little presents and silly toys to make her laugh.

When she was able to get out of bed, she walked down the hall on his arm. She was finally beginning to look a little more like herself, and Martin felt it was safe to start making plans. 'Jenny, I know you haven't said a word about us, but that's all I've thought about. I want to live with you. I want us to plan on getting married.'

She hesitated, then said, 'How would that work for us, Martin? We haven't solved anything. Have you spoken to your family about this?'

His silence gave her the answer.

'You see, that's just the problem, Martin. Being sick has given me a lot of time to think. Unless your family can accept me, Jenny McCoy, Catholic, I could never marry you.'

'My God, don't say that! I know they will accept you. They'll have to. But it may take time. Believe me, Jenny, everything will work out.'

'I really don't know, Martin,' Jenny said. 'I'm not sure.'

'Well, I am if you're willing to give it a chance.' He took her hand and held it gently. 'I leased an apartment in a building on Central Park West with a marvellous view. I bought furniture, and when I told them my bride had been ill, they promised immediate delivery. The super even arranged to have it painted in two days. I know you're going to love it.' He smiled. 'Incidentally, I hired a house-keeper so you won't have to pick up after me.'

When Jenny was released from the hospital, she agreed to move in with Martin at least until she felt stronger. She really had no one else to look after her and she was still too weak to resist. Besides, she knew she loved him.

She was very quiet on the ride home. Martin's apartment turned out to be everything he promised. The view was lovely and the rooms large, but she was startled to see how masculine the furnishings appeared. The walls of the living room were a deep blue. A wild piece of sculpture – a sunburst of jagged metal strips fused together at different points – hung over the leather sofa that flanked one wall, and an enormous glass coffee table sat on a thick copper carpet. Two large chairs in plaid corduroy sat like book-ends on either side of the fireplace.

Martin walked out onto the balcony with two glasses of champagne and said, 'Here's to us and to a new beginning.'

Jenny accepted the glass but she couldn't meet Martin's eyes.

As she lay next to him that first night, she *did* feel that she had come home. He did not press her to make love, indicating that he would wait until she felt stronger. For the next two weeks he cared for her patiently. Then one Friday she dismissed the housekeeper early, deciding to make dinner to surprise him. The following week she intended to go back to work and would have less time.

She laughed as she planned the menu. She was going to have Louisiana food: seafood gumbo, stuffed artichoke with crab, scalloped potatoes, green beans with slivered almonds, pecan pie. If she had anything to thank Cora Belle Collingsworth for, it was the times she had spent learning to cook in her kitchen. Jenny remembered the red bandanna that Willie May wore around her head and the white starched apron that she tied around her plump body.

Martin Had called several times to tell her not to overdo it, but her efforts had left her feeling more energetic and optimistic than she had for a very long time. By the end of the day, when she heard Martin's key in the latch and ran to greet him, she didn't feel the least bit tired.

'God, you smell delicious,' he said as he kissed her.

She took him by the hand and led him to his favourite chair. 'Let's have a drink.'

'Great.'

'Let me fix it this time, okay?'

'Fine.' She looked radiant tonight, he thought.

As she handed him his drink and seated herself on the ottoman by his chair, he glanced into the dining room, where the table was set with crystal candleholders and a centrepiece of pink roses. 'I hope you haven't tired yourself.'

'You know I'm almost happiest when I'm cooking,' Jenny said. 'Sometimes I think I should have gone into haute cuisine instead of cosmetics.'

'Is the kitchen the only room where you can be happy?'

'Don't be devious.'

But he was pleased to note that she was smiling.

After dinner Jenny sat gazing at Martin across the table. She had never loved him so much. Then, with a shadow of uncertainty in her voice she said, 'Martin, I want so much to marry you. You're the only man I'll ever love. Now and for always.'

Martin took her in his arms. 'Oh my dear, sweet Jenny. It's been such a tough road for us.' *And will continue to be*, he couldn't help thinking. There was still the ordeal of confronting his parents, but he shoved the thought aside, not wanting to spoil the moment.

There was an extra tenderness in their lovemaking that night as if all they had suffered had only brought them

133

closer. With each kiss, each caress, Martin found himself knowing that Jenny was the most important person in his life.

The next morning at breakfast Martin watched as Jenny broke his soft-boiled egg in the cup, buttered his toast, and poured his coffee. She looked irresistible in her violet taffeta dressing gown. He knew the moment had come; he would have to go West and see his parents. The thought of that painful meeting must have showed in his face, for Jenny looked up from her plate and said, 'What's wrong, Martin?'

'Not a thing.'

But she persisted. 'I know you. Something's bothering you.'

'Well,' he sighed, 'I've thought about this very carefully. I'm going to San Francisco as soon as I can make a reservation.'

Jenny caught her breath. She had no doubt that Martin's decision was anything but an act of commitment, but still the idea terrified her. He was so close to his family. What if once he left her, they forced him to change his mind? What if he never came back to her? Yet she knew he had to go. It was the only way. 'How long do you think you'll be gone?'

'About a week. I haven't seen them since I came to New York. But you're not to worry. You must believe me. Everything will work out.'

'I do believe you,' she said. That much was true, but when she heard Martin make his reservation with United Airlines for a five o'clock flight that afternoon her heart sank. As she packed Martin's suitcase, she wondered if she should go with him. Not to see his parents, but to give him, perhaps, the moral support he needed. Then she realized that if she did go, it would be more to quiet her own fears than to give Martin support.

As they stood at the airport terminal, Martin said, 'I'll call you every night, darling, and don't forget if you need anything, call Dominic. I wish you would have allowed him to come to the airport with us. I hate the idea of you going back alone.'

With all the courage she could summon, she said, 'I didn't want anyone to share this moment with us. Martin, you will take care of yourself.'

'Yes, darling, and you too. I'll think about you every second I'm gone.'

Finally, in spite of herself, she felt the tears filling her eyes. 'It will be all right, won't it, Martin?'

He nodded. 'Yes, darling. You must believe that. Just trust me.'

'I do . . . I do . . . ' She wanted so badly to believe that.

When the boarding call came she looked at Martin, wanting to memorize his features. She had the feeling that this was as bad as seeing someone off to war: she might never see him again.

Sitting in the first-class cabin miles above the earth, Martin considered the different ways he could approach his parents. The task would be harder than Jenny's worst fears. He had already disappointed his family once: he had left his father's firm, choosing to live three thousand miles away. Every phone call filled him with guilt when his mother would conclude their talk with, 'Martin, when are you coming home? We miss you so . . . You should have come to your cousin Ronald's wedding. Sylvia was there . . . She's back from London. She's quite beautiful . . . '

Martin's answers were always apologetic, and when he hung up it was hours before the thought of his mother's reproachful gaze stopped haunting him.

It was ten hours before Martin's plane touched down in San Francisco. He hoped that because of the late arrival time his parents would not come to the airport, but they were waiting as he cleared the ramp. As he hugged them both he knew he would have to save his news for the next day.

A radiant Bess took his arm as they walked to the car. 'Oh, Martin, we're so grateful you're home.'

The next morning Martin slept late. He spent the afternoon trying to find a chance to catch his father alone, but events or his own faint heart intervened. In the evening, in addition to his uncles and aunts, Bess had invited Sylvia and her parents. Sylvia had, if possible, grown even more lovely, but Martin had trouble concentrating on what she was saying. A look in her eyes told him she knew he was suffering, and she made every attempt to steer the conversation away from him since he so obviously wished to be silent.

Soon after they left the table for the living room, Martin glanced at his watch and said, 'I'm really sorry to be so tired, but that flight was exhausting. If everyone would just excuse me . . . '

They all assured him it was fine that he go to bed. 'Of course we understand . . . ' 'Those flights are amazing, no wonder you need to get some sleep . . . ' 'Imagine crossing the country in ten hours . . . '

Martin hastened upstairs followed by those murmurs of concern for his fatigue. Once in his room he sat down at the desk and picked up the phone.

His heart leaped when he heard Jenny's voice but the conversation was stilted. Each was afraid to reveal their fears, which left them saying things they thought would please each other . . . 'I know everything is fine, dear . . . ' 'Oh yes, Martin, I had a wonderful evening with Dominic.' 'The flight? Wonderful . . . Of course I miss you terribly, but I'll be back before you know it.' Just bits of truths and half-truths.

When Jenny hung up it was with the same fears that she had experienced when she returned from the airport. Too depressed to eat, she had poured herself a drink and let herself give in to tears. She had not actually called Dominic. Instead she had just sipped several drinks until she had been able to fall asleep.

It was three days before Martin could mention the real

136

reason for his visit to his father, and in the end it was his father who created the opening. Martin had spent the day alone driving down the coast, and when he came home Williams, the butler, stopped him on the stairs. 'Your father has asked to see you in his study.'

Martin turned. 'Thank you, Williams.'

Julian was seated in his favourite leather chair to one side of the Georgian fireplace. 'Sit down, Martin,' he said, shocked anew by his son's drawn appearance.

Martin seated himself across from his father and gazed into the fire. Julian got up and poured two brandies, handing one to Martin. 'Son, we have to talk. Something's obviously disturbing you. You must tell me what it is.'

Martin remained silent.

'Whatever it is, Martin, I'll try and understand. I have before.'

But Martin couldn't find the courage to speak.

'I'm going to be perfectly frank with you,' Julian said. 'Even though I was hurt when you left the firm and went to New York, I realized that the war had changed you, that you needed time to find yourself. But I thought it would be a good experience for you and instead you come home looking worse than when you returned from Germany. Your mother is beside herself. We will do anything you wish. Surely you can confide in us.'

Running his hands through his thick black hair, Martin finally blurted out the truth. 'I've fallen in love, but there are problems.'

Julian hesitated. 'Is she going to have your child?'

'I wish she were; it might be simpler.'

'Is she in love with you?'

'Yes.'

'But you haven't known one another, I would imagine, for very long.'

'Is time the barometer? I've known Sylvia all my life.'

'Forgive me, Martin, but I thought love was something that grew. Of course, I come from a different generation.'

'I don't think love has changed so much.'

137

'I suppose you're right, Martin. But the point is, what do you plan to do about this woman?'

The lump in Martin's throat was almost too painful to swallow when he said, 'Marry her.'

'Then why have you kept it a secret?'

'Because she's Catholic.'

Julian slumped down in his chair. 'You're right. That is a problem. But you were also right when you said love has not changed so much from my generation to yours . . .' And then he astonished his son by explaining that when he was Martin's age he too had fallen in love with the wrong girl. 'I too was completely in love . . . ludicrous when I think back upon it now. But at the time, I was inconsolable. Marriage was out of the question. She would never be accepted. Ah, Martin, we have so much, but we can't always have what we want.

'I have my father to thank, God rest his soul, for setting me straight. Of course, I married your mother, and thank God I did. She belonged, she was right, and she fitted into my world. I knew she was the perfect woman to become the mother of my children.' Julian got up and poured another brandy.

'Martin, would you believe it, I can scarcely remember the girl's face. Quite accidentally I ran into this woman a few years ago and I would have passed her by had she not called out my name. We spoke, but it was like talking to a stranger. So I know what you're going through, Martin. I also know that it will pass. Can't you please believe that Sylvia is so right for you? If you were to marry, your affection for her could turn into love. The kind that I feel for your mother. There will be children, and before you know it, this other woman will fade from your memory.'

'You're wrong, Father. Our stories are not parallel. I can't marry Sylvia just because she comes from the right background. And I will not forget Jenny's face. That's her name. Jenny. I won't ever stop loving her. Father, you must believe me. I love this girl more than anything in the world.'

138

'Well,' Julian sighed, putting down his drink, 'what is it you want me to do?'

'Give me your blessing.'

He looked at Martin, filled with pain. He would do almost anything in the world for his son. Almost. 'You know what this will do to your mother, don't you?'

Struggling with his feelings, Martin answered, 'I know she'll be disappointed, but what should I do? Somebody's happiness has to be sacrificed, sad as that may be. In all honesty, Dad, should it be mine? The worst thing that I'm doing is marrying a girl that I love. It isn't her fault that she's not Jewish. I'm only asking you to please accept her.'

'That's asking a lot, Martin. I think we should go upstairs and see your mother. She isn't feeling well herself, you know. I don't mind telling you that these last few days have been a strain for her, not knowing what was wrong with you.'

If Martin could find anything to console himself it was that he no longer had to go on keeping Jenny a secret. Upstairs his father hesitated a moment, gathering his courage before knocking on Bess's door.

'Is that you, Julian? Come in.'

When they entered, Bess was lying on a chaise longue with a cold cloth on her forehead.

'I'm sorry you're not feeling well, Mother,' Martin said.

'It's just a headache, darling. I'm fine. In fact, I was about to get up for dinner.' Then she looked at Julian's white face and guessed they had come to tell her bad news. 'You've wanted to tell me something, haven't you, Martin?'

Slowly he answered. 'Yes, and I hope and pray that you will understand.' Then he told his mother what he'd just told Julian about Jenny.

Her cry seared him like a knife. 'How could you have deceived us so? Kept this . . . this woman a secret. Good God, Martin, have you no respect? And you want me to give you my blessings? Never!' she screamed. 'I will never accept her. This is the first time in our family that anyone has intermarried, and for you of all people to bring this disgrace upon us.'

'Mother,' Martin pleaded. 'You don't know what you're saying. You haven't even met her. She can't help being –'

'I don't care what she is. You can stop this before you break all our hearts. She's bewitched you.' Tears ran down Bess's cheeks. 'Why couldn't you love Sylvia? Why? She's worth –'

'I know what she's worth, Mother, but so is Jenny. Please meet her. Please.'

'Never, Martin.' She slumped back down on her pillows.

Julian looked at Martin and whispered, 'Let me speak to your mother.'

Feeling like a pariah, Martin walked out of the room and closed the door behind him.

Julian sat beside Bess, wiped her tears, and took her hand. 'Don't cry, darling. And listen to me, Bess. Even if Martin is a man possessed – and sometimes love can do that to you – he is still our son. Be wise, my dear. If we reject Martin now we will end up pushing him closer to this woman. He hasn't married her yet, so let us pray that he comes to his senses. But if he does marry her and we do not accept her, we will lose him.

Through her swollen lids, she looked at Julian. 'Do you really expect me to play along like that? I can't do it, Julian – not even for Martin.'

Julian's feelings were the same as Bess's, but he pushed them aside. 'You do not have to love her, Bess, but you must learn to tolerate her if she becomes Martin's wife. Do it now so that he can never hate you for standing in his way. I will support your decision, but I think my advice is correct.'

Bess wept softly. 'And what if Martin has children? They will be Catholic. How can I bear that?'

'Yes. But no matter what happens, we must not lose our only child. He's all we have.'

Bess lay silent for what seemed an eternity, then said quietly, 'All right, Julian. Have Martin come in.'

'Your mother and I give you our blessings,' Julian said when he found Martin standing in the hall. 'Go in, she'd like to see you.'

Filled with contrition, Martin said, 'Thank you, Mother. Is it all right for me to have Jenny come out? I want you to get to know her.'

Julian knew Bess was not ready for such a meeting. 'Not yet, Martin,' he said.

Martin was prepared for that answer. It was asking a lot at one time. At that moment it was enough just to have his parents accept the concept of Jenny.

Chapter Thirteen

Martin flew back to New York, pleased with his partial victory and hoping that Jenny would understand that his parents had done the best they could for the time being. Later when they met and came to know Jenny he knew they could not help but love her. His heart leaped when the plane landed and he saw Jenny running towards him.

Kissing him over and over again, she said, 'Do you know what an eternity is?'

'Yes, a minute away from you.'

When they reached the apartment, he realized that she had done everything to make his homecoming beautiful. The vases were filled with white roses, stock and lilies. The candles on the table made the crystal glasses gleam. The champagne hissed as Jenny poured the bubbling liquid. He decided that he would not tell her the details of his talk with his parents until they'd finished eating. He lifted his glass. 'To you, my love. May this be the beginning of a wonderful long life together.'

'I hope so. But, oh God, Martin, just love me.'

He took her in his arms and, in that extraordinary moment of reunion, they gave themselves to each other with an unbearable need for reaffirmation.

Afterwards came the time for questions. Jenny simply had to know where she stood.

'Martin,' she said, 'you've said very little to me except that your parents gave you their blessings.'

'Well, darling, that's what we wanted.'

'Of course,' Jenny said slowly. 'But you said nothing about their wanting to meet me. When I asked if it was all right for me to fly out, you were so evasive.'

'No, not at all. My mother just hasn't been feeling too well.'

'You mean she really wasn't up to meeting me. You don't have to answer, Martin. I knew that, but they're going to have to meet me eventually and, Martin, I'm not going to marry you until they do.'

'But they have accepted you, dear,' Martin said. 'They gave us their blessings.'

'Not us, you. You're their son and they'd do anything for you. But, Martin – I won't be patronized.'

Martin got out of bed and paced the floor. 'Goddamn, Jenny, what do you want? They've done everything they could for me.'

'Yes, but not for me,' Jenny persisted, knowing she was being unreasonable. 'Until they meet me I'm not going to go on living this way. It's a sin, Martin. Don't you understand that? We have to get married.'

'Well, I'm not quite ready for that!' Martin shouted, exhausted by the storm of emotion he'd experienced in the last few days.

'You never were!' Jenny jumped out of bed, ran to the bathroom, and slammed the door. Sitting on the edge of the tub, she wondered how the fight had gotten so out of hand. He had just come home. This was not the way she had planned it. She dried her tears. She would apologize to Martin. But when she opened the door she saw his robe on

142

the floor and her heart began to pound when she realized he'd left. Throwing herself on the bed, she burst into tears again. She'd lost Martin; she knew she had lost him.

When Jenny had run into the bathroom, Martin, exasperated, decided he simply wasn't up to coping with her tantrums that night. He threw on his clothes and went down the elevator and outside, where he walked until he found a quiet bar.

Sliding into a booth, he ordered a scotch and soda. When it came he sat thinking about Jenny's reaction, deciding that she had been unreasonable. He had done everything he could, but he wasn't going to abandon his parents, not even for Jenny. They needed time to adjust to the situation. He had all but destroyed them by not confiding in them sooner. He'd never forgive himself for that.

But as his anger ebbed he began to understand Jenny's feelings. Until they were married she felt as though she were committing a mortal sin. She needed his parents' acceptance.

He got up, hailed a cab, and went back to the apartment. When Jenny heard his key in the latch she rushed out of the bedroom into his arms, kissing him over and over saying, 'I'm sorry, Martin. Please forgive me. I behaved like a stupid child. Of course this was hard for your parents. Oh, Martin darling, please love me.'

He placed his finger against her lips. 'Don't say any more, there's no need. This has been impossible for you and I know it. But if we're going to have a happy life together, it's important that my parents be happy also. You and I have to be a little patient about this, Jenny.'

'Oh, I will, Martin.'

'Thank you, darling. Forgive me for losing my temper. As soon as I get caught up in the office we'll go away for a long weekend.'

That night, Martin lay awake in the dark, staring up at the ceiling. He had missed Jenny so, and yet lying beside her he could find no peace. It wasn't just his parents that troubled his thoughts. For the first time in months the faces of the wretched Jews who had been liberated from the camps in Germany and Poland came back to haunt him. He too was a Jew but he knew so little of Judaism.

Early the next morning, before going to work, he visited the shabby little synagogue on Hester Street. He wasn't sure why, but the Lower East Side seemed to hold out the promise of some answers to the truths for which he searched. He wanted Jenny, but he did not wish to abandon his heritage. He hoped that in this small schul, where the old men spent their mornings and their evenings, his past would reach out to him and provide some solutions.

Hearing the ancient prayers, Martin felt soothed even though he did not understand their meaning. He prayed for forgiveness from his parents, from Jenny, from his great-grandfather Ephraim, who had left everyone he loved so his offspring could grow up in freedom. But as Martin left the schul and took a cab uptown to the office, he wondered if Ephraim had envisioned a freedom which allowed his great-grandchildren to marry Catholics.

After three weeks of long hours at the office, Martin felt he had caught up enough to take a long weekend with Jenny in Vermont. Dominic cheerfully lent them the Vermont farmhouse he had bought at a bargain price during the war.

When Jenny and Martin brought their bags inside, they found that Ned, who took care of the house during the winter, had left an ample supply of logs for the fireplace. His wife, Lucy, had carefully dusted every surface, stocked the larder, and filled the house with pots of chrysanthemums and huge vases of pine branches and juniper berries. When he had left, she gave a last glance around, thinking that it was a perfect setting for newlyweds. Dominic had told her Martin was coming on his honeymoon to ensure their privacy and because he really hadn't known what other explanation to make.

After dinner on Friday evening, Jenny lay in Martin's arms, gazing into the roaring fire. Martin felt more peaceful than he had in months. Getting away was just what they needed. They made love over and over that night, wishing that these moments would last forever.

The next morning, after a breakfast of country fresh eggs and biscuits, they dressed and went outside. The earth was blanketed with new-fallen snow. The pines and firs sparkled under a cloudless blue sky.

Martin found an old toboggan in the barn, and they trudged up a hill behind the house, startling a deer into flight with their voices. As they careened down the hill, the snow stung their faces, and they only burst out laughing when the sled came to a halt and tipped them over. Martin thought Jenny looked adorable, her cheeks glowing in the cold crisp air.

'This is the best fun I have ever had in my life,' he whispered, 'and it's because of you. I can't imagine what life would be like without you, Jenny.'

'You were so right about our getting away,' Jenny said. 'It's as though a whole new world has opened up for us.'

For a moment they were silent. Then he helped her to her feet and righted the sled. 'Game for another try?'

'Naturally, since I'm carrying the sled.' He made a snow-ball and tossed it lightly at her chest.

She laughed, packed snow in her mitten, and aimed at his face. It landed on his chin.

'You want to play rough, huh,' he said, ducking her next snowball and scooping up his own ammunition.

They raced to the top of the hill, Martin still dragging the sled. She reached the top, breathless, and called out, 'See, I told you I could beat you.'

'That was dirty pool.'

He reached out and wrestled her to the ground, and together they rolled down the hill. When they reached the bottom, he was on top of her, pinning back her shoulders. Their laughter echoed in the silence.

'See, I told you you couldn't beat me,' he said, his breath steaming against the cold air.

'Okay, you win.'

He gave her a kiss and pulled her to her feet.

After lunch, Martin got Ned's permission to harness his chestnut gelding to the old sleigh. Martin held the reins as the trotted through the countryside. Jenny was delighted until they passed a Catholic church and she remembered how long it had been since she had gone to confession. A shadow crossed her face, but fortunately Martin was too busy handling the horse to notice.

When they reached the general store, Martin hitched the gelding to the iron post and helped Jenny out. He saw her excitement as she looked about at the old village.

When they entered the store, there was a group of men chatting around the potbelly stove. The proprietor got up and walked behind the counter.

'Afternoon. You're not from around these parts, are you?' he said in his clipped Yankee accent.

'No, but we're staying at my friend's house.'

'And who would that be?'

'Dominic Gatti.'

'The fella who bought the Calvin Walsh place a few years back. And this is the missus?' Mr Swanson added. 'Lucy told me that you were up on the honeymoon. She's a mighty fine-looking woman.'

Martin looked at Jenny and smiled. 'I think so too.'

'Now what can I do for you?'

'We're going to look around, if you don't mind.'

'You do that,' Mr Swanson said, going back to the game of checkers.

Jenny was delighted. Even though it was only make-believe, this was the first time anyone had acknowledged her as Martin's wife. It did a lot to salve the hurt she had felt when Martin had told her he would have to go home without her this year for the holidays. To take her with him would be ill-timed, he'd said. But next year she was certain she would go as his wife.

The night before leaving to go back to New York, she prepared a special dinner for the two of them. Later, as they sat in front of the fire, he gave Jenny a gold and diamond bracelet. Her present to him was a pair of gold cuff links made in the form of a calendar. A small ruby marked November the fifth, the day he had asked her to marry him.

Putting them back in their box, he drew her to him saying, 'You're the love of my life, darling, and right after I come back from California, we will set our wedding date.'

'What about meeting your family, Martin?'

'I think it best for them to come to New York to meet you. It will be easier that way, without the rest of the family around.'

Jenny was hurt for a moment, but she brushed the thought away. 'I'm going to try and make them love me, Martin.'

'I know you will, darling. And it won't be that hard; I'm not the only one in the family with good taste in women. Now let me get you some mulled wine.'

Jenny looked up at him. There was more than courage in her smile, there was peace.

Marriage. 'After the first of the year,' Martin had said.

Chapter Fourteen

It was as if the gods were jealous of their happiness. No sooner had they gotten back to New York than the phone rang. Martin started when he heard the sound of his mother's voice. 'Darling, thank God you're home at last,' she sobbed.

'What's wrong, Mother?' he asked.

'I don't know how to tell you, but your father has had a heart attack. A very severe one.'

Martin couldn't believe it. He had spoken to his mother this afternoon, just before leaving Vermont, and everything was fine. And his father had seemed so healthy when he'd been out there last. If anything, it was his mother's health that had concerned him. 'I don't understand. When did this happen?'

'About two hours ago. Sylvia and I have been calling you ever since.'

Groping for words, Martin sputtered, 'Where . . . I mean what hospital . . . '

'He's at home.'

'At home? Why isn't he in the hospital?'

'Because he refused to go,' she sobbed.

'Why didn't Dr Silverman insist?'

'Because he understood your father's fear. He's afraid that if he goes to the hospital, he might never come home.'

'I'll get a flight as quickly as possible,' Martin said. 'I'm so terribly sorry I wasn't there with you.'

'Oh, darling boy, just come home as quickly as you can.'

'I will. I love you,' he added. He hung up, wondering if he would ever again be able to tell his father he loved him.

Jenny felt as if her whole world were crashing down around her. Just a few hours ago it had seemed as if their future was assured. And now the Fates had intervened. Jenny had a terrible premonition that the moment Martin reached San Francisco his parents would keep him from returning to her. And she couldn't let that happen.

'Martin, would you like me to go to California with you? I don't mean to meet your parents. I'd just like to be there in case you needed me.'

But Martin was so upset about his father that he scarcely heard her. Sensing her hurt, he said, 'Darling, I would love to have you with me, but under the circumstances I don't feel that it would be fair to you.'

Jenny wanted to cry, but she controlled herself. This was not the time to dissolve. When Martin was gone there would be time for that. 'Call the airlines,' she said, 'and I'll go fix us some coffee.'

When it was time for Martin to leave for the airport, she

clung to him. He had insisted it was too late for her to drive him there. 'I'll be here if you need me,' she said, holding him to her.

'I'll be back as soon as I can,' Martin promised. 'And then I'll never leave you again.'

From the moment he entered the Woodside house, Martin was filled with a sense of foreboding. The heavy drapes in the living room windows were pulled shut; it was as though the house itself were in mourning. When he held his mother in his arms, he knew that things were very bad.

'Oh, dearest boy, I'm so grateful that you're here.' Then, before Martin could say anything, she added, 'Dr Silverman just left. He thinks your father is a little better today.'

Martin nodded. 'I want to see him.'

'He's been waiting . . . I told him you were coming.'

Martin walked up the wide stairs to the second floor, pausing at his father's bedroom door. Then he turned the knob and quietly entered. Everything Julian loved was there, photographs in silver frames, pipes and trophies, the collection of a lifetime. But his father – now shrunken and still in the big bed – was no longer the same man. The heavy oxygen cylinders stood by the bed in obscene warning.

Martin felt his eyes fill with tears. How could his father be dying? He should have had years ahead of him. Time to see his grandchildren born, to play with them. Pulling up a chair, Martin suddenly wondered if Julian would have ever dangled Jenny's child on his knee. Then concern for his father blotted out all other thought.

After a few minutes, Julian's eyes fluttered open. 'Have you been here long?' he asked, his voice little more than a whisper.

'Not long, Father. Just a moment or two.'

Julian sighed. 'My dear Martin, these months must have been so painful for you, feeling we had not really accepted your choice. I was not there to comfort you as I should have been. But here you are at my side when I need you. Help me sit up, so I can see you better. Ah . . . that's good. Martin, I feel I must say this. If anything happens to me . . .'

Martin tried to still him but Julian continued.

'You mustn't be foolish, Martin. I won't leave before it's my time, but I know that when I go, it will be very hard for your mother and for you since you will have to take on certain responsibilities. What I'm saying is don't allow this to become an obligation that will stand in the way of your own life. Do you understand what I mean, Martin?'

Martin would never forget his father's words. He was giving him more than his blessing. His father was leaving him a legacy of love. 'We will talk more in the morning,' Julian said haltingly. 'Help me to lie back.'

Martin sat for a while listening to his father's shallow breathing. Then Julian began to gasp and the colour left his face. Martin rushed out for the nurse, but by the time they returned Julian was gone.

Martin stood for a moment, tears streaming down his face. 'I loved you, Father, even though I disappointed you. I just wish I had been able to tell you how much I cared.'

He went to find his mother. She was sitting in the library with Sylvia. The moment Bess looked at him, she knew. 'He's gone.'

Martin nodded. Without a word, she left the room and walked upstairs to sit by Julian's bedside. For over an hour she wept there, but as the family began to gather she pulled herself together, drawing on some secret well of strength. She made all the arrangements and would not accept a word of consolation. What were words in view of a loss like hers?

According to Jewish law, Julian was buried at the earliest possible date, laid to rest next to his parents, next to Ephraim himself. Standing in the crypt, Martin had a sudden vision of himself lying in alien earth, next to a Catholic wife. Then he brought his thoughts back to his mother, who stood rigidly erect, listening to the Rabbi. When he had finished kaddish, Martin touched Bess's arm.

She seemed lost in a reverie. 'Mother, I think it's time to go.'

They left the small chapel, going out into the dismal December afternoon. Bess lingered briefly, watching the heavy bronze doors being closed. 'Sleep well,' she whispered, 'my love . . . my life, until God wills that I join you.'

That night, Martin called Jenny. He was grateful she didn't press for details of the funeral. She just told him she loved him and asked hesitantly when he might be coming home.

'I can't really say, dear. It's a difficult time for my mother, as you can imagine.'

Yes, Jenny knew. She had gone through it when her mother died, but in a very different way. Alone. She still felt alone and needed Martin terribly, but all she said was, 'Whatever you feel is right, Martin. I love you, please remember that.'

'I will, darling, I will.'

Chapter Fifteen

At first, Martin imagined that once the household calmed down and the details were worked out with the attorneys he would be able to go back to New York. But he soon realized that there would be no chance of that. It would be much longer before he could get away. Martin had been named executor of Julian's will, and there were endless details to be handled.

He called Dominic and arranged a leave of absence, apologizing for all the time he had taken off. Dominic said to relax. Martin's acquisition of the soup account had put

151

the Gatti agency in the big league. Even if Martin stayed away for a year, he still would have earned his keep. Martin wished that his conversations with Jenny could go as smoothly, but meantime he turned to the problems at hand.

The bulk of Julian's estate had been left to Bess for her lifetime, but Martin was made trustee. That was in itself an awesome responsibility and Martin found the time passing with no sign of his business obligations relenting. It seemed his father had accomplished in death what he could not in life: Martin was fast taking over the family business. Through this time his mother depended on him more and more. Although she seemed unable to share her grief or express her feelings, she was increasingly unable to let Martin out of her sight.

The one bright note in the oppressive atmosphere was Sylvia. She was almost able to make Bess laugh. When she spoke about the past, she made Bess recall only the happy times. As far as her attitude to Martin was concerned, she seemed to have fallen back into the easy relationship they had enjoyed in their teens.

When she joined him in the study one night after dinner – she had moved in with Bess again as she had during the war – Martin's guard was down. He needed to talk. Sensing this, Sylvia fixed him a scotch and soda. 'You know, Martin,' she said, handing it to him, 'silence is *not* golden, it's destructive. You're living with all kinds of ghosts. Certainly you should be able to share your thoughts with me.'

Martin sighed. 'It's tough, Sylvia.'

'Revealing one's self always is. But you know, Martin, I would never judge you.'

Martin got up and replenished his drink. 'I feel so guilty about my father, Sylvia. I can't come to terms with it,' he said, going back to the couch.

'Now wait a minute, Martin. You're not responsible for your father's death.'

'I know that. But I neglected him over the last year. He was really hurt when I went to work in New York. And you know how he must have felt about Jenny.'

'Martin, you're being very hard on yourself. Don't you understand that your father really wanted you to be happy? He may have been upset that Jenny was Catholic, but he certainly understood. Now may I make a suggestion. I really think it's time for you to get on with your own life.'

'When my father was alive, I would have been able to,' Martin said. 'But now I can't bring myself to leave my mother here, alone.'

Sylvia took a large swallow of her drink, wondering why she was trying to send Martin back into another woman's arms. She knew she didn't want him to stay if he would be unhappy. Taking a deep breath, she said, 'Stop trying to fill your father's shoes. Marry Jenny. If you feel you must stay with your mother, bring Jenny out here to live.'

'But you and I both know that my mother hasn't accepted her, and in her present condition, I doubt whether she is well enough to cope with that situation.'

'So what do you intend to do? Is it fair to Jenny to keep postponing her?'

'I don't quite like the way you phrased that. My intention was to marry after the first of the year, but certainly she can understand that under the circumstances I can't put my own wishes first. Dammit, Sylvia, my mother is my responsibility and I simply can't abandon her.' Martin got up and began pacing the floor. 'I'm so confused, Sylvia, I don't know what to do. I want to do what's right for both Jenny and my mother. I feel as if I'm being pulled apart. Please, Sylvia, what do you think I should do?'

'If you really love this girl, then your place is with her,' Sylvia said, her voice a knife in her own heart. 'Your mother will survive. We all are left with scars, but time heals many of the wounds. And your Jenny isn't going to be content much longer with phone calls. A month is a long time to wait, and even "I love you" can start to sound hollow if always over the phone.'

Martin knew Sylvia was right. He decided he would face his mother the next day.

Back in New York Jenny was even more impatient than Sylvia suspected. With every passing day she became more uncertain of Martin's commitment. She was so afraid that he would sense her annoyance that she had taken to writing him letters. That way she could tear up complaints she would have regretted later.

In the letters she mailed, she expressed only her fondest thoughts:

My dearest, she would write, *I've been thinking of you all day. Darling Martin, I keep remembering the little things that I could do for you . . . Honey, New York is covered with snow. Yesterday we had the worst blizzard in thirty years . . . Darling, the promotion at Macy's was simply wonderful – fire engine red lipstick is going to be the rage come spring. Dearest Martin, it's so terribly lonely without you. When will you be back? I love you.*

Martin's response was always a telephone call promising to call again the next day, to return as soon as he could.

But as the days moved on slowly, phone calls no longer sustained her. Her loneliness overwhelmed her and she became increasingly depressed. Her anxieties finally forced her to a decision. It was nearly dawn when she finished the last draft of her letter.

Dearest Martin,

I know it's been a terrible time for you, but it has been equally difficult for me. I have sat here, night after night, drowning in my loneliness, wondering where our life is going. Today has been the most devastating of all, since I have thought of nothing else but you, and where I fit into your life. I have reached a crossroads. You belong to a totally different world, one in which I would never fit.

If you truly loved me, you would have allowed me to share your grief – but you have shut me out. If you love someone, and are unable to help them in their sorrow, you feel useless. You and I both know that we are lost to each other. I'm going away because I love you, Martin. It is the only way. I hope and pray you do not lose yourself.

With all my love,
Jenny

Martin read the letter in a state of shock. Frantic, he picked up the phone and called the apartment, but Jenny was not there. Suddenly the words . . . *I'm going away because I love you, Martin*, stung him with such force he thought he might pass out, as though he'd been punched in the gut. In a state of panic, he called Dominic to see if he could reach Jenny, but Dominic said she'd quit her job and given up her lease on the little apartment she had insisted on keeping until their marriage.

Martin read Jenny's letter over and over until he'd all but memorized it. Could it have been over a month since he had seen her? What a fool he'd been. Even Sylvia had warned him to return to New York. Now he'd lost Jenny. He picked up the phone and called Dominic again.

'Call the best detective agency in the city. I don't give a damn what it costs. I'm going to find her.'

But as the weeks passed with no trace of Jenny, his hopes of success faded. He flew back East to search himself, but with no better results. While there he spent a long time talking with Dominic. In the end, both friends agreed it would be best for Martin to quit the business. He could not ignore the debt he owed his father. The time had come for him to assume his rightful place as a partner in Roth, Seifer, Roth, Stearn & Hines.

Even as Martin closed his apartment and handed over his agency accounts to Dominic, his mind was filled with memories of Jenny. Everywhere he walked in the city images of her laughing face rose to haunt him. How could he have let her get away?

His last night in New York, when no trace of her had been found, he went out with Dominic and got very drunk. *Oh God*, he thought as he threw himself across his hotel bed, *I loved her so much. Why couldn't she have been patient? Didn't she understand that while I owed her my heart I still owed my parents my heritage and loyalty too?*

When he woke to catch his plane, his face was wet with tears.

Book Two

Chapter Sixteen

All through the spring back in California, Martin could not stop thinking of Jenny. He was glad that picking up his father's clients kept him so busy. His mother fretted as he left the house at six, only to return after dinner. Many times he would come home to see Sylvia and Bess playing cards. Though Sylvia was always around, she never foisted herself on him and he was grateful for the attention she paid his mother, attention that he could find neither the time nor the emotional strength to offer. The only antidote to the pain of Jenny's leaving was work, and his goal each day was to exhaust himself so that when he finally went to bed he fell asleep instantly.

As spring blossomed into summer, Martin found himself besieged with social demands. He received numerous wedding invitations and rather than argue with Bess found it easier to call Sylvia and go. Sylvia never made any demands and seemed to respect Martin's grief. If either Bess or Sylvia's mother got their hopes up, they were wise enough to keep their thoughts to themselves.

Martin was aware that he and Sylvia were regarded as a couple by their friends. They were usually seated together at dinner parties and often asked out as a pair. Martin became increasingly comfortable in Sylvia's presence.

For a long time he prayed that Jenny would call or write, but he realized he could not live out the rest of his life with mere hope. He wanted a home and children. He wanted the stability his parents had enjoyed. He knew he would never feel for anyone the unreserved passion he had experienced with Jenny, but maybe, as his father had said, there were other kinds of love equally satisfying.

It was at about this time that he began to see Sylvia in a different light. She was right for him in a way Jenny never could have been. He began arranging to go for walks with her in Muir Woods, sail on the Bay, picnic on the board-walk in Sausalito. By the end of the summer everyone seemed to take it for granted that they would marry, and Martin found himself sharing the assumption.

One night when they were finishing dinner at Trader Vic's, Martin reached across the table and took Sylvia's hand. 'I love you, Sylvia.'

She looked away and fumbled with the sugar. 'Do you really, Martin? I mean really? I have the feeling that you're still as much in love with Jenny as ever.'

Don't lie, he told himself. 'Sylvia, I can't deny that Jenny was important to me. Maybe she will always be part of my youth, but I'm ready to grow up now and I want the kind of life you and I can build together.'

'But losing her still hurts, doesn't it?'

'I can't say it doesn't but it's gotten to the point that I can look at our affair objectively. I suppose there's not a lot of logic about love, but at least now I can see that if we had married we probably wouldn't have been very happy. Believe me, I want to live with you. I need you.'

She didn't answer.

'Of course,' he said. 'I haven't even asked if you'd have me. I'm not much of a bargain, I grant you, but for what-ever it's worth, I want to marry you and spend the rest of my life trying to make you the happiest lady in the world.'

She started to cry. Leaning over the table, he lifted her face and kissed her. 'Please marry me, Sylvia.'

This was a moment she had dreamed about for so many years. Marrying Martin was something she wanted more than anything in the world. And, if he had asked her before Jenny, she would have been filled with joy. Now her happi-ness was shadowed. She wanted Martin to be so very, very sure. What if Jenny turned up sometime in the future and he left her? She looked at him for a long, contemplative moment. 'I will marry you,' she said. 'But let's keep our engagement a secret for a while. I mean from everyone, even your mother and my parents. I think we should be together for a while to make sure it's what we both really want.'

Martin felt strangely rejected. 'If that's what you want. I would have thought that we could have gotten married in a couple of months. After all, we're not exactly strangers.'

'In a sense, we are,' Sylvia said. 'This will be a very different relationship. We still have loads to learn about each other.'

'I guess you're right,' Martin grudgingly admitted. 'How long do you want to wait before telling people?'

'Until next spring,' Sylvia said firmly.

And that was the way they left it. People could talk all they wanted, but Sylvia and Martin would not confirm the gossip for another six months.

In the end, Martin was glad they waited. The secret gave them time alone together – time to forge a romantic bond in addition to their friendship.

As Sylvia said, 'Once we are formally engaged we'll never have a minute to ourselves.'

Martin used the time to good advantage, learning to appreciate Sylvia for who she truly was. The best thing he discovered was that they were so much alike. They had the same tastes and enjoyed the same ways of spending their free time. Even in little things like taking long walks or eating strawberries and cream for breakfast, their likes meshed. Martin was aware that he and Jenny would never have been so conjugal. Their future would always have been filled with uncertainties. He wondered why it had taken him so long to realize how right Sylvia was for him, with her quiet logic, her attention to detail, her sense of humour that could lift him out of a dark mood. He discovered dimensions in her that he more than admired.

Their only point of disagreement was where they should live. Martin asked if she'd like to rent an apartment or buy a house right away. 'I don't really want a house of my own,' she surprised him by saying. 'I've decided the most wonderful thing we could do is live with your mother.'

'Darling, you can't be serious. There's no house in the world big enough for two mistresses.'

'Well, your mother and I are the exception to the rule. Of course I haven't mentioned anything to her, but it would be best for all of us. Think about it, Martin.'

There wasn't really any need to think about it. Martin knew in the long run Sylvia and Bess would win.

The minute the wedding was announced, Bess felt a sense of purpose enter her life. She had suffered terribly when Martin had announced he was marrying Jenny McCoy. Now Bess's only sorrow was that she could not share the triumph with Julian. It seemed that God took but He also gave.

She blessed Sylvia's mother for letting her give the wedding at the Woodside house.

'I don't mind it a bit, Bess, since she's always been more your daughter than mine. Just don't come crying to me later about how tired you are!'

And suddenly it was as if their period of mourning had ended. There were so many parties given for them that Sylvia and Martin were kept in a constant whirl. Sylvia was involved in long days of trousseau shopping, bridal fittings, and decisions about the wedding. She and Bess had to select the menu, choose the photographers, pick the flowers, and buy the gifts for the wedding party.

They decided to have the wedding itself in the large salon. The furniture would be taken out and the two hundred and fifty guests would be seated in rows of gilt chairs set up on either side of an aisle. Bess also insisted that the chuppa, the traditional wedding canopy, would be magnificently adorned with roses, lilies of the valley, carnations, and white satin streamers. Gold candelabra would be placed on either side, and two giant flower-filled urns would adorn the altar.

Even though it would be June, Bess was afraid to set up an outdoor tent. She decided to have the reception in the white and gold ballroom, since the Woodside house was old enough to have one built with magnificent proportions.

As the elaborate preparations continued, Martin felt more and more in the way. Finally, he said to Sylvia, 'Darling, you are so involved with all this, would you mind terribly if I flew to New York to see Dominic? I have felt so guilty about the way I left the agency. There may still be some loose ends he'd like to go over.'

For a moment, Sylvia thought her knees would buckle. Had he heard from Jenny? Was this trip a pretext? Then, with gentle wisdom, she said, 'Of course not, darling.'

As Martin rode into Manhattan from LaGuardia, he couldn't help thinking of Jenny. Although he reminded himself that his only motive for coming to New York was to see Dominic, he kept remembering the times he had picked Jenny up at the airport. He could almost see her now running across the tarmac, her hair blowing in the wind. He could almost feel her in his arms. Guiltily he reminded himself he was engaged to Sylvia, but the images continued to torment him.

He was grateful when the cab stopped in front of the Waldorf.

'Will that be all, sir?' asked the bellhop when he'd shown Martin his room.

'Yes, thanks,' Martin said, giving him a dollar. After the door had closed, Martin looked around the room, remembering the hotel he had stayed in when he first moved to New York. This time his mother would have approved.

After washing up he went downstairs to the bar. He'd told Dominic he would be in too late to have dinner, but the truth was Martin wanted some time alone in New York to think. As he sipped his scotch, he wondered why he had given himself a free evening, why he had really made the trip to New York. One reason he hadn't admitted to Sylvia was to finally sublease his apartment on Central Park West. All these months he'd been paying rent, but it was only now he could admit to himself he'd been hoping Jenny would return. Well, such dreams would have to end. He'd call the renting agent in the morning and make arrangements.

He finished the last of his drink and went out the lobby to Park Avenue. He started to walk, deciding he'd stop to eat when he came to a restaurant that appealed to him, but in every window he passed he seemed to see Jenny's face. Unable to bear it any longer, he hailed a cab and gave the Central Park West address. Tonight he would give in to his memories. Then tomorrow he'd sign the sublease the realtor was holding, visit Dominic, and spend the next few days buying a wedding gift for Sylvia and concentrating on his future.

But would he be able to forget? he wondered as the cab came to a halt before his old building. Riding the elevator, he felt Jenny's ghostly presence at his side, and once inside the apartment he pictured her everywhere he turned, smiling at him when he walked in the door, struggling over a new recipe, and with him in bed. They had been so happy. They had never even said goodbye properly. And now he remembered all the words he'd left unsaid.

He didn't know how long he sat in the empty bedroom which had held so many of his dreams. It was after nine when he finally went back to the street and found a cab. Too emotionally exhausted to think of eating, he went straight back to his hotel and went to bed.

Before he fell asleep, he remembered his father's kindness, his mother's joy in his wedding next month, and Sylvia, who had waited so patiently for him to sort out his life. He promised himself he would spend the rest of his life making her happy. He would be the most devoted of husbands. He would never cause her a moment's grief. He appreciated all her virtues, and together they would build a life that would be a proud testament to his parents, Ephraim, and all the Jewish men and women who had struggled to live in freedom. He would live happily with wife and children who believed in his God and his past.

Even with this resolve firmly in his mind it took Martin several hours to fall asleep.

The next morning, though, he felt better. He visited the

realtor and spent the afternoon in Dominic's office outlining some of the accounts he had in mind for the company to chase and certain plans the agency might adopt for expansion.

That evening he went back with Dominic to his apartment. Martin couldn't get over how successful his friend had become. He had moved to a large apartment on Riverside Drive, employed a Filipino houseboy, and was currently living with a French model named Coco.

Dominic had come a long way from the poor Italian section of New Haven, and he'd done it all on his own. The thing that amazed Martin the most was his friend's self-confidence. Dominic never seemed to question life or where it was taking him. He was obviously fond of Coco, but when they broke up he'd cheerfully find a replacement who'd make him equally happy.

'Drink up,' Dominic urged. 'Coco's spending the night at her sister's. We can really tie one on.'

Martin laughed. 'You never change, do you. Always ready for a good time.'

'And why not, Martin? Life's short. You've always taken it too seriously. Come on, old buddy, this will be your last trip East as a free man.'

'Maybe that's what's bothering me. Look, Dominic, the thing that haunts me is the fact that Jenny just disappeared. If I knew she was all right, I think I could put her out of my mind.'

'Well, that bothers me too. But you have to remember Jenny grew up in the school of hard knocks. She's tough. She was vulnerable where you were concerned, because she loved you. But I wouldn't worry too much. She's a survivor.'

'God, I hope so. I just wish I could have done something for her.'

'Well, there wasn't a hell of a lot you could have done. You never could have married her.'

Martin looked away. 'How can you be so sure? You told me once that if I loved her, I should fight for her.'

165

'Well, did you?'

'What the hell do you mean by that? Of course I did!'

'No, you didn't, old buddy. Not really. After your father died, she felt abandoned.'

'What the hell could I have done?'

'You could have sent for her. Or come back here.'

'You don't know what you're saying. My mother was in such a state of shock, she wasn't quite ready to cope with a gentile daughter-in-law.'

'And maybe you weren't ready for a gentile wife. Now do yourself a favour, Martin. You can have a long, fruitful life with Sylvia. She comes from the same background, and from everything you've told me she was made for you. Opposites may attract, but I don't think they live together happily. Now go home, Martin. Forget Jenny. Otherwise you'll just end up destroying your marriage.'

Dominic's logic was so airtight Martin couldn't argue. He relaxed and allowed himself to enjoy the evening.

Two days later when Dominic saw Martin off on the plane – a beautiful emerald cocktail ring from Tiffany's in his pocket – Dominic's last words were, 'Learn to enjoy life, Martin. See ya at the wedding.'

Chapter Seventeen

The day of the wedding had arrived at last. Bess was almost as happy as the bride. Both women were about to see their dreams fulfilled.

Bess came into the bedroom as Sylvia was fussing over her hair. The maid had already zipped up the tight scalloped bodice and straightened the full skirt over its petticoat. The silk was trimmed all over with circles of lace with small pearls sewn in the centre.

'I wanted to see you before you officially become my daughter, but after all these years no words could make us any closer. You've brought me untold joy as I know you have to Martin.'

Sylvia embraced Bess. 'I promise you I'll make Martin happy.'

'I know you will, my dear,' and she took the heavy strand of pearls from a velvet jewel box and slipped them over Sylvia's head. 'These were given to me by Martin's grandmother on my wedding day. I pass them on to you with the same love. Wear them in joy, my dear.'

Bess stood back and watched as the maid lifted up the yards of Valenciennes lace veiling.

In his old boyhood room Martin, fortified with brandy, was struggling with his pearl studs. When he finished getting the last one in, he began to fuss with his white tie, nervously pulling it loose.

'Here, let me help you do that,' Dominic said with a deft tug. 'All you have to do is relax, old buddy.'

'Relax? How can I? I'm scared to death!'

'Well, you won't be for long. Listen, you're one lucky man to have a girl like Sylvia. She's fabulous. What the hell did she ever see in you?'

'Thanks. That really helps a lot, Dominic.'

'Well, you needed a little pep talk. It's time for the best man to lead the groom to the altar.'

The music had begun. The two friends watched as the bridesmaids walked slowly down the centre aisle and took their places. Then the organist paused and began the wedding march.

A regal Sylvia walked down the marble staircase, her long train held by her thirteen-year-old niece, Linda. The pearls around her throat gleamed and her arms were filled with fragrant white roses and lilies of the valley.

At the entrance to the salon she was met by her father. Linda adjusted the veil, then retreated down the aisle.

Sylvia took her father's arm and waited while two little flower girls in long white organza dresses strewed the aisle with rose petals. Then the youngest cousin, Ephraim Roth, walked down the aisle, dressed in short black velvet pants and a white silk blouse, nervously bearing the rings on a white satin pillow.

Finally, Sylvia and her father started down the aisle between the two rows of flower-filled standards towards the altar. Sylvia was oblivious to the admiring whispers. 'Isn't she beautiful . . . ' 'And people thought she'd end up an old maid.' 'She certainly snagged the most eligible bachelor in San Francisco.'

A hush fell as they reached the canopy. Her father hugged her briefly and whispered, 'We love you,' then handed her over to her husband-to-be. Sylvia and Martin stood side by side while the Rabbi spoke the vows. Martin promised to love, honour and cherish; Sylvia promised to love, honour and obey. Then Martin crushed the traditional wineglass under his heel and the Rabbi pronounced them husband and wife.

When Martin lifted her veil to kiss her he couldn't believe how beautiful she looked. In that moment he adored her without reservation.

Bess had not cried during the ceremony, afraid if she allowed herself to miss Julian for a moment she would never be able to stop sobbing, but Sylvia's mother had wept joyously.

As the two families stood in the great hall greeting their guests, Bess was again overcome with Sylvia's poise. She began to enjoy herself, although her eyes darted about making sure the champagne was correctly served in the fluted glasses and the trays of canapés were circulated quickly.

When everyone had toasted the newlyweds, Bess began urging people into the ballroom. The bride, groom, and members of their immediate families were seated at a long table in the front while their other guests were placed at round tables for ten. Bess looked about her and smiled.

The white damask cloths gleamed with silver and crystal. Tall epergnes filled with white gladioli, roses and stock filled the air with a delicious scent.

Seeing the room in all its glory, Bess laughed, remembering her sleepless nights and frantic debates with Mr Maiard, the caterer. They had finally agreed to skip any shellfish even though none of the guests were kosher and settled on a pâté en croute, soupe aux cerises, and pheasant with wild rice and artichoke hearts.

Just before the wedding cake was served, the waiters came out with a parade of ices carved in the forms of hearts. Then the six-layer cake was wheeled out and Martin and Sylvia cut the first slice. After several more toasts the band struck up for the dancing.

When Sylvia and Martin walked onto the floor the guests began to clap. Few had seen a more handsome couple, nor one that seemed to have such a bright future. Later, Dominic claimed Sylvia, saying, 'You could almost talk me into marriage, Sylvia. You're my idea of a perfect lady, and I think that Martin is one lucky dog. Would it be out of order to give you a word of advice?'

'Please do,' said Sylvia, hoping he wouldn't speak of Jenny McCoy.

'Be patient.'

Sylvia wasn't quite sure what that meant, but she said, 'I will . . . and thank you for being a good friend. To both of us.'

Suddenly it was midnight. Sylvia and Martin were spending their wedding night in the suite Bess had moved out of after Julian's death, redecorating it for Martin and Sylvia as soon as her son had agreed to live at the Woodside estate.

To avoid wedding night pranks Martin and Sylvia pretended they were going East that night to start their month's honeymoon. Instead, after leaving under a shower of rice, they carefully circled the estate and then, turning off the car's lights, came down the driveway leading to the garages. Giggling like mischievous conspirators, they tiptoed through the servants' hall and up the back stairs.

Martin opened the door and carried Sylvia over the threshold. When he put her down, she looked at the old four-poster bed. On either side the burgundy draperies had been tied back with silken cords. A small fire glowed, warming the cool June night. The maids had left a bucket of champagne by the bed and turned down the spread, revealing the white satin comforter.

For a moment each was haunted by unwanted memories. Champagne had always been Jenny's drink – their drink – and her face suddenly seemed to float before Martin. As if she could read his mind, Sylvia found herself wishing that she had been her husband's first real love.

Martin popped the cork on the champagne and poured Sylvia a glass. 'To you, my dearest. May our life together always be as happy as it is for me tonight.' And as he spoke Martin honestly believed his words were the truth.

'I hope so, Martin,' she said, touching his glass with hers.

They sipped the wine in front of the fire in silence. When they finished, Martin went into the dressing room that had been his father's while Sylvia put on her nightgown in Bess's old dressing room.

She was so nervous as she lay in the huge bed waiting that she felt as if Martin were a stranger and she herself a virgin. Perhaps it was because she'd only had that one, brief encounter with him before the war. She started as Martin came towards her and turned off the lights. Only the fire illuminated his face as he bent over her and gently kissed her lips. She took his face in her hands and forgot her fear, embracing him without restraint. To his surprise he found himself overwhelmed by her touch and soon all restraints vanished as the two of them became one. For the rest of the night their joy was unshadowed either by memories of the past or fears for the future.

Martin awoke early the next morning and lay watching his bride sleep. He saw her as if with fresh eyes. She was, if possible, even more beautiful asleep than awake. *God, how lucky I am*, Martin thought. *How lucky I am to have a wife such as this.*

Sylvia stretched languidly and, opening her eyes to discover Martin, smiled.

'Did you sleep well?' he asked, taking her in his arms.

'Like a contented kitten.'

Marriage is an extraordinary thing, Martin thought. Knowing he belonged to another human gave him a unique sense of peace. Caring for Sylvia, watching over her happiness, would give his life a new purpose.

Tightening his arms around her, he kissed her urgently and her breath quickened as she guided him again inside her.

'You've made me very happy, Sylvia,' he said afterwards, and he prayed that today would set the tone for the rest of their lives, while Sylvia vowed to be a good wife who would never burden her husband with self-doubts or silly jealousies.

At that moment the Sevres clock on the mantel chimed. Martin, darling, it's eleven o'clock. Good grief – there's so much to do before we leave.'

When he came back from his shower she was sitting brushing her hair, which fell in loose waves over her blue satin gown.

'Let me look at you,' he said, taking her hands and turning her towards him. 'You're beautiful,' he said, 'and I love you.'

Sylvia wanted to believe that Martin had fallen in love with her at last, but all she said was, 'I hope it will get better and better and better with time.'

'I'll settle for the way I feel now. In fact, if you don't watch out, I'll carry you off to bed again right now.'

Smiling, she said, 'I'm afraid you'll have to use some restraint. Here's the maid with breakfast.'

As they sat waiting, Sylvia said, 'I don't remember swallowing a thing last night, but God, your mother outdid herself.'

'I know. Funny thing about human nature, nobody knows what they can really do until the time comes. After my father died, I thought she'd never pull herself together, and suddenly she has developed the strength of a lion. Some of that was your doing, Sylvia.' He took her hand. 'You know Bess loves you better than she does me, don't you?'

'She has every reason to,' Sylvia laughed. 'Now, darling, finish up and get ready.'

Bess and Dominic were waiting when the newlyweds came down the stairs. Sylvia was wearing a mauve wool dress with matching shoes and bag. The sable coat, which had been a wedding present from Bess, was draped over her arm.

The first person she embraced was Bess, thanking her for the lovely wedding. Then she stood in front of Dominic. Her look said, 'I will always take your advice. I've been patient.' Aloud she said, 'Thank you for coming, Dominic. It certainly wouldn't have been the same without you.'

Bess stood on the cobbled drive for a long time after Edward drove them out of sight. Tears streamed down her face, but when she walked back inside she was smiling.

The car took Martin and Sylvia to the airport where they were to catch a plane East to board the *Andrea Doria* the following day.

This time, when Martin walked across LaGuardia air field, he faced no ghosts. Grasping Sylvia's arm, he felt as if he were arriving in a strange city. The bridal suite at the Pierre was exquisite, and that night, as they walked the streets of Manhattan, Martin saw no faces from the past mournfully staring at him from the store windows.

They dined at Le Pavillon and later danced until three at the Starlight Roof to Guy Lombardo's band and that night they made love with a wild passion Martin hadn't suspected Sylvia possessed. He knew in those moments how much she loved him and vowed again never to hurt her.

In the morning she poked him awake, and getting out of bed without even reaching for her nightgown laughed and said, 'I'll race you to the shower!'

They reached Pier 44 just in time to hear the call, 'A

visitors ashore.' Martin and Sylvia quickly found their assigned stateroom, where their trunks already waited, then hurried on deck where they were caught up in the excitement of departure. The giant whistles shrilled as clouds of confetti fell on the crowds from the dock. Martin and Sylvia began waving back, laughing. It was a marvellous moment.

Back in their stateroom, Sylvia said, 'Oh, Martin, I'm so happy we came. Sometimes I think I'm dreaming. I adore you so . . .'

'Well, I should hope so. Now you rest and I'll make arrangements for the late dinner sitting. Remember now I'm your husband and if you obey me,' he said joking, 'nothing will come between us.'

Sylvia felt an unaccountable chill as she looked at him. 'I hope so, Martin,' she said, but he was already out the door.

The first night out Sylvia dressed in white chiffon and wore Bess's pearls and the emerald ring Martin had brought from New York. Seated at the Captain's table, Martin realized as if for the first time how openly other men stared at her. Suddenly he was filled with pride.

Sylvia was oblivious to the stir she caused. She had eyes only for Martin, her husband. To her he was the handsomest man there.

Later that night, Sylvia said tentatively, 'Martin?'

'Yes?'

'Can I talk to you about something?'

'Anything.'

'Please come closer. Yes, that's better . . . I have a confession to make.'

He smiled in the dark. 'Wow – that *does* sound serious. I'll try to be generous.'

'Martin, be serious, please.'

'Sorry, darling. Go ahead.'

She took hold of his hand. 'When we got married I wasn't quite sure if you really loved me.'

'Well, do you have any doubts about it now?'

'I guess what I'm really asking is, you really don't have

any regrets, do you, Martin?'

He answered quickly. 'Good God, no, Sylvia! How could you think that? You're the best thing that has happened to me. You must know that. You've given me a whole new sense of purpose.'

Purpose, she thought a little sadly. What about the fire and passion – the sorts of feelings he evoked in her? Then she remembered Dominic's advice and was silent, letting Martin show in the best way he knew how that he deserved her.

The five days on the *Andrea Doria* sped by and Sylvia could hardly believe it was time to leave the ship when they docked in Southampton. She felt that she and Martin had been living in a dream, isolated and protected from all intrusion, but Martin left her no time for regrets.

A car picked them up and drove them straight to the Connaught, plunging them into a pre-war opulence that fascinated Sylvia. Dowagers sat in the lobby chatting over tea and cucumber sandwiches. Mustachioed, irritable ex-officers looking like Colonel Blimp filled the salon, and everywhere she turned Sylvia found someone wanting to know if there was anything Madame needed.

As they drove through the streets sightseeing, the war intruded. Even in exclusive Mayfair the perfect rows of Georgian houses were interrupted by an occasional bombed-out lot, and the new American Embassy towered over Grosvenor Square as if to shout the new balance of world power.

They saw Westminster Abbey, visited Parliament, watched the changing of the guard and marvelled over the Crown Jewels guarded by the Beefeaters in the Tower of London.

Sylvia began to tire, but Martin insisted they spend a few days in Paris before going on to Venice, where he promised they would rest.

'After all, it is a city made for romance,' he said.

As it turned out, Martin was as pleased to leave Paris as

Sylvia. The Champs-Elysées, the sidewalk cafés, the Louvre were all enchanting, but the Parisians themselves seemed resentful of Americans and went out of their way to pretend to ignore their requests or to not understand even Martin's excellent French.

Venice, however, lived up to both their dreams. It was, as Martin had promised, a city made for lovers. Sylvia felt as if she had been transported to another century where her most extravagant fantasies could come true.

The first night she stood on the balcony of their room and looked out at the Grand Canal, watching the gondolas slip past in the moonlight. She heard the sound of the boats sliding through the water and listened as the gondolier began a song that must have been written hundreds of years before. Sylvia imagined the passengers were aristocratic Venetian ladies from the distant past, escorted by their dashing lovers to some secret rendezvous hidden in the maze of canals.

She could almost see them . . . the embroidered silk gowns, the flowing black or scarlet velvet cloaks – the jewelled masks which stood between them and the wrath of jealous husbands.

'Sylvia?'

Martin's voice called her back to the present.

'Yes, darling,' she answered, turning around.

'Enjoying the view?'

'Oh, yes, I've never been so excited in my life. I think this is going to be the best place we've ever been. The weather is so warm and it's all so romantic.' She walked over and found him in the beautifully carved rococo bed. That night their passion seemed to reach new heights.

Early the next morning, Sylvia quietly slipped out of bed, dressed, and went down to breakfast alone. It was only seven o'clock, but she didn't want to miss a moment of *bella Venezia* . . .

There was no one in the dining room except the maître d' who was mildly startled that an American lady would be up so early for breakfast.

175

Sylvia chose a table looking out at the Grand Canal. A small motorboat was tied up at the pier unloading produce.

How incredible, she thought. *Like a delivery truck!*

After her breakfast of rolls, black coffee and *formaggio*, Sylvia went for a walk. The narrow streets were still deserted except for vendors getting ready for the tourists. Here and there shopkeepers were washing down the sidewalks in front of their stores.

Cats rummaging through the garbage cans stopped to peer at her. One arched its back and snarled. 'Don't be so disagreeable. It's too beautiful,' she scolded them aloud. Sylvia felt as if she were in love with the world. Laughing at herself, she tossed her straw hat up in the air, shouting into the empty street, 'Oh, Venice, I'll always remember this time!' Then walking rapidly, she returned to the hotel.

As she entered their room, she found Martin had just finished dressing. 'My God,' he said, 'what time did you get up this morning? From now on, Syliva, if you're going to disappear please leave me a note.'

'Were you worried, Martin?' she asked, secretly pleased.

'Yes . . . a little.'

'I think that's charming, but I'm a big girl now.'

'Be that as it may, this is a foreign country, and young women can't be too careful.'

She smiled, thinking, *Oh, Martin, you should have known the perils I survived all the years you were away*, but all she said was, 'I love it when you're protective.'

'Where were you, anyway?'

'Downstairs, having breakfast.'

'So early? I just called room service. Now you're going to have to sit and watch me eat. Then maybe, if you're very good, I'll let you out of this room long enough to see a little of the city.'

She laughed as Martin took her in his arms.

At twelve o'clock they found themselves seated at a sidewalk café in St Mark's Square. The overfed pigeons strutted nonchalantly around their table until as if stirred by a single thought they took off into the air, almost blanketing the sun.

Sylvia watched as they finally settled on the other side of the Square. 'Oh, darling,' she said, 'I'll remember this all my life. I'm so happy that this is one city we're both seeing for the first time together.' She didn't add that in London she had occasionally found her pleasure clouded by memories of that dreadful year of self-imposed exile.

Martin took her hand and said, 'Yes, I know. Now I'm going to take you for a ride you'll never forget.' He led her back to the Grand Canal, where he hired a gondola for the afternoon.

They lay back in each other's arms and watched while the palazzi and churches slid by on either side of them.

That night in Harry's Bar, Sylvia said tearfully, 'Darling, I just feel so sad we're leaving tomorrow. Do you think we'll ever come back?'

'Of course,' Martin said. 'We can come back once each year on our anniversary.'

She reached over, took his hand. 'God, I really hope so, Martin.'

By noon the next day they were on a train bound for Rome. After they were settled at the Excelsior and began sight-seeing, Sylvia sensed that Martin was no longer enjoying himself. He seemed distant, withdrawn, as he had been when Jenny first broke off their affair.

But Martin wasn't thinking about Jenny. All he could remember were the days right after the Italian surrender, the children rummaging in garbage cans, and thirteen-year-old girls selling themselves for a candy bar.

He tried to exorcize the images with a frantic schedule. For the first time since they left the *Andrea Doria* they stayed up late. They danced almost until dawn, and when Sylvia woke still tired at noon, Martin presented her with a long list of places he'd arranged for them to visit: the Forum, the Coliseum, the Pantheon, the Baths at Caracalla. They even went across the Tiber to Vatican City to visit St Peter's and the Vatican Museum. They didn't get back until after five. Sylvia expected they would have an intimate dinner in the hotel, but Martin announced they had reservations at a well-known nightclub. Sylvia was on the verge of protesting when she noticed his tense expression. Uncertain what was troubling him, she decided to go along and hope the show would cheer him up. Patience, Dominic had recommended, and patient she would be.

For a while in the dark, smoke-filled nightclub, Martin seemed to regain his spirits. He laughed loudly at the Italian jokes Sylvia could not follow, but she noticed that he was drinking more than usual, and when he thought she wasn't looking, his face was drawn and blank. Sylvia was almost asleep when Martin finally suggested they go. All the way back to the hotel she tried to guess why Martin seemed so depressed. Her first thought was that something had reminded him of Jenny, but then she decided that was foolish.

As soon as they reached the Excelsior, Martin stripped off his clothes and flung himself on the bed. Sylvia went into the bathroom, turned on the taps, added bubble bath, and watched the tub fill. After she immersed herself in the soothing water, she lay back, looked up at the ceiling, and tried to think.

If knowing someone for a very long time meant that they would achieve a perfect union, then she and Martin should have had total compatibility. But that wasn't true. She had known Martin all her life, loved and adored him, but there was a part of him she didn't understand at all. Every time she had tried to break down that barrier and see what lay inside, he had stopped her. The fact that they were now married hadn't changed a thing.

Lying among the bubbles, she forced herself to put her own fears aside, reasoning that no matter what it was that bothered her husband, he needed her. She dried herself, walked into the bedroom, and snuggled down beside him. In spite of the fact that she felt him tense as she moved closer, she kissed him passionately and whispered, 'My darling Martin, I do adore you so.'

178

Sylvia had no way of knowing that the ghosts that had haunted him since the war had left him impotent tonight. She had probably thought sex would cheer him up, but for the moment it reminded him of too many sweating bodies and too much cheap perfume.

'I'm sorry, Sylvia, but I'm very tired.' He regretted the words of rejection the moment they left his mouth. But, as happens with people who are unable to reveal their weaknesses, Martin found himself imprisoned by them.

Sylvia suddenly remembered the night when he'd first come home from the war, when she had stolen into his room and tried to make love to him. He had said almost the same thing. *'I'm sorry, Sylvia.'*

She sat up slowly and took Martin's hand. 'Do you really love me?'

'Dammit, Sylvia, why do you ask me that?'

'Because I suppose I need reassurance.'

'About what?'

'That you love me, Martin.'

'Well, I wouldn't have married you if I hadn't.'

Trying to keep from crying, Sylvia said, 'You've become so remote in the last few days. Sometimes I do think you have regrets about marrying me.'

With more irritation than he meant, Martin snapped, 'What are you trying to say, Sylvia?'

'I think you're still in love with Jenny McCoy.'

Martin sat bolt upright, angrier than she had ever seen him. 'Goddamn it, Sylvia, I'm not going to spend the rest of my life feeling that every time I upset you, it's because of Jenny. I never want you to mention her name again. I want to forget her.'

Trying to maintain what little dignity she had left, Sylvia got up and went to the bathroom. She was certain now that Martin was in love with Jenny. The tears rolled down her cheeks, and for a long moment she wanted to die. Then she washed her face in cold water and sat on the rim of the bathtub. *Be honest at least*, she scolded herself. *He was in love with her, and at times I'm sure he's torn between you*

179

and her, but you're his wife. You're here, she's not. For God's sake be smart and make the most of it.

Alone in the bedroom, Martin cursed his outburst. He might just as well have slapped her. Contrite, he got out of bed and tried to open the bathroom door, but it was locked. He knocked.

No answer.

'Darling, I'm sorry.' He waited.

'Sylvia, please open the door.'

No response.

He went back to bed, wishing he could undo the hurt he had caused her. Dammit, he was always wounding the people he loved best. He was trying to decide what to say to her when she opened the door and came back into the bedroom.

He looked up as she seated herself on the edge of the bed. Softly, she said, 'Please forgive me if I offended you.'

He reached for her hand. 'It wasn't you, Sylvia.'

'Do you want to talk about it, darling?'

He hesitated. Could she really be made to understand what a strain it had been on him being back in Europe. Could she accept the fact that even the pleasures of a honeymoon could not erase the terrible memories of the war, which Italy in particular reawakened? Or would she be insulted or think him weak? Everywhere they had gone, he had seen a million ex-GIs, laughing, talking, drinking, holding hands with dark-haired Italian beauties. They had fought in the war, too, but seemed to have made peace with the past. Even the Italians seemed to have picked up their lives with their usual zest. What was wrong with him that he alone could not shake off the sad recollections?

Staring at Martin's ravaged face, Sylvia suddenly glimpsed the truth. She was able to put aside her own insecurities and think only of her husband. The problem wasn't her, it wasn't secret comparisons with Jenny, it was simply that it was too soon for Martin to enjoy Europe without feeling guilty. She thought very carefully before speaking.

'Darling, you know how I have adored our honeymoon,' she said. 'But you know, I think playing tourist is getting a little boring. I don't mean you, dearest, you'll never be boring. But I think maybe it's time to go home. How would you feel about that?'

He put his arms around her and drew her close. 'I love you, Sylvia,' he said huskily. 'I don't know what I've done to deserve you.'

Once again Sylvia realized that her patience and her uncanny ability to guess Martin's wishes had helped her choose the right course of action. She hoped she would never lose that gift.

Chapter Eighteen

The trip home was an exhausting one and the pair spent only a night's stopover in New York. The flight from Europe was delayed and they were able to snatch only a few hours' sleep before it was time to dress and return to LaGuardia to board their plane to San Francisco.

Sylvia in particular had a hard time shaking the effects of the trip. Tired and listless, she barely had the energy to unpack and give Bess and her parents their gifts before collapsing into bed.

On Friday, the fourth evening after their return, Bess gave a small family dinner to celebrate their return. Martin came home early from the office to find Sylvia still undressed and resting on their bed.

'Are you all right?' he asked, knowing she would normally be downstairs helping Bess.

'Yes,' she said, forcing herself to get up and start her bath. 'I don't know what's wrong with me. And here you were the one who said Europe had been tiring.'

Later, after a meal she barely touched, she looked around the living room and asked if anyone minded if she excused herself. Martin quickly leaped to his feet.

'Are you sure you're feeling well?' he asked, gazing at her drawn face.

'I'm fine. It's just the effects of the flight. I still haven't adjusted to the time change.'

'Are you sure?'

'Of course. Let me run on upstairs.' She cheerfully said goodnight to the other guests, but once outside in the hall Sylvia thought she was going to faint. Beads of perspiration broke out on her forehead, and she clung to the newel post, waiting for the sensation to subside. Finally she felt a little better and continued on to her room, where she got into bed and fell asleep almost immediately.

The next morning, when she came downstairs, Martin and Bess had already finished their breakfast. 'My God,' Sylvia said. 'I can't believe I slept this late! Why didn't you wake me up, Martin?'

'Because you seemed to need the sleep. How do you feel this morning?'

She was really still a little sick, but she answered, 'Fine now.'

Bess asked quickly, 'What do you mean? Were you ill?'

'No, not exactly. I just felt rather strange . . . '

'What do you mean, "strange"? What were the symptoms?'

'Mother, I think you're making much too much of this.'

'Be that as it may, you didn't answer the question. I asked you for the symptoms . . . '

'Well, slightly nauseated.'

Bess smiled. 'Oh, my dear. Let me see if we can get an appointment with Dr Friedman.'

Before Martin could object, Bess had dialled the doctor's number, which she knew by heart. He said he could fit Sylvia in at two o'clock.

All during the ride into the city Bess kept her happy

suspicions to herself, but once the nurse ushered Sylvia into the inner office, Bess anxiously paced the waiting room.

After the examination, Dr Friedman asked Sylvia to dress and come into his consulting room. 'Well, my dear,' he said smiling as she sat down, 'I do believe you are going to be a mother.'

'Are you sure?'

'Almost certain. Of course, we will run a test to be sure.'

Sylvia was so overcome with happiness that she scarcely paid attention to Dr Friedman's initial instructions. She did hear him say, 'A first child at thirty requires a little more rest, a little more caution.' She looked at him with unspoken concern.

'Dr Friedman, I must have this child. It must be healthy.'

'Well, we really don't have anything much to concern us, but I would suggest that you not exert yourself. No strenuous exercise, a rest in the afternoon, no cigarettes or alcohol. And watch your diet. It's not so easy to lose weight after the baby at your age.'

'That sounds easy,' Sylvia said smiling.

'Now let's go outside and tell your mother-in-law,' Dr Friedman said. 'I know how excited she will be.' He put an arm around Sylvia's shoulders and walked her back into the reception room.

'Well, my dear, it seems that you're going to be blessed with a grandchild. My congratulations to you and Martin. I'm sure that Sylvia is going to come through this splendidly.'

Bess wanted to telephone Martin immediately but Sylvia insisted they wait until he came home from work. By six-thirty, though, when he still hadn't returned, she was sorry she hadn't called the office. When she heard his car in the drive she went out through the French doors, ran down the path and threw herself into Martin's arms.

'Darling, guess . . . '

'Oh my God, it's true! Are you sure?'

He held her as though she were extremely fragile. 'Sylvia, I didn't know I could feel so happy. Having a child means more to me than almost anything in the world.'

'Oh, Martin, I just want to make you happy.'

'You have already. You've made me happier than I have a right to be.'

That night he held her in his arms with a mixture of tenderness and desire that he had never felt for anyone before. She was going to be the mother of his child. She was going to fulfil his destiny and in doing so make him whole again.

Life over the next months settled into a quiet routine. Both Martin and Sylvia were early risers. Most mornings, she put on a casual dress and the two of them had breakfast alone, since it was Bess's habit to sleep late and to have breakfast in bed.

Sylvia loved the morning room. It was filled with plants and ferns of all sizes. The little table was lacquered green and the chairbacks painted with bright flowers so that even in winter it felt like spring.

When they finished breakfast, Martin would drive into the city, leaving Sylvia to a leisurely round of activities. She would call her parents, visit a while with Bess, and then often meet a friend for lunch. It was a lazy time, but she knew it was good for the baby and didn't feel guilty even when a nap consumed most of the afternoon.

Martin watched happily as Sylvia moved from loose shifts to actual maternity clothes. Though both her mother and Bess encouraged her to indulge herself, Sylvia watched her weight carefully. She took her vitamins obediently and, in addition to her calcium tablets, drank three glasses of milk a day. She was nervous about gaining more pounds than she could easily lose after the baby was born.

Until her eighth month Sylvia was superstitious about letting Bess furnish the nursery. Dr Friedman kept assuring her they were fine, and when Sylvia finally saw the old-fashioned bassinette Bess had chosen – tufted in white satin and trimmed with tiny blue bows – she became as excited as her mother-in-law.

When Martin saw the blue bows, he laughed, saying, 'What if it's a girl?'

'I don't think it will be,' Sylvia said. 'I think you're going to have a son, Martin. But if it isn't we'll change the bows to pink.'

Earlier Sylvia had been afraid something might happen to the baby. Now she relaxed. She even let her mother send over her old brass crib, still as bright as the day that Sylvia had first slept in it, and enthusiastically joined both the older women in shopping for a layette. Towards the end of her eighth month Sylvia began interviewing nurses. She finally hired a widow in her middle forties who came with excellent recommendations.

One morning, a couple of weeks later, going down to breakfast, Sylvia tripped on the last step. She managed to hold on to the banister as she fell, and seemed more frightened than hurt, but everyone was relieved when Dr Friedman arrived and confirmed that she was fine. At one o'clock that night, however, her waters broke. Not having the slightest idea what to do, Martin called his mother, who came rushing into the room. In spite of her great anxiety, Bess managed to stay calm as she called Dr Friedman and Sylvia's mother, and then arranged to have the bedding changed.

Dr Friedman arrived in less than half an hour. After a quick examination he said he didn't think there was any need to rush to the hospital. Sylvia could rest a while until the contractions became more regular. He said he wasn't tired and he'd wait for Bess for a while downstairs.

Martin pulled a chair over to the bed and took Sylvia's hand. 'Are you in much pain, dearest?'

'No, at least not too much. The pains are still too far apart to be severe.'

But when Dr Friedman came upstairs an hour later, she gripped his hand tightly, moaning as the contractions became sharper and more frequent.

'Just relax, Sylvia,' he said. 'And try to breathe naturally. You're too tense . . . Now that's a good girl. I think for your comfort I'm going to take you to the hospital by ambulance. That way you won't have to get up.'

Sylvia tried to follow the doctor's instructions, but the next pain was so sharp that she screamed and clutched Martin's hand so tightly her nails broke the skin. She was desperately trying not to scream again when two medics entered the room with a stretcher.

Sylvia felt herself being lifted, transferred to the stretcher, then carried down the stairs, where the attendants slid her into the ambulance. Martin climbed in after her and they took off with sirens wailing. She was aware of Martin crouched over her in the ambulance. The next thing she knew she was being shifted from the stretcher to a narrow white bed, able to think only of the next shaft of pain awaiting her. This one was so sharp that she bit her lip until it bled.

'I'm here, darling,' Martin said.

Then Sylvia heard the doctor suggest, 'If you'd just wait outside, Martin, until I've examined Sylvia.'

As Martin bent down to kiss her, Sylvia whispered, 'You will come back, won't you?'

'Yes, as soon as the doctor allows it. I'll be right outside your door, darling.'

Throughout the night her labour continued, and as the pain wore down her resolve, she found herself screaming more and more often. Now it hurt not just during the contractions but consistently and without relief. Martin stayed with her in the labour room except for the brief moments when she was being examined.

By two o'clock that afternoon, Martin was beside himself. 'You can't let her go on suffering like this,' he said. 'I know you believe in natural childbirth, but nothing seems to be happening. I don't know how much longer she can stand the pain.'

Dr Friedman said he would make one more examination. When he came out he asked Martin to come back into the room with him to speak to Sylvia. 'I'm going to arrange for a caesarean,' he said.

In spite of her pain, Sylvia cried out, 'No, I can wait. I can stand it.'

'Sylvia, you're in no condition to make that decision.'

Grabbing his hand weakly, she whispered, 'Please, please, doctor. I'll die if anything happens to this child.'

'Nothing will happen. Please believe me.'

'I won't go,' she gasped, perspiration running down her face. 'No one can make me go . . .'

When he saw the look of determination in her eyes, he agreed to wait just a little longer. He was now sorry that he had encouraged her so strongly to consider only natural childbirth.

Another hour passed and she became almost too tired to cry out. Martin, frantic, sat with his head in his hands. The few times he went out to the waiting room his mother and Sylvia's parents tried to reassure him, but it did little good. He had stopped worrying about the baby and just prayed that Sylvia would be all right. At that point she was his only concern.

By seven o'clock the baby's head was ready to emerge, but Sylvia was so weak that Dr Friedman regretted having let her talk him out of the caesarean. Keeping his fears to himself, he arranged to have her taken to the delivery room. Martin went out to wait with the parents.

It was a breech birth and even the delivery itself took longer than usual. Finally, twenty hours after Sylvia's waters broke, the baby was born. At first the cessation of pain was all she cared about. Then she heard a small cry and a wave of pure joy washed over her.

'It's a boy, Sylvia,' said Dr Friedman, placing the baby on her stomach while he delivered the placenta.

Sylvia looked down at the tiny form. Except for Martin she was never to know a greater love. This was truly the culmination of her marriage: the flesh of their flesh.

They took the baby away to be weighed and washed. Sylvia was moved to a stretcher to be wheeled to her room while Dr Friedman went out to tell Martin the good news.

Still in his surgical garb, he walked into the hall, took off his glasses, and said, 'Martin, you have a son.'

Martin was transfixed. Bess gripped his shoulders, saying, 'Oh, dear God, Martin, I remember the day you were born. And now *you* have a son!' Tears ran down her face.

'How is Sylvia?' Martin asked.

'Fine. The labour was too damn hard. How she came through it, I really don't know. I'll tell you now, it was touch and go for a while. But she'll be good as new in a few days. Right now she's more tired than anything else.'

'Thank God! When can I see her?'

'They're taking her to her room now. Just give her a few minutes to tidy up and you can go up. But don't stay long. She's exhausted.' He turned to Bess and the Lowenthals. 'I think the rest of you should wait until tomorrow. Sylvia really needs to rest.'

The Lowenthals nodded and began to gather their things in preparation to going home.

'I'll wait here,' Bess said to Martin. 'Then we can drive home together.'

Martin went up to Sylvia's room and sat by the edge of her bed. She looked up at him, blinking away happy tears. She felt that their son was her final triumph over the phantom Jenny.

Martin too was overcome with emotion. If he and Jenny had had a baby his joy could never have been so complete. Jenny's child would have belonged to the Church. This tiny boy was a true Roth and could carry on his father's heritage. Gently he leaned over and kissed Sylvia on the lips.

As he straightened up, Dr Friedman came into the room, his coat over his arm. 'I think you should leave now. Sylvia is very tired. And you, young lady – I'll see you and your son in the morning.'

Although Sylvia was exhausted from her long ordeal, after Martin had left, she asked if they would bring her baby from the nursery. She could not get over the miracle of him.

The nurse reassured Sylvia that the baby would be returned to her at seven o'clock. Reluctantly, Sylvia resigned herself to the long wait, but before she knew it, it was morning and the whimpering child was laid at her breast. He sucked for a few minutes, but Sylvia knew that he was just getting colostrum. Her actual milk would not come in for another day.

At twelve Bess arrived, followed soon after by Sylvia's parents, who had brought with them flowers for their daughter and a silver rattle, a Teddy bear and a football 'for when he's older' for their grandson. After leaving the presents, Bess and the Lowenthals went down to the nursery, where they were instantly convinced that their grandchild was brighter, better looking, and more perfect than any of the other babies.

'No doubt about it,' Mr Lowenthal said, beaming.

When Martin arrived they were back in Sylvia's room discussing names. 'I really thought we'd call him Julian, after my father,' Martin said.

Bess's face lit up. 'Oh, I'd love that. But would you mind?' she said, turning to the Lowenthals.

'Of course not, dear,' Sylvia's mother said. 'It's what we expected if Sylvia had a boy.'

Martin smiled again, happy that there was no conflict, that the families were of one mind. Sylvia leaned back on her pillows, almost overcome with happiness.

It was not until some days later that she discovered a small cloud on the horizon. Although baby Julian had been nursing every four hours, the fluid in Sylvia's breasts was steadily decreasing. The nurse attached a small breast pump, trying to start the flow, but little came. When she saw the baby was getting no milk, she left the room and returned with a bottle. Realizing that she would not be able to breast feed, Sylvia burst into tears. She was certain the problem resulted from her strenuous dieting. She continued to weep even when the nurse settled the baby in her arms and showed Sylvia how to hold the bottle so he didn't get any air. Almost at once, the baby stopped fussing and sucked contentedly.

When he had had his fill, the nurse took him in her arms

to return him to the nursery and said gently, 'I think he'll have to be bottle fed from now on.'

Sylvia bit her lip. 'Maybe if I take a lot of nourishment I can do it . . .'

'Dr Friedman will know what to do.' The nurse went out, leaving Sylvia regretting every calorie she had denied herself during her pregnancy. *A baby should lie at his mother's breast*, she thought, *instead of sucking on a rubber nipple. Damn. Damn that diet. Damn my thirty years. I should have had my first baby at twenty.* She worked herself up into a real stew by the time Dr Friedman arrived.

Concerned at her emotional state, he did his best to calm her down. 'Children do as well, and sometimes even better, on the bottle,' he said, but he only upset Sylvia more by confirming the nurse's prognosis.

'I don't believe that,' she sobbed.

'But it's true. And besides, we really don't have any other choice.'

'What would happen if I took more nourishment? Isn't there anything I could take to help me produce enough milk?'

'I'm afraid it wouldn't make any difference at this point.'

Sylvia realized that Dr Friedman was unaware that, in a sense, he had created her problem by recommending the diet. But remembering his kindness over the last eight months, she decided not to pursue the matter. 'Well,' she said, drying her eyes, 'if that's the case, at least I want to give him his bottles.'

'Only during the day. The nurses will handle the night feedings.'

'No,' she insisted, 'I want my son brought to me for all his bottles, day or night.'

Dr Friedman looked at her and laughed. 'You're incorrigible. Now, Sylvia, let me examine you.'

He wasn't at all pleased when he saw the toll the long labour had taken on her uterus. It had not tightened as fast as he had hoped. When he was done he pulled out a chair and sat down.

'Sylvia, I have some instructions which must be carried out to the letter. You know, my dear, you can be very stubborn.' He smiled, shaking his head. 'I want you to have very few visitors during the next week. And I want you to put on some weight . . . '

'I promise,' she said and smiled back.

'Fine. Now get some rest and I'll see you tomorrow.'

Soon after, Martin came in and kissed her softly on the lips. She drew him closer. 'Motherhood has not transformed me into a saint. You can do better than that.'

'I can do much better than that . . . ' He kissed her again – a real kiss this time, filled with the love he felt for his wife – and sat down.

'How are you feeling this morning?' she asked, seeing that he obviously hadn't slept well.

'Fathers always survive.'

She smiled, 'Martin, isn't he beautiful?'

'Like his mother.'

'You mean I look like a little red lobster?'

Martin laughed. Then his face became serious. 'Look, darling,' he said. 'I've spoken to Dr Friedman. I really want you to rest.'

She reached out and took his hand. 'Oh, Martin, I'm so full of love, how can I feel tired? You've given me so much.'

'No, darling, it's the other way around. You've given me a son, *our* son. Now rest.'

'Will you be back soon? Please?'

'If you promise to eat, and nap, and not talk too much. Otherwise it's solitary confinement.'

For the next few days even her mother and father visited only briefly. Bess just stuck her head in from time to time announcing grandly, 'I'm going to see my grandson, Julian Roth the Second.' It was just a year since her husband had died, and Bess found it especially significant that the baby was born at this time.

At last the day came for Sylvia to go home. Martin stayed home from work and, when Sylvia was comfortably settled in their bedroom, he spent the rest of the afternoon

191

watching his son. He was enchanted by the little face that looked so much like both himself and his father.

At dinner that night Bess's pleasure at having her grandson home was so great that Martin silently congratulated Sylvia once again for having persuaded him to live in Woodside rather than buying a house of their own.

As the months passed, Julian grew into a chubby, happy baby. Except for a little colic and some hard times with his first teeth, he was an easygoing, cheerful soul. He smiled at Sylvia, Bess, his nurse, even strangers, but his favourite person in his small universe was Martin. His mother and grandmother and nurse were there all day. Martin's company was special.

On Sunday mornings, Martin would get up early and bring Julian into the big four-poster to play. The proud father would hold his baby boy up in the air while little Julian kicked and laughed. Then he would sit him up and pretend to carry on a real conversation. Julian would gurgle and try to imitate his father's sounds.

Sylvia never tired of watching them together. She was still crazy in love with her husband and thought that his prematurely greying hair had made him handsomer than ever. And it seemed as if Martin loved her more than ever, too. The smallest holiday became an excuse for indulgence as he brought her a new ring, a bracelet, earrings. When she protested, Martin just said that the mother of his son deserved the best.

On Julian's first birthday, Sylvia had a small party for the family in the garden. Julian sat in his highchair, pounding on the attached tray with his spoon while his two adoring grandmothers vied for his attention. At one point Bess pulled him up to give him an exuberant hug, but when the baby caught sight of Martin at the head of the table he stretched out his arms and screamed for his father.

'If ever there was a daddy's boy, he is,' laughed Bess, placing the baby in Martin's arms.

Sylvia observed the scene smiling. Then she stood up and

aised her hands to get everyone's attention. 'I have an announcement to make,' she said, turning to her husband and son. 'I think you, dear Julian, are going to have a little competition in the fall.' Martin looked at Sylvia for a long moment, then returned Julian to Bess and walked over to his wife. 'Darling, how wonderful.' He looked around the flower-filled garden, saw his proud relatives, heard Julian's happy laughter. His heart filled to overflowing and he vowed he would never let anything happen to hurt his family or endanger their happiness.

Chapter Nineteen

On December the twenty-sixth, Sylvia delivered a baby girl, weighing just under seven pounds. After much persuading, she had agreed to a caesarean, so the baby's time of arrival was known well in advance. She was spared the long ordeal of labour, but she also missed the excitement of hearing her daughter's first cry. Sylvia was back in her room before she regained consciousness, and she didn't see Martin until the next day. He seemed delighted to have a girl and handed out cigars to all the doctors. When Sylvia suggested naming the child after his favourite grandmother, Amanda Roth, he seemed as pleased as he had when she'd named Julian after his father.

Martin was pleased and as the babies grew he knew he had little cause to complain about the pattern his life had taken. The brokerage prospered, the family was healthy, and Sylvia seemed to have accepted the role of suburban mother. If sometimes Martin felt life proceeded on too even a keel, he kept such thoughts to himself. Only occasionally did he allow himself to question his life, and that was when he felt the children were growing away from him.

Between the nurse, Sylvia and the maids, Martin felt as if he were losing the special closeness he'd enjoyed with Julian. He began working longer hours the year Amy was born and sometimes days passed when he wouldn't see his daughter. He begged Sylvia to keep the children up later, but she didn't like to upset their routine.

Goddammit, they're my children, Martin sometimes felt like saying, but he didn't, although sometimes sitting at the table with Bess and Sylvia he felt a surge of restlessness. Was it less than two years since Julian's first birthday, when Martin had felt he was the luckiest man in the world? Now sometimes he envied Sylvia's apparent contentment, envied and resented it at the same time.

One night after the children were in bed, Martin and Sylvia settled into their favourite chairs in the library. Martin had taken out the stock market report and barely heard Sylvia's rundown of the day's activities until she said 'If you could have seen how excited Julian was.'

Martin poised his index finger on the quotation on US Steel and looked up with sudden interest. 'Sorry, I'm afraid I missed that. Who did you say was excited?'

'Julian.'

'Oh? About what?'

'Going to nursery school. The one your cousin Jane is sending Mark and Deborah to. Of course they are in kindergarten but Julian will be in the same group as Joe and Nicole and –'

As though he had been struck, Martin shouted 'You are sending Julian to school? For God's sakes, he is only three.'

Sylvia was shocked by his outburst. Suppressing her own anger, she said quietly, 'Jane sent the twins when they were only two.'

'I don't give a damn what my cousin Jane did, she can do anything she damn well pleases, but I don't believe in regimenting children that young. Let them grow up, fo

God's sake.'

'But you don't understand Martin. I feel Julian needs to play with other children. In fact, the other day when Jane stopped in after school, Julian asked Mark if he wouldn't take him.'

'Why in the hell didn't you discuss this with me before?'

'Well, darling, that's what I'm doing now.'

Well, she was, but Martin sensed the decision had been made. Knowing he was being unfair, he said crossly, 'All right, Sylvia, but the answer is no. Julian is entirely too young to be sent away to school.'

Sylvia bit her lower lip, trying not to smile. She knew Martin was having a hard time realizing that Julian was no longer a baby. She expected this was partly because he had never become as close to Amy. Trying to keep her patience, Sylvia said, 'He is not exactly being sent away, Martin. He will be in school from nine to eleven-thirty. It will be good for him. He'll grow up being a very lonely little boy if he is only surrounded by adults.'

Martin felt as if he'd been pushed into a corner. In her sweet, compassionate way, Sylvia sounded as if the sacrifice were entirely for Julian's sake. Martin didn't believe it. He felt that Sylvia followed whatever his cousin Jane suggested. As the mother of four, Jane's advice was sacrosanct and for all he knew maybe she was right. But the thought of Julian going off to school filled Martin with a nameless sadness. For the first time he wished they lived in San Francisco so he could walk Julian to school in the morning before going to the office. Well, there was no use arguing. He would look like a heel if he tried to stop her, and he was damn well sure his mother's allegiance would be with Sylvia. His mother always sided with her.

'Well, where in the hell is this school?' he asked sullenly and Sylvia knew that was his way of giving his consent.

Martin insisted on driving Julian on the first day, but afterwards he was sorry he had gone. Something very precious died in Martin when Julian let go of his hand and

195

ran off to play with the other kids. He didn't even look up when Martin pecked him on the cheek and said goodbye. If Martin had ever been asked to pick a time when the first blush of happiness left his marriage, he would have siad the moment he left Julian at school. But he knew that was unfair. It wasn't Sylvia's fault the boy was growing up.

Over the next year Martin frequently went to work late, dropping Julian off first, and he often called home at twelve to make sure the boy had returned safely. He saved all of Julian's crayoned pictures and had them matted and framed as if they were Picassos. He even hung some in his office and would point them out to visitors saying, 'By God, the boy is really good, for a three-year-old.'

No one was surprised that Martin's favourite was a scribbled figure captioned 'Daddy.'

One night Julian sat on Martin's knee, describing a new picture, showing off all the brilliance Martin insisted the boy possessed. 'Look, Daddy, the sky is blue and the tree is green, the moon is yellow and the house is white. And look there's a daddy walking up the path with his big boy,' and he pointed to two figures who were almost the same size.

'Do you like it, Daddy?'

'I love it, Julian, but don't you keep wishing to grow up. Stay a little boy just a while longer – for my sake. Okay, Julian?'

'Okay, Daddy.'

Although Julian said he was willing, time was not. Somehow, before Martin knew it, Julian turned six and one morning he and Sylvia went to enrol the boy in the Menlo School, which was a day school through ninth grade. Instead of remembering his own happy days there, Martin felt bereft.

Later that afternoon he sat in his office and couldn't concentrate on anything. He stared out the window at the bridge, but even that elegant span of metal failed to raise his spirits. His life felt so empty. The children seemed to have less time for him. Both were busy with their own playmates, and even Sylvia suddenly seemed involved with a bunch of silly charities. He felt as if he were living on the edge of everyone else's lives, even his mother's. Hell, no one was paying him much attention. He didn't want to feel sorry for himself, but he did.

Yet Martin didn't complain, which in many ways was unfair to Sylvia. As far as she could see their marriage was as happy as ever. They never fought. They rarely argued. But Sylvia was aware that Martin was less than content. Of course she did not have much time to dwell on the problem. She had been raised to believe that children were the most important thing in marriage and, after all, Martin said he was happy.

Sylvia pushed the vague concern aside and continued to fill her days taking the children to the orthodontist, to dancing lessons, tennis lessons, horseback lessons, swimming lessons. She was elected to the school board to help supervise the curriculum and worked hard getting a local Congressman who favoured safe streets and better schools elected. All this would help her children's future.

She didn't neglect Martin, for no matter what she did during the day, she was always home by five to shower and dress for his homecoming.

Their friends considered them the ideal couple. They went to the opera, the theatre and charity balls. They supported several San Francisco galleries and were active members of the country club. If Martin was bored by the conversation at the golf course or by the inevitable game of gin after dinner at the club, he showed his feelings only by an occasional prolonged silence.

He would sometimes watch Sylvia's placid acceptance of her own routine with envy. She didn't seem to mind the constant driving. She said that she'd resented being consigned to the family chauffeur when she was a girl and was determined her children would not be similarly neglected. She was convinced that that was one of the reasons she did not feel close to her own mother. No, she told Martin when he questioned the hours she spent in the car, she was happy

197

to drive. It gave her a chance to talk with the kids.

'Don't you get bored?' Martin once asked her.

'No.' She enjoyed her days. She was content being the loving mother, devoted wife, obedient daughter-in-law. She planned their life carefully. That's why it was so perfect. They were the lucky couple, weren't they? Ask anyone.

Anyone, that is, except Martin Roth. He was jealous of Sylvia's tranquillity, and decent enough to be angry with himself for begrudging her her enjoyment of the small things which filled her life.

Reading the paper one Sunday in April when Julian was about nine, Martin looked out through the French doors to the garden and was filled with an indefinable yearning. It was spring. The flowers were bursting into bloom, filling the air with a heady fragrance. The seasons were changing, life was racing by, and Martin felt as if he were being left at the side of the road, a passive onlooker. Stepping outside, his feeling of frustration grew. Why had he allowed himself to be stifled? Why did he let his wife and mother control his life? The fact that the accusation was unfair just made him angrier. He knew in the beginning he'd encouraged Sylvia to run his home just as his mother had run his father's. He had believed that this was all he wanted. He had been certain that any other longings would be satisfied by the children. Well, they weren't, and he found himself furious at Sylvia whether it was her fault or not.

Tossing down the paper, he walked upstairs, just past Julian and Amy's rooms to the bedroom he shared with Sylvia. He stood for a long moment observing her. 'Hi, darling,' she said when she realized he was there. 'What have you been –'

'I want you to get the children ready to go to the house in Tahoe,' he said impulsively. Maybe a change of routine would put him in a better mood.

Sylvia, shocked by the anger underlying his request, wasn't sure how to respond. 'Martin, darling,' she said finally, 'it's too early for Tahoe and the children are –'

198

'I don't give a damn, Sylvia – it won't hurt them if they miss a few days of school.'

'Darling, I really don't understand any of this.'

'That's just the trouble,' Martin said. 'Why do you need to understand? Why can't we just once do something because I feel like it? And I feel like going to the Lake.'

'Martin, I think you are being unreasonable. I can't get the house ready that quickly, and besides I want to find out why you are so angry.'

Martin clenched his fists before answering. Good fathers and husbands controlled their tempers, but suddenly he wasn't sure if he still wanted those two roles. Still he would try. Taking a deep breath, he tried to explain, praying that Sylvia would understand the need for excitement and adventure that he couldn't express, that he was trying to assuage with this small, unplanned family trip.

'Sylvia, I am not angry. At least I'm trying not to be. I just thought it would be a good idea if we could get away. What would be so dreadful if you and I went up without the children and let Bess bring them up in a few days?'

'Really, Martin, as much as I would love that, I think we should be here when the children get out of school. If you think about it, darling, you'll see that's the right thing to do.'

Martin didn't care about doing the right thing, but the idea of a spontaneous little vacation had been ruined anyway, so he decided to give in. 'You're right,' he said. 'We'll go when we planned.'

'I knew you would agree, Martin, darling.'

Martin spent the next two hours hitting tennis balls as hard as he could from the ejector.

On the fifteenth of April, precisely as planned, Martin checked twelve pieces of luggage into the car to drive to the airport. They always flew to Tahoe because Amy got carsick on long trips. They reached the airport in plenty of time only to discover the plane had been delayed by fog, which did little to improve Martin's spirits. He snapped at Sylvia when she suggested coffee and yelled at Julian when he refused to play cards with his sister. At Sylvia's urging he agreed to take Amy to explore the airport shops, but when they came back with enough bubble gum, Hershey bars and comic books to last a lifetime, Julian began asking, 'When are we going to leave, Dad?' until Martin blew up, shouting at his son to shut up until they were on the plane.

'Martin, I don't think it at all necessary to speak to Julian that way,' said Bess, for once breaking her own rule about interfering.

Sylvia tried to stay out of the argument, but as Martin's voice rose she tried to calm him, whispering that Julian was still a little boy and they would be going soon anyway. Martin realized that he was acting childishly, but his bad mood didn't lift until they finally landed in Reno.

Almost from the moment they arrived, Martin felt as if he had been let out of jail. As soon as the children had gone to bed he drove Sylvia down to the Cal-Neva lodge, where she played roulette and Martin shot craps. Then they danced until one in the morning and caught the last show of the Hawaiian revue. By this time Martin was a little drunk. Sylvia was still acting wary, uncertain of his temper, when he announced she had never looked better and he couldn't wait to get her home to bed.

The next morning he was up at eight, rested as if he'd had a full night's sleep. He left Sylvia in bed and went down to breakfast, where he was thrilled to find he had the children to himself.

Boy, they are gorgeous kids, he thought as he looked at them over the rim of his coffee cup. 'Dad, can we go on the higher slopes today?' Julian asked, seeing Martin's good spirits.

He looked at them for a moment. They were damn good skiers, better than most kids their age, but he knew Sylvia didn't think they were ready for the advanced trails. 'I don't think so, Julian, not this year,' he said.

'Why not, Dad?'

Amy chimed in, 'Yes, why not, Dad?'

'Because I really don't think you're quite ready for it.'

Upon which Julian protested, 'I'm not a child any longer and I've been skiing since I was four.'

'Me, too, Daddy,' Amy said.

What they said was true and like most indulgent fathers he found it hard to say no. 'We'll just go up and tell your mother,' he said, giving in.

Sylvia was yawning as they came into the room. 'How did you sleep, dear?' Martin asked.

'Just great,' she said. Then, noticing the kids, she added, 'Have you all made plans for the day?'

'Well, the children are anxious to get in some skiing.'

'Darling, would you forgive me if I didn't join you? I'd like to be lazy today and I think Mother wanted to go into the village a little later.'

'I wish you would,' Martin said. But before he could say more to persuade her, Julian and Amy pulled him from the room. Julian figured the less time they spent around their mother the less likely she was to find out they were planning to try the upper slopes.

It was only a short drive to the ski area, where they took a gondola to the top of the mountain. The kids were beside themselves with excitement and Martin had to restrain them so that he could check their bindings.

Finally they were ready for the descent. Amy quickly manoeuvred her way in front, shifting from side to side with neat parallel turns. She felt very grown up and hoped she could stay in front of her father and brother for the whole run. She concentrated on turning just at the top of each mogul, trying to maintain her speed. Then she looked back to see how far behind her brother was. The moment of curiosity proved disastrous. The edge of her ski caught on some ice and she lost her balance, still going over thirty miles an hour. She toppled over and over until she hit a snow bank.

Martin saw her fall and his heart nearly stopped. He skied up to her and when he saw she was unconscious he yelled for Julian to get the ski patrol. Lifting her head

201

gently, he implored her to wake up, speak to him.

Slowly she opened her eyes, but there was no recognition in them. He wanted to die. Martin had no idea how long they were there, but it seemed like an eternity before the ski patrol arrived with the sled.

'She is going to be okay, Dad,' Julian said as the medics lifted her. Martin put his arms around his son, grateful for the boy's attempt to comfort him. They waited until Amy was bundled into the sled, then followed the patrol down the mountain.

At the Squaw Valley emergency room Martin called Sylvia. When she heard Martin's voice on the phone, she knew something was wrong.

'Sylvia,' Martin began, 'don't get upset. Amy has had a little accident.'

Swallowing hard, she asked what had happened. 'Well, she hit her head. But I'm sure she'll be all right.'

'Where *are* you?' Sylvia asked.

He told her and she said she'd be there immediately.

Martin and Julian were waiting in the hall when she and Bess arrived.

'Where is she?' Sylvia asked, trying to hold back her tears.

'She's been taken upstairs.'

'How badly is she hurt?'

'The doctor told me she has a slight concussion.'

'Concussion?' Bess and Sylvia said at the same time.

'Yes,' Martin almost whispered.

'How did it happen?' Sylvia asked.

'We were coming down from the Gun Barrell,' Julian began.

'Gun Barrell?' Sylvia gasped. 'I can't believe you took the children up there.'

Bess, who rarely criticized her son, couldn't resist saying, 'Martin, that was totally irresponsible.'

'Get off my back, Mother!' Martin snapped. 'I'm worried sick as it is. I don't need your recriminations.' With that he walked away, leaving Sylvia to find out where

Amy's room was. She started upstairs, still furious. Skiing with the other families wasn't enough for Martin. He needed to show his children what a free spirit he was. Never mind if they were not ready for the upper trails. When she reached Amy's door she braced herself for the sight of an unconscious child, but when she went inside she found Amy propped up in bed with a big bandage around her head. 'Hi, Mom,' she said.

Sylvia almost fainted with relief.

'How are you, darling?'

'Great, Mom. I just got a bump on my head.'

'Are you sure? You're not just saying that?'

'No, Mom, really.'

The doctor confirmed that the Roths had a great deal for which to be grateful.

After a few days of observation, Amy was sent home as good as new, but the accident left Sylvia and Martin with scars that didn't heal so quickly. Though they didn't discuss it again, Sylvia felt he had foolishly risked the children's lives. For his part, Martin resented her silent accusation. Even Julian sensed the tension. One night at dinner he rose to his father's defence, answered the unspoken question by saying, 'You know, it wasn't Daddy's idea to come down Gun Barrell and it wasn't his fault Amy had an accident. She was doing great, in fact she was in the lead.'

Sylvia felt ashamed of her attitude, and when they flew back to San Francisco she tried to leave the incident behind her, but she knew it had made one more crack in the now battered façade of their marriage.

Chapter Twenty

As long as he lived Martin would always remember the day Julian graduated from high school. For the first time he realized how hard it must have been for his own parents to see him grow up and go off to college. Sitting in the bright sun, Martin took Bess's hand and squeezed it as he watched his son walk up and receive his diploma. Seeing the gesture, Sylvia smiled. Martin seemed happier these days, less restless, or so she liked to believe. But if she had been able to read his thoughts this bright June day she might have felt less serene.

As the headmaster began his speech, Martin could not believe that it had been decades since he had sat on the same platform facing the audience at his own graduation. Where the hell had his life gone? In September it would be Julian's time to set off for Yale but Martin knew he would have a much easier time. With no quotas, and admissions based mostly on grades and college boards, it was unlikely that Julian would find himself in a suite filled with tweedy anti-Semites who thought college was just a place to play sports and drink beer. But even with all of his problems at Yale, Martin would eagerly have relived those years. His mother stirred at his side and he glanced at her, shocked to see how much she had aged in the last months. She was approaching seventy now, and that fact frightened him too.

In many ways Martin knew himself to be a lucky man, but he found himself more and more often forgetting where he was and reliving the past. And the past meant Jenny. Despite his best intentions he kept remembering their year together in New York. He saw her running across the room to him, bending over the stove, throwing back her head in uninhibited laughter.

As the band struck up 'Pomp and Circumstance', Martin dragged himself back to the present, feeling as guilty as though he had actually been with Jenny, kissing those red lips and brushing back her thick, wavy hair.

As Julian started off the stage, Martin wanted to cry out to him, *Enjoy it, son, it goes so fast.* Was it really only eight years ago he had been playing Little League, only five years ago they had gone trout fishing without either Amy or Sylvia? Martin blinked back tears as he made his way through the crowd to congratulate his son.

Two years later, when Amy graduated, Martin found the memories even more overwhelming. Tuning out the headmaster's dull speech, he let a kaleidoscope of pictures run through his mind: Amy at five, whizzing past him on her new two-wheeler, 'Look Dad, no hands'; at six, swimming the length of the pool; at eight, going camping and falling in the poison oak; at thirteen, winning the piano competition and coming home on top of the world, convinced she could do anything.

That night when Amy came into his study to show off her long white prom dress, Martin had trouble believing that this was the same little girl he had watched grow up. He kept remembering how he had walked the floor with her when she had scarlet fever. Could this be the same child in floating chiffon with her hair twisted up on her head, soft tendrils framing her face?

'How do I look, Dad?'

Not Daddy any more. 'Like my beautiful princess. Who gave you the orchids?'

'Mark Rosenthal. He's taking me tonight.'

Martin realized he should have known. She and Mark seemed to have been going steady since the cradle, but now they were no longer little.

'What time will you be home, darling?'

'I don't know, Dad, about one, maybe.'

'No "maybe", Amy. I want you home on the dot or you'll turn into a pumpkin courtesy of your old dad.'

205

Later, playing bridge, Martin had trouble concentrating on the game. When he did the unpardonable and trumped Sylvia's ace, his cousin Jane said, 'Martin . . . are you with us tonight?'

Sylvia laughed. 'I'm not sure. I think Amy's graduation really got to him. He just can't admit that Julian and Amy aren't children any more.'

'You mean they've grown up and he has the growing pains?' teased Jane.

'Something like that.'

'Well,' said Jane, 'I'm going to let my birds fly. When they're all gone, I'm not going to mind a bit. Arthur and I will enjoy being a couple again. I think that's the best part of getting older.'

That made a lot of sense to Sylvia, but seeing Martin's frown she remained silent.

Two days later the Roths flew to Europe for their summer vacation, where they were joined in London by Julian, who had left from New York a week earlier.

As they toured all the famous spots in London and Paris, Sylvia was eerily reminded of Martin's withdrawal on their honeymoon. He said all the right things, chose the best restaurants, tried to make sure the children were enjoying themselves, but it was obvious his heart wasn't in it. On their honeymoon, Sylvia knew that it was the war which cast a shadow on their trip. This time she wasn't sure. She only hoped and prayed he would find words to tell her.

When they headed for Italy she knew the time had come to take action. While everyone was out shopping one afternoon in Rome, she headed for an exclusive lingerie shop on the Via del Angelo. When she left with the little gaily wrapped package in her hand, she could hardly wait for the night to come. Martin sensed her unusual excitement all through dinner.

Finally the kids went to bed and Sylvia went to the bathroom to undress. She took a long time and Martin, hearing the water running, realized she was taking a bath.

When she emerged she was wearing a short lace nighty which clearly revealed her nipples and the dark triangle between her thighs.

'Jesus Christ, you look like a whore,' Martin shouted. As she raced back to the bathroom Martin lay back sullenly on the pillows. Did she think he needed that to get a hard-on? Then his anger subsided and he felt bad. She had just been trying to cheer him up and he had made an ass of himself.

'Sylvia,' he called, 'I'm sorry. Come back to bed.'

There was no answer. Sylvia was staring at herself in the mirror. She did look like a prostitute. No wonder Martin had been upset. Sex gimmicks, pornography – he had never been interested in any of that, and certainly those things had never been necessary to initiate their lovemaking. His forty-fifth birthday had been especially traumatic, and in his present state of mind her prank had probably made him think she doubted her own appeal.

She knew some of the women at the club had made a play for him, showing by a smile, a gesture, that they wouldn't at all mind being seduced. In fact, a few had been more than obvious. Maybe she was taking Martin for granted, but she would have bet her last dollar that he had never cheated on her.

She washed her face, took a deep breath, and came back into the room dressed in a simple white nightgown.

'Darling, I want to apologize. However, dear, I was just teasing because I know how down you've been. I wish you could tell me what's bothering you.'

He looked at her, wondering how the hell he could explain. She deserved the truth, except he wasn't certain what the truth was. He sighed. 'I don't know if I can.'

'After all this time, Martin, don't you know you can tell me anything? Why should there be any secrets between us?'

'It isn't a question of secrets. It's that some things are tough to admit, especially to ourselves.' Swallowing hard, he said, 'OK, here's a confession: I used to think that fear of ageing was only a female trait. The truth is, men are just as

207

frightened as women. Not just for the wrinkles. In fact, vanity has nothing to do with it. Nor does sex. Crazy as this is, everything seemed to hit me so suddenly. Seeing the children all grown up made me feel as though I had lost my usefulness . . . my function as a father. I know there's no logic in any of this, but our lives were so consumed with them through the years that I feel as though I've come to a crossroads.'

It was strange, Sylvia thought. She had known Martin all her life but would never have guessed that he had such deep-seated fears of ageing. He was so extraordinarily handsome, more so now than ever. He was right, Sylvia thought: logic had nothing to do with it.

'I can still hear the sound of her laughter,' Martin continued, 'that day I took her to the circus and she saw the clown. Where the hell did the years go? Suddenly I turned around and she's all grown up. It seems a whole chapter of our lives has closed on us. God, Sylvia, I don't know how to say this, but I really feel over the hill.'

Sylvia wasn't sure what to say. She wanted to reassure Martin by saying that the two of them could have fun alone, but she wasn't certain he would agree. After all these years, the old insecurities came flooding back to haunt her. Maybe Martin would not be happy living with her now without the children. She looked at his sad face and forced herself to put her feelings aside.

'You know what your daughter said?' Sylvia said, forcing a note of gaiety into her voice.

'What?'

'That her father was the most handsome man she'd ever seen in her life.'

In spite of himself he smiled. 'Did she?'

'Yes. Do you remember being eighteen? You don't know if you really want to finish growing up or slide back into childhood. It's a funny age.'

'So is forty-seven.'

'It shouldn't be. Especially when a man looks like you,'

she said, tilting her head back. 'Do you know what I want right this minute?'

Suddenly he did. Off came the white silk nightgown and he proceeded to show her . . . and especially himself.

Later, when he got up to turn off the light, Sylvia whispered, 'You're getting better with age, darling. Keep it up.'

At nine the next morning, Amy came into the living room of their suite at the Excelsior Hotel. She found Julian dressed and ready for the day's excursion, but the door to her parents' room was closed. That was unusual, she thought, especially when they had planned the day for sightseeing. 'Where are the folks?'

'Sleeping.'

'How come? We were supposed to go to the Catacombs early.'

'The Catacombs have been here for thousands of years.'

'But we won't. I'm going to wake them up.'

'I wouldn't do that, Amy.'

'Why? Everything closes down at two for their crazy siestas.'

'I know . . . that's why the Italians have so many children.'

'You mean the folks . . . ' Amy's sophistication dropped away.

'That's what I mean, baby sister. Now let's go down to breakfast, hop a bus, and strike out on our own.'

'But they won't know where we've gone.'

'I'll leave a note.'

Sylvia blinked the sleep from her eyes, then looked at the clock. It was late, already eleven-thirty. Hastily she put on her robe and went into the sitting room, expecting to find the children and apologize for spoiling their day, but the room was empty. Then she saw the note propped up against the lamp. 'Dear Mom and Dad, when in Rome do as the

Romans do. *Molto amore*. We'll be back at three. Love, Julian.'

Sylvia blushed. She was the one who had advocated sex education, but when your children knew *all* about what their parents did behind closed doors . . . She showed the note to Martin, who just laughed.

For the rest of the trip he devoted himself to his family's pleasure. They did everything tourists do: visited the Catacombs, the Coliseum, the Vatican. And Martin made certain that everywhere they went Sylvia had an excellent time.

But when the time came to leave Amy at school, he was devastated. He felt all the weight of his almost fifty years. The night in Rome had cheered him for a time, but like most people, Martin was a victim of his moods, and as they left Europe he felt heavy with depression.

All the way home on the plane to New York he chastised himself for wallowing in senseless self-pity, but when he dropped Julian back at Yale he felt as though someone had shot a cannon through him, leaving a hole so big nothing would ever fill it up. Once again he spoke to himself like a Dutch uncle. He had to stop all this nonsense about disenchantment. Who the hell did he think he was? He had more than any man had a right to. And it was time to stop mooning over his youth. Everyone gets old, and he was not even fifty yet. He was going to enjoy the time he had, and by God, make sure Sylvia did too.

Martin was as good as his word. Despite long hours at the office, he improved his golf, spent more time with Sylvia at the opera and the theatre, and insisted she drive into town once a week to meet him for lunch.

The first time she came in he chose the St Francis, and that afternoon instead of going back to work he took a room and they spent the rest of the day in bed. It was as good a way of recapturing lost youth as any.

Sylvia was happier than she'd been in months. She went on a diet, lost the five pounds she'd put on in Europe, and carefully planned their social life around the people Martin liked best. Even Bess noticed a lift in her son's mood, and if either of the two women closest to him noticed an occasional artificial note to his gaiety, they both thought it wiser to say nothing.

Growing up was different for everyone. Particularly at forty-eight, particularly for Martin Roth.

Chapter Twenty-One

Back in America with Julian at Yale and Amy now at school in Switzerland, Sylvia hoped they could sustain some of the joy they had experienced in Rome, but although Martin tried to fulfil her expectations, life settled down to the old routine. They went out, they entertained, Martin worked even longer hours in the office. Despite his best resolutions his fiftieth birthday when it came depressed him greatly. Sylvia gave him a party and he found himself inexplicably angry with her. How could she celebrate middle age?

But like it or not, time passed. His mother was in her seventies, in the best of health. Amy came home from Davos with the profound announcement that after graduation she was marrying the tennis pro she had met in Monte Carlo. For once Martin put his foot down. No more tennis pro, no more Switzerland, no more Europe. That September Amy was packed off to Wellesley, relieved if anything that the romance had been ended, though she would not give her father the satisfaction of saying so.

Martin himself was probably more upset than his daughter. He remembered the pain of his separation from Jenny, but consoled himself by saying that eighteen wasn't twenty-eight and that a tennis pro was hardly good husband material.

He was less lucky dealing with Julian's choice of mate. Julian had been graduated from Yale with honours and been accepted by their law school when he called home to say that he was engaged to Sarah Storey. He brought her home over the summer to visit. She was very elegant, very Vassar, very Episcopalian, and very Beacon Hill. To Bess's dismay she had made it clear that her parents had forgiven Julian for the bad taste of being born a Jew and were very grateful that somewhere along the line one of his ancestors had had the good sense to change the family name of Rothenberger to Roth.

Bess moaned in private, but Martin and Sylvia consoled themselves that under the Old Boston veneer the girl seemed smart and friendly and very much in love with Julian, which in Sylvia's eyes made up for a multitude of sins.

The wedding itself was an elaborate affair in the garden in the centre of Louisburg Square. It was a strain on all of the Roths. The minister, a thin, disagreeable young man, made no concessions for the Jewish bridegroom, and Martin stood watching the pretty blonde bridesmaids troop into the garden, wondering what his father would have said if he were alive. Was it worth it, Martin thought suddenly, giving up Jenny, always doing the right thing? His son had cast away all traces of his religion to marry this pretty, slender gentile with her New England ways. For a moment the pain in his heart was more than he could bear. His eyes flickered to Amy, who was looking ravishing as the maid of honour. Who knew whom she would want to run off with next? They had saved her at eighteen, but would they be able to forestall a misalliance at twenty? Martin sighed. What good had his toeing the family line of tradition and heritage done? For the first time he felt old, without hope.

When the Roths returned home after that curious wedding it was with heavy hearts. Amy had cheerfully returned to college, and Bess declared she needed a week's rest after all the travelling, leaving Sylvia alone to face Martin's gloomy looks across the breakfast table. To see him so withdrawn was almost more than she could bear. It wasn't only the wedding, she knew that. He seemed to be fighting the years, unwilling to sit back and enjoy this time alone together. The truth was they had a lot to be grateful for. Amy was doing well at Wellesley and Julian certainly worked hard and seemed responsible. If anything, his new in-laws had made him a little stuffy. Sylvia found herself annoyed with Martin. There was no reason for him to be so gloomy.

That night when Martin sat down to dinner she said, 'I think it would be so good to get away together. Just the two of us. No parents, no friends. Would you like that?'

Would he like that? Well, after the tensions of the past weeks it might help. 'Okay, let's go up to the Lake tomorrow.'

Sylvia closed her eyes. Everything was going to be all right. Wasn't it?

The drive up to the mountains was a silent one. When they did talk all they seemed able to discuss were the children. It appeared they had lost whatever mutual interests they had shared. Well, this weekend would be a new beginning, Sylvia resolved.

Moving closer to Martin, Sylvia took hold of his right hand. This holiday was what they needed. Married people needed time alone. She hadn't understood that well enough over the years. It had always seemed so important to do things as a family. But today she knew better. For all of her devotion, they essentially could only fix themselves. Children were selfish by definition. That's what growing up was about. Learn to care for other people. Well, soon Julian would have children of his own. The important thing now was to cheer Martin up and save her own marriage. Hopefully this weekend in Tahoe would be a new beginning.

They did all the things they had done in the past: walked in the mountains, had drinks before the fire, rode horses down into the valley. They were kind and polite to each

213

other, but nothing seemed to rekindle the old sense of romance. Both knew it and both were miserable.

It wasn't anybody's fault, Sylvia thought. Something had happened to their lives. As she got ready for bed that night she decided that the air was very chilly even for Lake Tahoe.

Chapter Twenty-Two

It was the month after the trip to Tahoe that Martin ran into Jenny. It had been Sylvia's regular Wednesday in town. As he left to meet her, his age weighed heavily upon him. On his way out of the office, he realized that most of the brokers were in their twenties and early thirties. He had once been the youngest in the firm. In fact, he had been referred to as 'the kids'. But the men of his father's time had either died or retired. The world belonged to the young.

Outside, the bustling Yuletide crowds made him feel lonelier than ever. It had been the Christmas season when his father died; Christmas when he had broken up with Jenny. Frankly, he would be happy when the holidays were over.

As he sat across the table from Sylvia at the St Francis he hoped the glow provided by two double martinis would conceal his depression. He was relieved when she didn't seem to pick upon his mood and wasn't aware that he was only half listening to what she was saying. Something about the party that night and reminding him not to be late. Then he kissed her goodbye in front of I. Magnin's.

Two minutes later he had caught sight of Jenny and his life was turned upside down. All his feelings for her returned. It was as though the last twenty-five years had never existed. She aroused sensations within him he hadn't experienced in that many years. Nobody else had ever made him feel that way.

The next day in the office when he picked up the phone in his sweating palm to call Jenny, a wave of guilt swept over him. Not once during his marriage had he been unfaithful to Sylvia, unless one counted his thoughts of Jenny. But Martin knew that he was going to have an affair with Jenny. He knew that he couldn't help it. He also knew that was a lie. Of course he could help it. All he had to do was let her get on her plane for Hong Kong without calling her, he thought as he finished dialling. Just hang up. Martin was about to when he heard Jenny's voice.

'Hello,' she said in her lyrical voice.

'It's me, Jenny – Martin.'

She laughed. 'I would have recognized the voice. How are you, Martin?'

'Fine. Can we meet?'

She paused. 'I asked you yesterday if you thought it was wise. Have you thought about it?'

'About nothing else. Somehow I don't feel like being wise at this point. I want to see you, Jenny.'

'All right. Where shall we meet?'

'If it's all right with you, the Fairmont.'

'That's fine.'

When Martin saw her in the lobby waiting for him he knew how much he'd missed her throughout the years. She was still incredibly beautiful. They went into the Cirque Room and ordered drinks.

'I still can't get over meeting you yesterday, Jenny.'

'It was an extraordinary coincidence, wasn't it?'

'I often wonder about coincidences. Is it fate or happenstance?'

Jenny laughed. 'Well, I wouldn't get that philosophical. Now tell me about yourself, Martin.'

'What do you want me to tell you?'

'Well, there must be a few things that have happened over the last twenty-five years. Are you married? Do you have children? Most of all, are you happy?'

'I am married and I do have children. I'm not so sure though how to answer your last question. There have been times that I have been very happy with Sylvia – that's my wife – but there have also been times when all I could think of was how much I missed you.'

Jenny looked at Martin over the rim of her glass. 'And I thought you'd forgotten me.'

Martin motioned the waiter to bring fresh drinks. 'I've never stopped loving you, Jenny,' he said.

'I'm not sure if I believe that.'

'It's the truth. Whatever else you think, believe that.'

Jenny smiled. 'You may think it's the truth, but when the time came to choose between me and your family, your family won.'

'I never really made a choice, Jenny, and I was still very young. I know I behaved badly after my father died and I've suffered because of it.' He reached across the table and took her hand. 'You know, I never stopped wondering where you went. For the longest time I tried to find you. What did you do, Jenny?'

Jenny twirled the olive in her glass and without raising her eyes said, 'I don't think I am going to tell you today.' Martin was silent and for a few minutes they sat sipping their drinks and carefully avoiding the other's gaze. Finally, as if shaking herself out of some private dream, Jenny looked up and smiled.

'Well, Martin, it has been great seeing you, but I have a million thing to do between now and the time my plane leaves.'

'Jenny, I can't let you go,' Martin said, uncertain how to persuade her to stay. 'Not this time.'

'I'm afraid you can't stop me,' she said, smiling gently.

'Jenny, I'm no longer a kid. I love you and I don't believe fate let us meet again just to say goodbye. You can't walk out of my life again.'

'I think you're a little confused. It was you who walked out of my life. Now really, I must dash.'

'Don't punish me, Jenny.'

216

'You've already done that, Martin, to yourself.'

'You really hate me, don't you?'

'No, strangely enough, I don't. There were times that I did but not any more.'

'Please, Jenny, give me a chance to make up for the past.'

Jenny smiled. Years ago she would have thanked God on her knees to have heard those words, but she was no longer naive enough to believe him. He was a married man with two children. How could he possibly erase the pain of the last twenty-five years? 'I don't think so,' she said, getting up. 'But thanks for the thought.'

Martin rose and helped her on with her coat. When they reached the lobby they stood facing each other for a long, awkward moment.

'How can I get in touch with you?' he asked, wanting to take her in his arms.

'That could be difficult since the job I have now involves so much travel.'

'You mean you're just going to vanish from my life?'

'I'm afraid so, Martin. Stay well and happy New Year.'

He watched as she walked towards the elevator that would take her to her room. He remained frozen for a long time after the doors closed, the image of her face still before him.

How he walked to his car he couldn't remember. The next thing he knew he was behind the wheel, driving aimlessly, reluctant to return home. When he finally stopped near the Coit Tower, he turned off the engine and looked out at the dark, churning Bay. The bleak, overcast day reflected his mood. What was there left for him to savour if Jenny held no part of his future? The children were gone, and he wasn't sure what he felt for Sylvia at this moment except an enormous sense of guilt. He started the car and began driving back towards the Fairmont. This time he was not going to let Jenny run away without putting up a fight.

In her hotel room, Jenny was trying to pack. She would take something from the closet, fold it, then put it aside. It was impossible to concentrate. After taking her evening dress out of her suitcase for the third time she gave up and lay on the bed.

Meeting Martin had shaken her more than she had revealed. Just seeing him brought back not only the memories of their affair but of the terrible time after he had left. She had never been so miserable in her life and she would never let herself be hurt in the same way again.

Wiping her eyes, she got up, undressed, and turned on the shower. She first ran the water as hot as she could stand it, then turned on the cold. When she began to shiver, she got out and rubbed herself dry with the big terrycloth towel.

Still too upset to pack, she put on a robe and poured herself some vodka over ice. Closing her eyes, she let the past wash over her.

She had never recovered from her affair with Martin. She had gone through all kinds of hell trying to put her life back together, but the truth was she had never stopped loving him – not when she wished to die, not when she cursed him, not at any point in the lonely years since he had gone back to San Francisco. If only he had loved her enough to put her above his family. If only he had married her as he had promised she would not have had so many incidents in her life to bitterly regret. She had changed after he abandoned her, hardened. At times over the years she had forced herself to remember what a nice girl, a good person, she had been when she met him. But that girl was dead. Jenny had deliberately buried her, deciding that if it meant killing off some of her better impulses, the loss was worth the protection this new, cruel shell afforded her.

She remembered one night getting drunk in a bar and waking up the next morning with a strange man next to her. She could hardly believe this was Jenny McCoy, the girl who was determined to leave Biloxi and make herself a success.

When she'd fled New York, she'd also given up her job, and the one she landed in Chicago meant taking a step backward. She had been crushed and bitter, no longer able to lose herself in the excitement of work as she had before meeting Martin. She wasn't making excuses. She was just too unhappy to pull herself together. Her performance suffered and she failed to get the hoped-for promotion. Since her salary was so much less than the one she'd earned in Manhattan, she ended up taking a room in a boarding-house in the wrong part of town – quite a departure from the elegant Central Park West apartment she had shared with Martin.

The morning she had woken up next to a stranger was when she hit bottom. Still half drunk, she staggered to the bathroom and looked at herself. Her make-up was smeared and her hair hung limply about her puffy face. Disgusted, she turned back to the young man who the night before she thought had resembled Martin. He was sprawled naked across her bed. In the harsh morning light she saw that the resemblance was the product of too many martinis. He was pale, probably from spending so much of his time in sleazy bars, and flabby from too little exercise. The hair which had appeared thick and wavy was now plastered down over a small bald spot. God, she couldn't even remember his name. With a shudder she went to the window and looked down the eight floors to the sidewalk.

If she'd had the courage, she would have jumped, but either fear or the spectre of committing a mortal sin prevented her. When she turned away from the window, she discovered a core of strength she hadn't known she still possessed. She was going to survive.

She dressed and hurried out of the room. Without stopping to analyse her motives she went to the train station and bought a coach ticket to Biloxi. Then she went back to her room, where she was pleased to find that the young man had gone, stealing only her radio. She flung her clothes into her suitcase and went back to catch her train.

Little Jenny McCoy had failed up North. Maybe she never should have tried, but now at least she was accepting her defeat and going back where she belonged.

Biloxi scarcely gave Jenny a sense of homecoming. She had been away too long. Her first summer back was almost more than she could bear. She had never known such heat such dust, or such discomfort. She would have left but unable to find a job, had soon run out of money.

The morning she walked into the Biloxi commercia bank she had eaten little for two days. Standing before the manager's desk trying to fill out a job application, she was overcome with dizziness. She put a hand to steady herself but it was no use. She fell to the floor in a dead faint.

She came to on a couch in the bank president's office. As her eyes fluttered open she was aware of someone sitting at her side, holding her hand.

'Are you feeling a little better?'

Jenny wasn't sure, but she nodded yes.

'My name is Cyrus Worthington, and I must say you caused us all a fright.'

'I'm sorry,' Jenny said as she tried to sit up.

'I really think you should rest for just a bit,' Cyrus said gently forcing her to lie back down.

Jenny focused on the man looking down at her with such concern. Despite a thickset figure testifying to a fondness for good Southern cooking and a face flushed by a steady diet of mint juleps, Mr Worthington presented a very distinguished appearance. Thick grey hair was neatly parted over a broad forehead, and his even features were set off by a handsome smile.

Jenny was not aware that his concern was dictated by the throbbing between his heavy thighs or that some of his sexual predilections had made the most popular madam in town ban him from her parlour. All Jenny saw was that he seemed kind and that if she played her cards right he might offer her a job.

Patting her hand in the most paternal way, he said, 'I understand, my dear, that you are looking for employment.'

'Yes. I have excellent recommendations, Mr Worthington.'

She told him that she had been born and raised in Biloxi, had left to attend Hunter College, and then stayed on in New York to work first for the Gatti agency and then Elmo Cosmetics. Both companies would vouch for her competence.

'Well, Jenny,' he said, smiling, 'we'll check as a matter of form, but I'll be very surprised if my manager doesn't call you tomorrow offering you that job.'

'Thank you,' Jenny said. The job would take care of the future, but she still had to get through the next twenty-four hours. Her rent was paid until the end of the week, but how could she go another day without food? Gathering her courage, she said hesitantly, 'Mr Worthington, I know this is an unusual request, but do you think that you could make me a small loan? I'm completely without funds and you could withold the amount from my first pay cheque.'

'I think that could be arranged,' said Cyrus, pleased to learn the girl was utterly penniless. 'How much do you need?'

Jenny wanted to ask for fifty dollars but she decided twenty-five sounded more reasonable. As long as she didn't have to wait two weeks for her first cheque, she'd be fine.

Cyrus took out his wallet, thrust the bills into her hand, and then insisted she have a cup of coffee before she left.

Back in her room, after enjoying the first satisfactory meal she'd eaten in weeks, Jenny decided that perhaps the worst was over. She'd been so frightened the last few months about securing the necessities of life, she had hardly thought of Martin. Now, as she drifted off to sleep she wondered if he'd recognize the new Jenny. The one who worried about paying for her next meal, who had decided to survive no matter what the cost, who took on the world armoured with a determined selfishness and lack of concern for other people.

The first month she worked in the bank, Cyrus kept a respectful distance. She would see him welcoming visitors to his office, going out to lunch, or occasionally staring at her legs when he thought she wasn't looking. Then one evening when she was working late totalling up her deposit slips, he came over to her teller's cage.

'When you're done, Jenny,' he said, eyeing the manager, who was waiting to close, 'stop by and see me.'

Jenny finished up and went over to Cyrus's office, hoping that she was not about to lose her job.

'Sit down, my dear,' he said, motioning to a chair. Jenny decided he would not look so relaxed if he were about to fire her. 'I wanted to tell you what a fine job you're doing,' he said. 'It was a lucky day for us when you fainted away here.'

Jenny thought that perhaps this was the time to mention a raise. Her salary was almost a joke.

'Mr Worthington,' she began softly, 'I want you to know how grateful I am to you. I really love working here, but I am finding it difficult to make ends meet. Do you think in the next few months it would be possible for me to get a raise?'

Cyrus smiled. He liked the modest way she asked. 'I'll mention it to the manager. I think you can count on an extra twenty a week at the end of your third month.'

Jenny was overcome with joy, though she was aware that even with the increase she would be making less than half her salary at Elmo. 'I do want to thank you, Mr Worthington, so very much.'

'Not at all, my dear. Now I wonder if you might do me the honour of having Sunday luncheon at my house.'

Jenny wasn't quite sure she wanted any personal relationship with Cyrus, but she wasn't about to jeopardize her job, so she smiled and nodded.

'I'll have my car come around for you at noon.'

On Sunday, Cyrus's driver picked her up promptly at noon and they rode about twenty minutes out of town before turning into an overgrown drive lined on either side with massive oaks that must have been over a hundred years old. Jenny felt an odd premonition of evil as she entered the large, shabby hall.

222

A black houseboy guided her straight to the dining room, where she found Cyrus standing before an enormous retracting table that would easily have seated twenty. The only other diner appeared to be an overweight teenager whose blank stare and protruding tongue gave Jenny the chills. The young girl was clearly a mongoloid.

'We eat very promptly here,' Cyrus said, apologizing for not serving drinks. 'My daughter must keep a strict schedule. She's diabetic.' He smiled at the girl, who shrank back against her chair.

'Now, Linda Mae, say hello to our guest, Jenny McCoy. Jenny, this is my daughter, Linda Mae.'

At his insistent look, the girl put out her hand. As Jenny leaned forward to shake it she noticed a dull blue shadow running along the girl's right cheek. A bruise? Following her gaze, Cyrus said, 'Our poor baby Linda Mae had a little mishap today. She tripped on the stair carpet. Well, don't you fret baby, Daddy's gonna have that tear fixed.'

Throughout the meal Jenny was touched by his tender concern for his daughter. He gently wiped her hand when she tried to eat her mashed potatoes with her fingers and gently substituted a fork. Jenny wondered why he had not thought to mention that he had an obviously retarded child, but decided it was probably too painful a subject for him to mention. Although gossip at the bank said his wife had had a nervous breakdown before she died over ten years ago, no one had mentioned the girl. Looking up as the houseboy served a rich pecan pie, Jenny smiled across the table and was pleased when Linda Mae smiled back.

Afterwards Linda Mae was taken upstairs and Cyrus and Jenny spent a pleasant afternoon on the veranda. Several times he looked as if he wanted to ask her a question, but each time seemed to restrain himself, creating an awkward pause in the conversation.

It wasn't until the next Sunday when Cyrus again invited her out to dinner that he was able to muster his courage and mention what he had in mind.

They were sitting over coffee in the drawing room when

he leaned forward and took her hand. 'Jenny,' he said, 'I have a favour to ask you. But you must feel free to say no. I don't want to put you in an awkward position.'

'Please, Cyrus. I can't imagine your doing that.'

He held her hand more tightly and for a moment Jenny felt uneasy.

'My dear,' he said, 'it would make me so happy if you would be friends with Linda Mae.'

Jenny didn't answer immediately. It was such an odd request. Finally, she found words. 'Of course I'd like to be of help,' she began, 'but Linda Mae and I are –'

'Worlds apart. I know that. But you are so kind, so sweet, you would be so good for her. She's never been close to anyone since her mother took sick. I think that's why she has made so little progress. Do you think you could find it in your heart to befriend her?'

Jenny hesitated. For the first time since Martin left her, she felt a small crack in the ice that had closed around her heart. Cyrus had been so kind to her. Maybe if she reciprocated, she would start building a future instead of just living in the past. Filled with genuine compassion, she said, 'I'll try.'

As the weeks became months, Jenny did reach out to Linda Mae, who began to flower under the attention. Her table manners improved and she was able to concentrate better on the simple tasks set by her tutor. She still remained clumsy and Jenny would frequently arrive to find her nursing a new black and blue mark, but she seemed so much happier, Jenny could not help being pleased and Cyrus was positively delighted.

After three months, when Jenny's visits had increased to three or four times a week, he asked her to give up her room and move in. 'You'll be well chaperoned,' Cyrus said and Jenny smiled, wondering what he'd say if he knew about her behaviour in Chicago. All she said was, 'Well, Cyrus, I'd like that. My little room is awfully depressing and this way I'll have so much more time with Linda Mae.'

*

One night after dinner, when she'd been living in the house for a couple of weeks, Cyrus sought Jenny out in the library.

'My dear,' he said, sitting in a chair across the room. 'I'm so glad this has worked out. It seems to suit you too. You look so much better than when we met. I hope that means you're happy here.'

'Oh, yes. You must know that. You've been so kind to me.'

He moved his chair a little closer. 'Not as kind as I would like to be.'

Jenny started and Cyrus realized he'd moved too quickly. He got up and went to the small bar near the fireplace where he poured them each a brandy.

Jenny, who had drunk very little since leaving Chicago, felt the liquor go right to her head. It was as if from a distance she heard Cyrus say, 'Jenny, my dear, don't be offended. What I was trying to say is that this house has come to life again since your arrival. Linda Mae is not the same girl and even the servants have responded to your charm. I don't quite know how to thank you.'

Unsure how to respond, Jenny just smiled and sipped her brandy.

Cyrus continued almost as if to himself. 'Having you here has brought me the only happiness I've known in years. What good is my money if I have no one to spend it on? Linda Mae can't be considered a real companion. Look around me. Everything is meaningless without you here to enjoy it. For the first time I realize how shabby I've let things get. A house like this needs an intelligent woman to restore its grace, just as Linda Mae needs a loving companion to help her fulfil even her limited potential. Oh, Jenny, Linda Mae and I would be destroyed if you left us.'

Jenny remained silent. She guessed where the conversation was leading, but felt powerless to interrupt the man who had been so good to her.

'I know I'm old enough to be your father, but I love you

225

and want to take care of you. Do you think in time you could return my affection?'

Jenny knew she should stop Cyrus before he committed himself further, but he had been kinder to her than anybody in the world. He had showered her with gifts. It was impossible not to like him, and more than once she had pretended that he was the father who had abandoned her. If she rejected his proposal she would have to move out, and she no longer believed she could survive alone. She remembered looking down from her eighth-floor room in Chicago, wanting to jump.

Forcing herself to look him in the eyes, she said, 'I already do care for you, Cyrus, but – '

'You needn't finish. I know what you're going to say. But, Jenny, one must be sensible. You have no family, no one to care for you. I can provide for you for the rest of your life. Sometimes security and peace of mind are more important than passion. The fever of first love can burn out. Respect and affection last. Jenny, please say that you will marry me.'

Jenny stood up. 'Can you give me some time?'

'Take all the time in the world, darling. I'll wait. Now you must be tired. Run on up to bed.'

Jenny hurried from the room, anxious to be alone to think. She ran upstairs without a backward glance and did not see Cyrus looking at her with barely disguised lust, or see his powerful hands balled into fists against his sides.

In her room with the pretty canopied bed and the new wallpaper Cyrus had insisted on hanging for her, Jenny considered her situation carefully. What had life brought her up to now? Her childhood had been spent with crazy Cora Belle, who had all but beaten her to death. She had built a career only to lose it by her impulsive move to Chicago. Her first real love affair with Martin had all but destroyed her. The more she thought about it, the more she realized that Cyrus was offering her the greatest opportunity of her life. Forget love. Look what it had brought her. If she married Cyrus, she would be a respected member of the community. She would never again have to cringe before the priest in the confessional. She could live the rest of her life in security and comfort with a man who had proven himself nothing but kind. What difference did it make if he wasn't tall and handsome like Martin Roth? She would be good to him, take care of his house, look after his daughter. Yes, she would marry Cyrus and she would make sure he would never regret asking her.

The next night after dinner Cyrus and Jenny went into the garden, leaving Linda Mae to watch television. He took Jenny's hand and guided her to the stone bench under the magnolia tree. Sitting next to her he said, 'It's lovely out here, like the garden of Eden. Whenever I feel upset or down I sit on this bench for a while and my problems seem to disappear. You have that same effect. When I'm with you the only feeling I have is happiness. I'm hoping that I will be able to enjoy such contentment the rest of my life. Have you thought further about my offer, Jenny?'

'Yes, Cyrus, I have. And I would be proud to marry you.'

'Oh, Jenny.' He took her in his arms, but when he kissed her, his tongue urgently parting her lips, she felt suddenly uneasy. She reminded herself that Cyrus was a good man and that physical passion had only brought her grief. Gently pulling away, she stood, saying, 'Let's go in and tell Linda Mae. You know this will make her so happy.'

Cyrus was determined to give Jenny the grandest wedding Biloxi had ever seen. The day after Jenny said yes he called Cartier and arranged to have his mother's diamonds reset into a stunning engagement ring. Then he insisted she order her wedding dress from the most expensive store in New Orleans. In the next six weeks painters and plasterers swarmed over the house, restoring its Southern grandeur. Cyrus planned to have the ceremony in the house and the reception in a tent in the garden. He was a little taken aback when Jenny said she had no one she wished to invite, but he didn't press and went cheerfully on with his elaborate plans with the menu, imported wines, and a string quartet.

227

As the day grew closer, Jenny became increasingly nervous. Some nights she woke up shaking, having dreamed she was back with Martin. Other nights she lay awake almost until dawn, trying to convince herself that she had made the right – the only – decision.

Finally the day of the wedding came. Jenny went through the ceremony and mingled with the guests as if in a dream. She made sure Linda Mae behaved and had all she wanted to eat, but aside from caring for the girl she left everything else to Cyrus. It was only when the last guest was ushered out and Linda Mae had gone up to bed that she felt a shiver of real fear.

As it turned out the premonition was well founded. Jenny's wedding night was more horrible than her worst nightmares. Either from too much to drink or fear that he would not please Jenny, Cyrus was initially impotent. Jenny tried to tell him that it did not matter, that they had all their lives ahead of them, but Cyrus became increasingly violent. She tried to get out of bed, but he forced her down, and pinned her to the bed. Bending back her wrists with his powerful hands, he took her with such force that Jenny, eyes pressed shut, prayed silently for it to end quickly.

At breakfast the next day he was calm, polite, and he acted as if nothing unusual had happened.

The pattern for their marriage was set. By day Cyrus remained the Southern gentleman – generous, charming and considerate – but by night he was a changed man. He would drink heavily, and when he didn't pass out, he would search for a victim for his frustrations – usually in the bedroom. Linda Mae was also subjected to his rages; it seemed Cyrus was not nearly as patient with his poor, retarded daughter as he had at first seemed. One morning, examining the purple bruises that streaked her own thighs, Jenny couldn't help but wonder if the mark on Linda Mae's face that Jenny had seen on her first visit had resulted from the girl's clumsiness or her father's fury. A chill passed through Jenny and she began to feel afraid.

Although she no longer believed things would get better, she continued to play the part of the successful banker's wife. She gave up her own job since it would not be fitting for her to remain a teller, and devoted herself to refurbishing the beautiful old house. But try as she might to keep up her side of the marriage, she found it increasingly impossible to protect Linda Mae – or herself – from Cyrus's violent temper.

After a month or more of nightly hell, Jenny began to despair. Several times, when Cyrus was at work, she packed her bags, only to unpack them again before he returned from the office. How could she desert Linda Mae? And besides, where could she go? For Cyrus was careful not to let her have more than a few dollars at a time for spending money. So instead of trying to run away, Jenny gave up on herself. Her hair often went uncombed for days, she stopped wearing make-up.

Just when she thought she could stand no more, Cyrus was the one who collapsed. He was brought home in an ambulance one morning, having suffered a massive coronary at the bank. For three days he lay in their big four-poster, surrounded by EKGs, oxygen tanks, and a battery of attending physicians. On the fourth day the medics removed the elaborate life-support system; Cyrus died without ever regaining consciousness.

All of Biloxi turned out for the funeral. Jenny sat stone-faced in the front pew, occasionally patting Linda Mae's hand. Cyrus's daughter seemed to be the one person who was genuinely grieved by his passing. Jenny was present because she had to be; the others were there for the spectacle of a funeral as grand as the wedding had been some months before.

A week after Cyrus was buried, his attorney visited Jenny to read the will. Cyrus's death had made her a very rich woman, but there was one catch: if Jenny were to inherit Cyrus's millions, she had to agree to two things. The first was she must continue to look after Linda Mae. Second, she had to keep the girl at home in Biloxi. If she failed to agree to either stipulation, she wouldn't inherit a dime. The choice was hers.

Jenny weighed her options carefully. Her dream had been to escape Biloxi and all its terrible memories. If she had guts, she knew, she'd chuck it all: the money, the mansion, her role as the rich man's widow, even Linda Mae. She would make a new start for herself somewhere else. She had done it before. But the events of the past few years had instilled a new timidity in Jenny McCoy. She was cowed by fears and anxieties that were unknown to the Jenny who had struck out on her own to go North to Hunter College. Given the prospect of another experience like the months in Chicago, Jenny knew what her choice would be even as she walked the grim-faced attorney to the door, saying, 'I'll have to let you know my decision in another day or two. I need some time to think.'

She called his office to accept the terms of the will the very next day.

Jenny tried to make the best of the new life Fate had brought her. She was good to Linda Mae and began to take better care of herself, but she couldn't shake the gloomy listlessness that enveloped her in this tiny Southern town. Days mounted up to weeks, weeks to months, and Jenny began to slip into a depression as severe as the one she'd suffered under the worst of Cyrus's tyranny. She began to regret having mortgaged her soul for security. And that was what she'd done. She again began to think seriously of leaving. The estate would hire a nurse for Linda Mae. But in the end, she couldn't give up the money. So for the next twelve years she lived as Cyrus no doubt intended: a demure widow, devoted mother to Linda Mae, chair-woman of various community charities. Jenny was not happy, but she wasn't unhappy either. She simply ceased to feel and just went through the motions of each passing day. Then Linda Mae took ill.

At first it was just a fever. The doctors were not concerned. But when it persisted for more than a day or two, she was moved to the hospital. Even round-the-clock care and the best specialists were not enough. Linda Mae died one April morning – the day the crocuses bloomed. It was the week before Jenny's birthday.

At her funeral, Jenny and a few servants were the lone mourners. As the polished mahogany coffin was lowered into the ground, Jenny wept, the first emotion she'd let herself feel in years. Although Linda Mae had kept her in Biloxi all these years, Jenny no longer resented her. In the end they had both been victims.

Chapter Twenty-Three

At last, Jenny was free. According to Cyrus's will, if his daughter died Jenny could live anywhere she chose. But suddenly, faced with this longed-for freedom, Jenny was no longer sure what she wanted to do. Once she might have tried to reestablish her career. But at forty, with more money than she could possibly spend, she lacked the motivation to go back and start at the bottom. Too much time had passed. Her youth was gone and the long years in Biloxi had drained her vitality.

She began to travel, diverting herself with long trips to Europe, the Middle East, and the Orient. It was as if she were trying to outrun a past that persisted in following her. But the past had a way of catching up with her, often when she least expected it. With the New York of her youth miles and years away, she'd find herself reminiscing about her brief affair with Martin and yearning for the innocent girl she had been. These days if she found a companion she never let her get close. The walls she erected when she fled New York had become impenetrable.

Now as she stood on the balcony in San Francisco she was amazed that she had allowed the chance meeting with

Martin to move her so deeply. Their meeting made her realize how much she still loved him, and she bitterly resented the effect he'd had on her life even now.

She was brought out of her reverie by the telephone. Without answering, she knew who it was. *Let it ring*, she almost screamed. Then quickly she picked it up. 'Yes . . . '

'Jenny, this is Martin. I have to see you.'

'Why?'

'Because I can't let you leave this way.'

'Where are you?'

'Downstairs in the lobby.'

She hesitated, glancing around the tidy room.

'All right, come up.'

Martin took the elevator to the tenth floor, where Jenny was waiting for him. When she opened the door, he hesitated, then said, 'I had to see you.'

'Why, Martin? When you went back to San Francisco you shut me out of your life. I remember your letters and our phone calls. I felt as if I were always being put on hold.'

'I was wrong, Jenny, but I've grown up. I have a great deal to say to you now.'

Jenny lowered her eyes, then looked straight at him, terrified of her own feelings. He still could get to her, after all these years. Struggling to appear calm, she said, 'I'm going to have a drink. How about you?'

'I don't think so.'

'Oh, why not?' she said cheerfully. 'You're among friends. If I recall, you take scotch and soda.'

Martin nodded.

'Do you know what I think? I think you're still hoping for something that will never work. It didn't before, when my only competition was your mother. Now you have a wife and children. Well, my friend, I've grown up too. I've learned to avoid situations where I can get hurt.'

Putting down his glass, he took her in his arms. 'Please listen to me,' he begged.

She wrenched herself away. 'No. I listened to you once

and it nearly cost me my life. Martin – I want you to go. Now.'

'But I love you. You're the only woman I ever felt this way about.'

'I'm sorry, but I'm not about to let you destroy me again. I've played the Phoenix once, and I don't think I can do it again. You've got to let me go.'

'I can't, Jenny. We have to talk.'

'Do you think talking will help? I want you to leave, Martin, before we both get in so deep I won't let you go.'

'What makes you think I'll want to?'

'History repeats itself. I may be a slow learner, but that's one thing I've come to know.'

'I love you, Jenny, that's all I know.'

'You don't know the first thing about me any more.'

'Then tell me.'

'That would take a long time. The last twenty-five years have been hard on me, Martin. I let myself become a victim. I won't let it happen again.'

'My God, Jenny, can't you understand that I was victimized too? Life made the choice for me – I never wanted to hurt you.'

'But you did.'

'I know – and I've lived with all kinds of guilt. But, darling, you've got to give me the chance to make it up to you.'

'How? I'm not going to play the backstreet mistress, waiting for the phone to ring. I can't live that way. I want to be seen with the person I love, not have to steal away for a few hours or an occasional weekend. Martin, I will not get involved with you as long as you have a wife.'

Martin took her in his arms again. This time she didn't twist away. 'When I left you today, I spent a long time thinking about my life. And I came to the conclusion that I can't have it both ways. I've had a good life with Sylvia. She deserved better than me. But I could never love her as she should have been loved. The memory of you always came between us. I know that now. This afternoon, when I realized that to have you would mean asking her for a divorce, it was tough. And I would be less than honest if I didn't tell you that I rejected the thought at first. Divorcing someone you've lived with for a very long time is a brutal thing. But the fact remains that I love you, Jenny. And I can't give you up. Not this time.'

Releasing herself from his embrace, she went to the bar and poured herself another drink.

'This is indeed a night of revelations, Martin. I'm touched by your wish to marry me. But divorces can take a long time. And I'm not quite sure that I want to subject myself to another period of uncertainty. You see, Martin, I've changed, too. Life does a great many things to destroy patience. And besides, in spite of what you say, I think you love your wife more than you realize. I really think I must go away as I planned.'

'Darling, how can you say that now? I beg you to give me a little time. I promise I'll speak to Sylvia about a divorce.'

'Speaking and doing are two different things. Twenty-five years ago you spoke to your parents. Will it be any different today if you speak to your wife?'

'I know Sylvia. She's an extraordinary woman, with enormous understanding.'

'Oh, my God, Martin – you *are* naive. Women are never understanding when their husbands want to leave them.'

'I know Sylvia. You must trust me.'

'I don't trust anyone any more, Martin.'

Martin winced. 'I guess I'm responsible for that, Jenny. I'm so sorry, but don't go away. Please stay.'

Sadly she walked over to the window and gazed out at the clear December night. In the distance was the silhouette of the Bay Bridge. Wherever she looked Christmas lights twinkled. If only she could believe Martin, she would be the happiest woman in the world. But trust was a word she'd erased from her vocabulary years ago. She had never wanted anything as much as she wanted Martin at this minute. She thought briefly of his wife, but realized there was no reason to worry about her. Sylvia had her family, the children, and she had been Martin's wife during the long years when Jenny had been alone. Sylvia wasn't her responsibility. And this meeting with Martin had been an accident. God would not have planned this just as a cruel joke. Jenny made up her mind: if Martin wanted her she would wait. Only this time she would stand firm and fight for him. She deserved some happiness in her life. And now she wanted Martin at any cost.

She started as Martin touched her arm. It reminded her of the time he had left when his father died. Yet in spite of all they had said to each other, she still feared her vulnerability, and the past hurts nudged her just a little. *Go slow, Jenny. Be sure, Jenny.*

'Let me get you a drink, Martin.'

He looked at her and smiled. 'Only if you tell me you're not leaving.'

She looked at him, making up her mind. 'I'll just go away for the holidays. It wouldn't be fair for you to leave Sylvia alone this week. Afterwards you can speak to her.'

Holding her close to him, he whispered, 'Oh, darling Jenny, I do love you so.'

Then, turning off the lamp, he kissed her passionately. He wanted more than anything in the world to feel her body yield to him as she had in the past. He wanted to touch her, excite her, rouse the passion that he had never forgotten. He pressed his lips against the sweet swell of her breasts and when she sighed with pleasure as he lifted her in his arms he forgot everything except his need for her. When he entered her he felt as if he had never known such exquisite joy. He held her tighter, feeling his excitement mount until together their passion was spent and she lay beneath him, her body damp with perspiration, her eyes glazed with satisfaction.

'Oh God, Jenny – I had almost forgotten what it could be like. When you come back we'll go away together.'

'I would love that, Martin.'

'I'm glad. I'll make reservations at the Beverly Hills

Hotel, and I'll call you when you get to Hong Kong. But
promise me you will come back.'

'I promise. This time I'm not going to lose you, Martin.'

Christmas at the Roths' was a joyous occasion. Even
though they didn't consider it a religious holiday and exchanged gifts on Chanukah, they still decorated a tree and
had a big family dinner. This year Julian came West with his
wife, and even Amy, whose birthday fell on the next day,
seemed happy to be home for the week. Only Martin had
trouble pretending to enjoy himself. He kept thinking of
Jenny alone in Hong Kong, and Sylvia, whose life he was
about to shatter. He called Jenny every morning on his
private phone, and Christmas morning her sad words
haunted him the whole day.

'I have to keep telling myself that next year we'll be
together. We will, Martin – won't we?'

Her demand made him angry on some level. He didn't
want to hurt Sylvia. But Jenny had been the scapegoat once
and she had no one except him. Sylvia had the children and
her family. Even his own relatives would take care of her.
He was the one who would be scorned by family and
friends, and he knew he wouldn't be able to justify his
actions except that, for once, he was entitled to think of
himself. Time was running out. If he didn't act now he
would never have another chance.

Still, Martin remained torn. Finally, late one night,
ravaged with guilt, he decided to call Dominic, even though
it had been several years since the two men had exchanged
more than casual hellos on holidays.

'Dom,' Martin said when his friend picked up the phone.
'I'm glad I caught you. With the three-hour time
difference, I was afraid you might be out on the town.'

'No,' said Dominic, who had married for the second
time. 'I've finally settled down. Betty never liked my wild
life-style and I've come to agree with her. Anyway, old
buddy, how are things? To what do I owe the pleasure of
this call?'

236

'Trouble as usual,' Martin said without hesitation. 'You've always given me good advice and this time I need it more than ever.' And he poured out the story of his chance meeting with Jenny and the devastating but euphoric effect it had had on him.

'I never really stopped loving her,' Martin concluded. 'When she comes back we're going away for a week to sort things out. Then I guess I'll have to tell Sylvia . . . ' His voice trailed off as he waited for his friend to applaud his decision. It was, Martin suspected, the real reason for his call.

Dom's response came as a shock.

'I wouldn't be so fast to change my life just because of Jenny's reappearance. Sleep with her if you must, but remember – even the first time around she demanded more than you could give.'

'Hey,' Martin said. 'I thought you were her friend. You once believed I should fight for her. I didn't, and she certainly hasn't had an easy life since I left her.'

'That may be true,' Dominic said cautiously. 'But tough times don't always make people nicer. You and Jenny were frequently at odds twenty-five years ago. Why do you think things will be smoother this time?'

Martin started to interrupt, but Dominic cut him off. 'Listen – Sylvia's quite a woman. Just be sure you don't throw away a great life for an infatuation which will leave you cold in a year. It may sound odd coming from me, but family means everything. Even though your kids are gone, your relationship with them will never be the same if you leave Sylvia. Take it from me. I've had a rough time with my own over the past few years, and Betty still has to put up with a lot. My advice is: shack up with Jenny if you must, but don't bust up your marriage.'

'I hear you, Dom,' Martin said. 'Believe me, none of this is easy. It just seems this is my last chance at happiness. If I don't grab it now, that's it.'

'Well, I'm with you whatever you decide. Just be sure you know what you really want,' Dominic said, ringing off.

Martin hung up, shaken, and tiptoed back to the bedroom where Sylvia slept undisturbed.

The next day Martin couldn't conceal the strain he was under. Sylvia tried her best to pretend things were as usual, but she did not know how to respond when Julian took her aside and asked, 'What's wrong with Dad, Mother?'

'I don't know what you mean, dear.'

'Oh come on, Mother, you can't be so blind. Do you think he's still so angry about my marriage?'

'Julian, don't talk foolishly. Whatever misgivings we might have had are long gone.'

'Then what do you think is wrong?' he insisted.

'I don't know. He says he's under a great deal of pressure at work. I'm sure that's all that's bothering him.'

Sylvia was considerably more disturbed about Martin's mood than she let on, but it wasn't the first time in their marriage that he'd been depressed, and he always seemed to come out of it. She decided the best thing she could do was wait for him to return to being the loving husband he'd been in the past. After twenty-five years of marriage, she knew when to give her husband time to work things out on his own.

She managed to get through the week putting the best face possible on things, but on New Year's Eve Martin was so withdrawn she could no longer hide her concern. He stood in the corner, watching the guests – friends he had known all of his life – without even making a pretence of joining in the festivities. When the bells rang out at midnight, Sylvia came over and kissed him, and though he responded she sensed he was just going through the motions. It was lucky she couldn't read his mind, because his thoughts were all with Jenny McCoy.

On January 2 Martin was up at dawn. Jenny was back in California and they'd arranged to meet that night in Los Angeles. Martin had told Sylvia he had a business conference, but when he boarded the plane he was overwhelmed with guilt. He still had not mentioned the possibility of divorce, and he wondered how long he could go on pretending things were all right. In the plane, he decided he would have to tell Sylvia the truth when he returned. He tried to blot out the image of her face. He knew he couldn't just erase a quarter of a century as though it had never been. Sylvia was part of his life. If only he could find a way to leave without hurting her.

'You know where I'll be,' he had said, despising his words as he said them. Her trusting eyes would haunt him.

'Yes, darling,' she had answered. 'If you decide that you'd like me to join you after all, you know I will.'

From the moment he landed in Los Angeles nothing went right. When he registered, the clerk handed him a note saying Jenny had missed connections in Hawaii. God only knew when she would arrive. He signed the hotel register Mr and Mrs and went up to his room. The moment the bellboy left, he called room service for a bottle of his favourite wine and turned on the tub. Half an hour later he was soaking in water as hot as he could stand, a glass of chablis balanced in the soap dish. As the tension drained from his body all he could think of was Jenny. How tender, how understanding she had been. He vowed to make up to her for the years after he left her in New York. Then he thought of Sylvia and wondered how he could spare her. She had been a good wife and mother. She had done nothing to deserve the pain he was about to cause her. He wondered what Bess would say. She would probably never forgive him.

He got out of the bath and put on his robe, still trying to sort out his thoughts, when he heard the knock. He assumed it was the waiter, who had forgotten something, but when he opened the door, there was Jenny smiling at him, her eyes shining.

'Oh, thank God!' he said. 'You're here.'

She laughed delightedly at the expression on his face. Scooping her up, he twirled her around until they fell on the bed, laughing as they pulled off their clothes.

For a while Martin could think only about how much he loved her, how beautiful she was. Making love with Jenny rejuvenated him. It was as though he were in his twenties again and his commitment to Sylvia had never existed.

Afterwards they slept, and when they woke he asked her what she would like to do that evening. 'I don't know, Martin. Stay here, go out – whatever you want.'

'I could spend the rest of the week in bed, but perhaps it would do us good to get out for supper. I hear Ma Maison is the new "in" place. Maybe we should try it.'

'Whatever you say, dearest. I'm just so happy to be with you.'

Although Ma Maison was filled with beautifully dressed starlets, Martin noticed that most of the men looked up and smiled as he took Jenny to her table. Her beauty still caused quite a stir. When they finished eating, Martin insisted on dancing until Jenny was ready to collapse.

'Martin, I'm not going to be able to walk tomorrow,' she laughed.

'In that case, I'm going to get myself another dancing partner.'

'You won't be happy with another partner. I've spoiled you for everyone else,' she whispered. 'And it looks like tomorrow we will just have to stay in bed all day.'

Martin grinned and went to get their coats.

Back in the hotel, they found the bed had been turned down, and according to Martin's instructions a bucket of champagne was waiting in the hall.

Jenny laughed as he popped the cork and the wine bubbled out.

'Darling, I love you so much. I don't care about the past. I just want to be with you for the rest of my life.'

Martin was happier than he had ever been. It was as though he were being given a second chance; as though nothing existed before she came back into his life. As he lay in bed waiting for her to come out of the bathroom, even his guilt at deceiving Sylvia faded. It was a miracle that he had found Jenny again, that she was with him again.

When the bathroom door opened and she came out

wearing a white nightgown with blue satin slippers, Martin thought he had never seen anything so beautiful. 'You're prettier than ever,' he said.

'Thank you, Martin. I've never felt quite like this before. Promise if I tell you something you won't laugh.'

'I promise.'

'When I bought this gown I told the saleslady I wanted something for a bride. That's the way I felt. This is the most important day in my life, even more important than our wedding day. Promise you'll never leave me.'

'Never,' Martin said, holding her close. And at that moment he meant it.

The next morning they had breakfast in their room. As Martin sat across from her, he realized that he had forgotten to call Sylvia. 'Jenny, I've got to call home,' he said nervously.

'Go ahead,' she said, discreetly going into the bathroom, 'I understand.'

For a moment, when the operator asked for the number, Martin almost forgot it. Then the call went through and Sylvia picked up the phone.

'Hello?'

It took him a long time to respond. 'Sylvia . . . how are you?'

'Fine, Martin, darling. How is the conference going?'

He swallowed hard. 'Fine.' *What do you say to someone with whom you've lived for twenty-five years?* 'I want to apologize for not calling yesterday.'

'Oh, don't be silly. I know what those business meetings are like.'

That was Sylvia – always so damned understanding. He tried to think of something else to say.

'How are you?'

Sylvia laughed. 'You've already asked me that. Listen, as long as you're going to be gone until the weekend, Mother and I are going to drive to Pebble Beach. Jane asked us to visit.'

It was impossible for Martin to keep up his side of the

conversation. Hearing Sylvia's voice over the wire realizing her calm, confident trust in him, he was over-whelmed by guilt.

'Yes, dear,' he said, recovering himself. 'I'll call you a Jane's.'

'Great. Now don't work too hard, don't skip lunch, and for heaven's sake, cut down a bit on those cigarettes.'

Dammit . . . If she just weren't so good to me.

'Sylvia,' Martin managed to say in parting, 'have a goo time and enjoy yourself.'

'I will, dear. I only wish you could come with us.'

After he hung up, Martin had trouble regaining his carefre mood. Jenny refrained from asking any questions, and by the time they went out for lunch Martin felt better. They went to Perino's and after a couple of martinis Martin managed to forget Sylvia and Bess and concentrate or enjoying himself. Later they stopped by Giorgio's, and Martin had a couple of glasses of white wine while Jenny modelled one magnificent gown after another. Finally she chose a two-piece velvet dinner suit. The short jacket had jewelled buttons down the front, and it came with a cowl-necked burgundy blouse. Jenny decided it would look smashing with black silk pumps and sheer, black hose.

That night Martin couldn't take his eyes off her. The black velvet made her skin shine like porcelain. He found himself forgetting Sylvia, believing that he was a free man.

'I adore you, Jenny,' he said, taking her hand. 'When I am with you, I feel as if I'm back in my twenties.' He took a small box from his pocket and held it out to her.

'Oh, Martin, what's this?'

She fumbled with the ribbon, tore the wrapping, and finally managed to open the velvet box. Inside was a ring set with a cabochon ruby.

'Martin, why . . . ?'

'Because you make me so happy. Besides, it's your birth-stone.'

'I love it, darling. But you don't have to buy me gifts.'

'It's to remind you how much I love you.'

He reached over, took the ring out of the box, and slipped it onto the fourth finger of her left hand. She held his hand for a moment. 'Martin, I'm going to cry.'

She took out a handkerchief and wiped her eyes. 'We're going to be very happy, Martin. I know it. Nothing is going to come between us. I won't let it.'

'You're right, Jenny. Things will work out. It will just take a little time.'

'I know. Oh, I can't wait for the whole world to see us together.'

'They will. In the meantime just love me a lot.'

Martin signed the cheque and helped Jenny on with her jacket. 'You know you're the most beautiful woman here.'

'You're prejudiced.'

'You're right,' he said. 'Now where to?'

'Anywhere.'

'There's a new club on Sunset Boulevard with dancing. Do you think you can keep up with anyone as young as me?'

She laughed. It was as though she were twenty again, too. They danced well into the early hours of the morning. Holding each other close as they danced cheek to cheek, neither noticed that the music had changed from slow to a fast swing beat.

'Hey, bud, get with it,' said a drunken dancer nearby as he twirled his partner.

Martin and Jenny only smiled sheepishly at each other.

Back in the hotel room he could barely wait for Jenny to undress. Pulling her towards him, he said, 'Do you know how you make me feel?'

'No,' she whispered, biting his ear.

'As if I could make love to you all night.'

He did make love to her for hours, and each time he climaxed he shouted, 'Jenny . . . Jenny . . . Jenny . . .'

Later she lit two cigarettes and handed him one. 'Oh, Martin, I do love you so.' She pulled him down to her and kissed his mouth, eyes, neck. She never wanted to let him

243

go. Then, steeling herself, she asked, 'Martin, when do you think you'll ask Sylvia for a divorce?'

Martin wished she hadn't chosen that moment to ask. He didn't want anything to spoil this night together.

Jenny saw the stricken look cross his face. She didn't want to hurt him, but this time she wasn't going to let him vacillate either. All the way back from the Orient she had known she shouldn't have returned to California. Instead she should have insisted he make a clean break and come East. When Martin didn't answer, she said, 'You're going to have to speak to Sylvia sometime. When do you think you'll do it?'

'After I get home, darling. But let's not think about it now. Let's just enjoy what we have.'

'Of course, darling – but you will tell her you're leaving when you get home.'

Martin hesitated. He didn't want to think of Sylvia or his mother right at this moment; he just wanted to savour these few stolen days. But despite himself, he remembered his conversation with Dominic . . . *Just be sure you know what you really want* . . . Well, much as he owed his wife, he believed he did know. He wanted Jenny – and this time he would fight for her.

The days sped by like seconds. Before Martin could believe it they were back at the San Francisco airport. Afraid they might be seen, he didn't kiss her, saying, 'I love you, Jenny. Everything will be all right.'

'I know, Martin, but you must tell her. Then we will really be together.'

He waited until she got a taxi, then walked through the long terminal to the parking lot for his car.

As he drove out to Woodside he kept rehearsing what he would say to Sylvia. By the time he got home he was so distraught he didn't put the car in the garage. Instead, he turned off the engine and sat wondering how he could possibly tell his wife he was leaving. They had known each other almost all their lives. What had she ever done to deserve such treatment? As a girl she had waited patiently through the war, Martin's year in New York, his affair with Jenny. As a wife she had been loyal and devoted. Whatever problems they'd had with the kids were no fault of hers. What reason could he give for walking out? That he felt their marriage had grown stale? Well, if it had, wasn't he really to blame? Sylvia had become so involved with her charities and volunteer work only when Martin had made it clear he would not fill the hours left by the children's absence. And Sylvia had obediently kept herself busy. In fact, when had she ever done anything without his approval?

Or was that itself the problem? Martin had married her because she was the right girl, because his mother adored her, because they envisioned a similar future. He had never pretended he felt about her as he had about Jenny. The very reasons for their marriage had left him with an unresolved longing for the irrational, the passionate, the forbidden. And now he was about to wreck her life.

He got out of the car and walked up the front path to the door. His heart pounded as he put the key in the lock and entered the large hall. He had a sudden image of himself as a child sliding down the banister and his mother chastising him: 'Little gentlemen don't do that, Martin.' Well, after tonight she wouldn't have to worry about his behaving like a gentleman.

Slowly he climbed the stairs and stood outside the door to their bedroom, a room that he already no longer considered his. In abdicating from his marriage he felt he'd have to set aside all claim to this house. He turned the knob and opened the door. Sylvia was in bed, eating an apple. Her face was sunburned from working in the garden, and there was a transparent layer of vaseline on her nose. Reading glasses perched somewhat unbecomingly on her nose. 'Oh, Martin darling,' she said, holding out her arms. 'I didn't expect you until later.'

'I decided to take an earlier plane,' he said, busying himself with some mail on the dresser to avoid her embrace.

245

She didn't sense anything wrong and said, 'I'm so delighted you did; how did your week go?'

'Fine, fine. Sylvia . . . would you mind if I went down and fixed a drink?'

'Not at all. In fact, I'll join you in a minute.'

Martin poured himself a scotch and went to stand by the French doors. He peered into the night as though he could find the answers out there. He still hadn't decided how to broach the subject of divorce when Sylvia entered the room. This time she did sense his tension.

'Martin, come and talk to me.'

He turned around and looked at her. Slowly he walked to a chair, sat down, and took a sip of his drink.

'What's wrong, Martin?'

He shook his head.

'If something is bothering you, don't you think it would help to discuss it? We don't do much of that any more.'

Martin remained silent.

'Please, Martin. Don't keep shutting me out.'

He simply couldn't tell her tonight. He'd call Jenny and tell her, and she'd have to understand.

'I'm going to bed. I'm really awfully beat. You'll have to excuse me, it has been a difficult week.'

'Darling, please give me a chance. Give us a chance. Talk to me about what's troubling you.'

He sank back into his chair. 'Sylvia, I love you. I always will. That's what makes all this so difficult.'

Her heart suddenly began to pound. 'What's difficult, Martin?'

'Sylvia, I don't want to hurt you. I don't know quite how to say this.'

'Say what?'

He began again. 'I have fought this – believe me, I really have.'

'Fought what?' she said, but even as she asked she had a terrifying flash of knowledge.

Martin still was unable to speak. He went over to the bar and poured himself a half glass of straight scotch. 'Sylvia, I don't want you to hate me . . . '

She folded her hands to keep them from shaking.

He paused, summoning courage, then almost inaudibly said, 'I met Jenny McCoy again, quite by accident. Sylvia, I still love her. All these years I pretended she was no longer a part of my life, but it wasn't true. When I saw her I knew I couldn't leave her again any more than I could tear my heart from my body. My only regret is hurting you.'

Sylvia thought she was going to faint. He'd been away with Jenny for the past ten days. She knew that whatever she said at this moment could affect the rest of their lives. She mustn't overreact. She was too stunned to tell him what she really felt.

'Would you mind getting me a drink?' she finally whispered.

When he brought it to her she took it with trembling hands and forced herself to sip it quickly.

Waiting until she thought her voice would be steady, she said, 'Well, Martin, where does this leave us?'

'God, Sylvia, I don't know how to say it, but I guess it won't be any easier tomorrow, or the next day. I want you to divorce me.'

Sylvia felt as if her world had collapsed. She had hoped even through her fear that Martin was just going to confess to a fling. She would have been upset, but she would have forgiven him. Instead he was telling her he was leaving. Well, she wouldn't let him. She just wouldn't. She could fight, too. She had won twenty-five years ago. Maybe she would again. For all she knew it was a phase – the male midlife crisis they were writing all those books about. Well, the trick was to stay calm.

'Martin,' she forced herself to say gently, 'give yourself some time to think. Don't act rashly. I'll try not to pressure you, but don't do anything impulsively.'

'Sylvia, you don't seem to understand. I'm not acting impulsively. I honestly need to be free. I feel so bad – worse than you'd know – but this really has nothing to do with you . . . '

'Nothing to do with me?' Despite her resolution not to lose her temper, she heard her voice rising. 'Then who *does* it have to do with? I'm your *wife*.'

Damn, Martin thought. *I'm handling this so badly.* 'What I mean is that it's nothing that you've done. You've been a wonderful wife . . . '

'Martin, don't our years together mean anything? You've always believed in family. Look how upset you were about Julian's marriage, yet you're ready to break up our home because you spent ten days with a woman you haven't seen in a quarter of a century.'

'Sylvia, I'm sorry."

'Sorry? I've put my life into this marriage. I'm not complaining, it's a fact. My first priority was to make you happy.'

'Please, Sylvia. I guess I never stopped loving her.'

'Oh God, Martin, are you telling me all these years in bed you were thinking of her?'

'No, no. You must understand me, Sylvia. I've loved you. I still love you.'

'Martin, don't make things worse. If you loved me you wouldn't be talking of divorce.'

He went to her and knelt by the couch. 'You're wrong. I do love you, Sylvia. If I could find a way to spare you this I would.'

She did not hear the rest of his words as she finally gave in to her tears. She didn't know how long she wept, but feeling Martin's arms around her restored some of her strength. She would not give him up easily. She would fight, but with the weapons that had served her in the past: patience, understanding, and the force of her love itself.

She sat up and asked Martin to freshen her drink. When he returned she was sitting up drying her eyes. With every ounce of courage she possessed, she made herself say, 'Sit down, Martin, and tell me what happened. I'm ready to listen.'

Martin told her everything, from how he had spotted Jenny right before Christmas after leaving Sylvia outside

. Magnin's. How he had fought with himself before calling her name, to how he had finally met her in Los Angeles.

'You've never stopped loving her, have you, Martin?'

'I think I have been obsessed with her. When she vanished I always felt responsible. There were times I was afraid she hadn't survived. If I let her go a second time, Sylvia, I'll never get over it.'

Sylvia swallowed hard before saying, 'Maybe you can go on seeing her for a while without leaving me. I'll try to be sensible, Martin, if you promise you won't act in haste. Make sure you're doing the right thing before you do anything that's irrevocable. You once told me that Jenny was a devout Catholic. I'm sure she has a high regard for the sanctity of marriage; it's not something she'd want you to toss aside carelessly.'

Sylvia wasn't really sure Jenny had any high regard for marriage, but she felt it was to her own advantage to speak of her in the best terms possible. Sylvia knew her years with Martin had given her a certain influence and she was determined to use it now.

Praying for strength, she said, 'Why don't you give yourself a chance to know her better. After all these years, you're almost strangers. Maybe you're just trying to recapture your youth. I don't know. I'm no psychologist. I'm just a woman desperately in love with her husband.' Then, feeling as though she were plunging a knife into her heart, she said, 'Live with her for a little while. See if what you feel is really love. Then in six months if you still want it I'll give you a divorce.'

Martin was stunned. Sylvia was everything a woman should be, all the things he had told Jenny she was. And dear God, if he could have willed it he would have loved her as she deserved. 'You could bear such an arrangement?' he asked.

'If I have to,' Sylvia told him, standing up. 'Look, Martin, I'm exhausted. Call Jenny or go to her if you wish. I want some time alone anyway.' She walked out of the room with her head high, but back in the bedroom she and

Martin had shared with so much pleasure she dissolved into tears. Going into the bathroom, she caught sight of herself in the mirror. 'You fool,' she said aloud. 'You stupid stupid fool. There isn't a woman in the world more stupid than you. You want him even though you know he married you on the rebound, even though he's still in love with her.' But the small voice of truth said: you have always loved him and always will. Even being second best was better than not having him at all. You won out over Jenny once, and with God's help you can do it again.' Then, putting Jenny and Martin together in Los Angeles, she lashed out: 'You bitch . . . you little Irish bitch. I won't let you ruin my life.' Picking up a bottle of bath salts, she threw it against the wall with all her might and watched it shatter into a million pieces. Then she slumped to the floor, resting her head against the cold tub. 'I love you, Martin. I love you. Please come back . . . please . . .'

When Martin called and told Jenny he was on his way back to the city, she rushed around to be ready. After ordering up champagne she took a quick bath and dressed in a bright red silk caftan. She was sitting waiting when she heard his knock.

She ran into his arms, but when she stepped back to look at him she saw his face was drawn, his eyes filled with pain. All her delicious sense of anticipation faded. She guided him over to the sofa. To ease the tension, she poured him a glass of scotch. The moment didn't seem right for champagne. *Poor Martin*, she thought. *Sylvia must have given him a dreadful time. Apparently she wasn't quite as understanding as he thought she'd be. Well, the worse she behaved the easier it will be for him to leave. And leave he will.*

Jenny had no intention of ever being deserted again. This time she would end up Mrs Martin Roth.

Martin sat staring at his drink, his face drained of colour.

Taking his hand gently, Jenny said, 'It must have been terrible for you. I'm sure these things are never easy, but

250

thank God it's over with. She knows.'

For some reason Martin resented Jenny's assumption that Sylvia no longer counted. 'Yes, she knows,' was all he said.

His tone frightened her. Trying to compose herself, she repeated, 'It must have been terrible for you, darling. Was she very angry?'

'No, she was very patient.' He took a sip of his drink.

'Tell me, Martin,' Jenny said, suddenly nervous. 'What happened?'

'Sylvia was very understanding. I don't know any other woman who would have acted so decently.'

Jenny wanted to turn the conversation away from Sylvia, but she had to know where she stood. 'Martin, it's very gallant of you to defend your wife, but you haven't told me what you both decided.'

'She thinks you and I should live together so that we are perfectly sure of one another and then she will give me the divorce.

Jenny tried to control her anger. No woman wanted another's permission to sleep with the man she loved, but she realized Sylvia had acted very wisely. She would have to do the same. 'That is very decent,' she said. 'In fact, her concern for you makes her sound a bit like a Jewish mother.'

Martin thought that was unfair, but he didn't say anything. Jenny had not had an easy life and it was understandable that she wanted everything to go smoothly. 'Jenny, she was a good wife. I don't want to hurt her more than I have to.'

'Martin, you have to be honest with me. You don't still love her?'

'Not in the sense that you mean. But you must understand, Jenny, that Sylvia's played a major role in my life. She's borne my children, cared for my home, even been like a daughter to Bess. I can't just turn my back on her and walk away. I still care for her as a person.'

Jenny knew she was being foolish, but she couldn't keep

herself from saying, 'Maybe you should have searched you[r] soul a little more carefully before you begged me to g[o] away with you. You can't have it both ways, Martin.'

Martin sat stunned. 'You haven't listened to one thin[g] I've said to you tonight, Jenny . . . '

'Oh yes I have, Martin. I've heard it all too well. Suppos[e] you try to understand me. This time I come first.' Despit[e] herself her voice rose shrilly. 'If you don't understand that you can walk out of that door and forget me.'

Jenny ran into the bedroom, threw herself onto the bed and sobbed. She still wasn't the victor. Sylvia was.

Martin hurried after her and lifted her into his arms. H[e] sat rocking her as though she were a little girl. 'Jenny darling, please – this is just very difficult for both of us. Yo[u] must know how much I love you. Let's not do this to on[e] another.'

She took Martin's handkerchief out of his coat pocke[t] and dried her tears. 'Martin, you must forgive me, but I fee[l] so frightened. I wanted you to ask for an immediat[e] divorce. She's playing for time. She isn't going to let you g[o] that easily, and I'm afraid she may not let you go at all. Fo[r] all you know she has some plan to separate us.'

Martin sighed. 'Darling, Sylvia is not like that. She is no[t] a calculating woman. Surely you can understand how upse[t] she must have been tonight.'

Difficult as it was for Jenny, she had to admit that Sylvi[a] had probably behaved better than she would have. N[o] woman gives up her husband without a fight, and Jenn[y] knew that once she married Martin, she'd never let him ou[t] of her sight. Quietly, she said, 'Of course you're right. [I] hope you will forgive me. But insecurity makes us do a lo[t] of things we wish we hadn't. How long do you think it wil[l] be before we can make definite plans?'

'Just let her get used to my moving out. In a few weeks I'[ll] talk to her again.'

That night Martin fell asleep with Jenny in his arms, bu[t] he didn't try to make love to her and she was too clever t[o] insist.

*

252

Over the next weeks Martin packed most of his winter clothes and moved them into a furnished apartment he and Jenny had rented on Russian Hill. He tried to avoid Sylvia's tearful gaze when he went downstairs with two heavy suitcases and was gratified that she kept her reproaches to herself. His mother showed no such restraint. She cried and shouted that Martin was crazy leaving a woman like Sylvia for a scheming shiksa.

'She was no good for you when you were in your twenties and she's no good for you now – only in your fifties you should know better.'

Bess railed on and on until in the end Sylvia had to calm her down so Martin could leave. On the whole his wife behaved very well, sometimes better than Jenny over the last few days.

Jenny was angry that Martin insisted their relationship remain a secret. Sylvia hadn't told the children yet and there would be time enough for their neighbours and friends to gossip when she actually filed for divorce. Jenny also was upset that Martin had only rented a comparatively small apartment. It wasn't that the rooms were not elegant, but thinking of Sylvia languishing in the opulence of Woodside heightened her annoyance. Nights when Martin came home she was often fretful and demanding. It was as though she wanted him to make up for all she had suffered since he had left her in New York.

Where he had expected bliss he found tension. When he thought he'd regained his youth, he seemed to be overwhelmed with cares. Sometimes the only moments of peace he knew were when he drove out to Woodside to talk things over with Sylvia.

Although they had not told anyone he had moved out, everyone in contact with Martin sensed that he was under terrible stress. He avoided lunch with his partners and snapped at his secretary until she threatened to quit. She was so upset she nearly complained to Sylvia one morning when Sylvia called to speak to Martin, but Mrs Roth sounded so sad, she decided to keep her problems to herself.

'Your wife is on the line,' she told Martin. 'May I put her through?'

'Yes, of course.'

He picked up the phone, wondering what she wanted. 'How are you, dear?' she was asking, as if everything were still all right.

'I'm fine,' he said mechanically. 'How are you doing?'

The truth was she was living in limbo. She had almost picked up the receiver a million times to beg Martin to come back. Each time she had stopped herself, knowing there would be time for that later if he still insisted on the divorce. Bess couldn't understand her. 'Sylvia, you can't be foolish enough to give Martin up without a struggle. You are just handing him a free rein, giving Jenny McCoy carte blanche so that she can become Mrs Martin Roth.'

But Sylvia kept her own counsel and didn't pressure Martin at all. Now she said softly, 'Under the circumstances, I'm doing much better than I would have expected. I called to ask if you were free for lunch today.'

'Yes, I'd like that.'

'Where should we meet?' There was no place Sylvia could think of that was not filled with memories. Certainly he wouldn't suggest the St Francis.

'Would Doro's be all right?' Doro's had no special significance, in spite of the fact they had been there from time to time. 'How's twelve-thirty?'

'Wonderful. I'll see you then.'

After hanging up, Martin sat staring at the silent phone for a long time. Then he buzzed the intercom and told his secretary to make the reservation at Doro's.

At twelve-thirty-five, Sylvia walked into the restaurant looking like a *Vogue* model. She had spent three hours achieving that effect – an hour at the hairdresser, an hour for a facial, and the rest of the time trying on almost every outfit in her closet.

'My dear Mrs Roth,' said the maître d', 'you look lovely

I believe Mr Roth is waiting for you at the bar.'

'Thank you, Alfred.'

Martin was seated at a small table. The dim lights only enhanced Sylvia's looks. Martin could not remember her ever looking more beautiful, not even on their wedding day. She seemed to have achieved a new serenity. He stood up and awkwardly brushed her cheek with his lips, thinking: *I can at least be civil – after all, we've been married for twenty-five years.*

They sat barely speaking, ordering a second round of drinks before the headwaiter came to escort them to a secluded banquette in the dining room. An enormous French menu was placed in front of them. Martin didn't bother to look at it because he always ordered a chef salad or broiled chicken. But Sylvia scanned the dishes carefully before ordering oysters, rack of lamb, and a tossed green salad. He was surprised, as she usually ate a very light lunch. He was still more surprised when she ate all the courses, leaving only the most minute portion on her plate. Barely touching his own meal, he stared at her out of the corners of his eyes. She seemed to be wearing her hair slightly differently and he detected a new perfume. It was as though she were subtly telling him that she was doing fine without him – and he wasn't at all happy at the news.

When the waiter brought the dessert cart she asked for an apple tarte and a double espresso. He watched as she took out a compact and powdered her nose. So far neither of them had said anything of importance, but he sensed the moment had come.

Sylvia put down her cup, praying she could maintain her composure. The whole lunch had been a charade. She just didn't want Martin to think she was beaten. The past two months had been a nightmare. She had decided she had lost, but when she told Martin she was giving up she didn't want him to feel sorry for her.

'Martin, I guess you're wondering why I wanted to see you today. I wanted to tell you that I've decided to go to Reno now. There seems no point in dragging things out.'

255

Martin looked down at his hands. 'What made you decide?'

'Martin, you and I have been much more than just husband and wife. We have known each other all of our lives. You've been my best friend. The two months you've been gone I've had lots of time to think. I could fight you on the divorce, but what would that accomplish? I don't want to force you to come back. If Jenny was just a passing fancy I could forgive that. But it seems you love her and want to be with her. I'm not looking for revenge. I want to do this quietly, with as much dignity as we can manage. The newspapers will have a field day as it is, and I know that a lot of my friends will lunch out on us for months. Bess tells me that I am stupid to let you off the hook this easily, but what's over is over. I must say that I think we had an awfully good marriage while it lasted. We had our share of problems and disagreements, of course. Who goes through twenty-five years of marriage without them? And the truth is, I probably took you too much for granted recently. The night you came home from Los Angeles you found me in bed with vaseline all over my face. Would it have made a difference if I tried to maintain a more glamorous image? I doubt it.' She took a sip of the cold coffee and said, 'The truth is, who knows how to make a perfect marriage? I certainly don't. And I guess we can't stay friends, but I do wish you the best of everything. You have waited a long time for Jenny McCoy.'

When Sylvia finished, Martin was close to tears. If she had fought he would have defended himself. If she had accused him he could have tried to justify his actions. As it was, he walked out into the cold March sunlight wondering for the first time if Jenny would be able to fill the terrible void that was left by the end of his marriage.

When Martin walked into the apartment that night he put his arms about Jenny and hugged her without speaking. He stood silently embracing her until she moved over to the couch and sat looking up at him, aware that something had happened. When he remained silent, she pulled him down beside her and said, 'Darling, do you have something to tell me?'

'I had lunch with Sylvia today,' he said abruptly. 'She's going to Reno.'

Jenny felt a surge of excitement: she was going to win. But noting Martin's serious expression, she concealed her joy and only asked, 'When?'

'Some time this week.'

'Oh, Martin, darling, I just love you so. And I hope you have no regrets?'

'None.' He lied, just a little.

'There are no words to tell you how happy I am,' Jenny said. 'Now we can stop sneaking around, take a nice apartment, go to the theatre, the opera.'

'Well,' Martin said, 'I've been thinking about that all afternoon. It would be very hard on Sylvia if we stayed in San Francisco. She's lived here all her life and is very active in the cultural community. Almost all the people we know are really her friends. Wherever we went we'd be running into them.'

Jenny could not believe what she was hearing. 'Are you ashamed of me?'

Martin winced. 'How can you ask me a question like that? Of course not. I just think it would be easier on us and kinder to Sylvia if we considered moving. My family and Sylvia's do occupy a certain position in this community. I can't take my happiness and flaunt it at them. Sylvia's going to live here. I won't stay and be a constant embarrassment to her.'

'You mean me. I would be the embarrassment.'

'No – for God's sakes, no. This has nothing to do with you, Jenny. It has to do with decency, dignity. I thought it might be wonderful for us to move to a villa in Rome, or on the Riviera, wherever you like, until this simmers down.'

As she stood listening to Martin, something within her snapped. She remembered all the agony she had endured in her life: her father's abandonment, the abuse she suffered

257

at the hands of a drunken mother, the years working for a paranoid woman who beat her, the months alone in Chicago, Cyrus's endless brutality. As though she were avenging her whole past, she screamed, 'No, Martin! I won't be dragged off and hidden. If you want me, you'll marry me here and acknowledge me publicly. I want everyone to know that I am now your wife. I want to shop where *she* shopped, get on committees *she* used to chair, be welcomed everywhere *she* was.'

'But, Jenny,' Martin said sadly, 'Sylvia was part of that society long before I married her. You must understand that her grandparents helped build this city, were a part of its culture. Do you see what I'm saying, Jenny? I don't want to be unkind, but your presence would drive her away from the only ties she has left. And besides, the women would snub you.'

'I don't care!' Jenny shouted. 'I want her to suffer. I want you to make up to me for all I missed when you left me in New York. *You owe me!*'

Martin flushed angrily. 'I don't want to marry anyone because I owe. Besides, Jenny, you and I are not the first couple in the world whose love affair broke up. What happened to you after that was not my fault. Look – I'm sorry I left you alone when my father died. The day I met you in front of Shreve's I knew I wanted to make it up to you. But I can't give you my soul. I don't owe you that, Jenny.'

She screamed as though she had gone mad. 'You do! You owe me everything. If you had married me as you promised, I would never have gone through the hell I did when I lived with Cyrus. And in that thing you call a heart, you know you're nothing but a lying Jew – '

Oh, my God, she thought, the second the words left her mouth. *I must be out of my mind. How could I have said that to him?* With tears streaming down her cheeks, she cried, 'Martin, darling, you must forgive me. I'm so sorry . . . You must believe me . . . I'm so sorry.'

Martin felt as though he had been struck between the

eyes; as though he were seeing Jenny for the first time. Swallowing hard he said, 'I'm sorry too, Jenny – for so, so many things.'

'Martin, let me make it up to you.'

'No, I don't think that's possible, Jenny. We've hurt each other enough.'

When he turned to leave, she stood in front of him and once again pleaded, 'Martin, I beg you – forget what I said. Forgive me. I love you.'

The Jenny of his youth was still dear to him. And it was for her that he had compassion. Taking out his handkerchief, he wiped her eyes. 'I'm afraid, Jenny, it just won't work.'

'If we try, Martin, it will.'

'No, I don't think so. Because a part of you hates me, Jenny. And that part has wanted to punish me ever since we broke up. I see that now. But try to forgive me, Jenny. And more important, try to forgive yourself.'

He turned and walked down the hall as Jenny slumped to the floor, sobbing. When the doors of the elevator closed, Martin leaned against the wall, trembling.

Without thinking, he found his car and began driving aimlessly around the rain-swept streets. After a while he found himself at the top of Telegraph Hill. He turned off the ignition and looked out over the Bay. The lights of the Golden Gate Bridge seemed to wink at him through the mist as though they knew more about Martin Roth than he did himself. What had caused him to chase this image he had of Jenny, this illusion of love, which had all but destroyed him? Maybe in order to understand he would have to go back to the beginning – after the war, when he was so uncertain about his life. He had been unable to figure out why he had survived the war, why he, a Jew, had been so privileged while six million had suffered and died in the camps.

Whatever the reason, Jenny had come along at a time when he was particularly vulnerable. She had fired his passion so that he felt he couldn't live without her. Even today he knew that she excited him to a degree Sylvia never could. His need for Jenny had been obsessive. But somewhere down deep in his soul, he knew that she had spoken the truth: he never really intended to marry her. He knew that all those years ago he hadn't asked Jenny to meet his parents because she would never have fitted into his life. She was right – he had lied to her, deliberately or not. And when he had seen her again last Christmas he had felt passion, but not love. It had been the vision of lost youth that had kindled something within him he'd thought was dead. Finally, he realized that the Jenny who had haunted him all those years was a figment of his imagination. He remembered Dominic's warning. The Jenny he lived with secretly never really existed. He had made her up. The only thing that had been real in his life was Sylvia – Sylvia, who'd always been there. She had shared the best and the worst of times. She had been the greatest thing that had ever happened to him – and he had taken her for granted. He shivered at the thought that he had almost lost her. Now he'd crawl if need be, beg for forgiveness, and at long last, love her as she deserved. He turned on the ignition and drove down the hill, towards home.

Sylvia had finished packing. She wiped her forehead and looked wearily at the luggage, all neatly stacked and snapped shut, and realized that all her hopes and dreams were buried within those small compartments. She remembered that Martin had bought the suitcases for their honeymoon, in Florence. She sighed, walked to the French window, and looked out at the moonlit garden. It didn't look quite as enchanting tonight.

Suddenly she felt her pulse race and her heart pound. Martin's car was skidding to a halt on the cobblestone driveway. She hesitated, then shouted with joy. She had won. He had come home to her. She knew it.

Sylvia ran down the stairs from her bedroom, across the vast hall, and flung open the door. She stood for a moment framed in the entrance. Then their eyes met and she ran to

260

Martin's waiting arms. In that extremely poignant moment of reunion no words were exchanged. There was no need for them, but their eyes were filled with tears of joy.

Susan Fromberg Schaeffer
The Madness of a Seduced Woman £2.50

Agnes Dempster is a beautiful woman destined to be severely wronged by life and love; her dreams, thoughts and actions propel her towards a horrific crime of passion she is incapable of preventing. In her search for an all-consuming love Agnes turns her back on an unhappy childhood, only to become infatuated with a man who will never make her happy, a man who pushes her to the brink of madness.

'A great many women have tried to write *the* feminist novel . . . *this* is the novel they've been trying to write' MARGARET FOSTER

Helen Hooven Santmyer
'. . . and Ladies of the Club' £4.95

From the chaotic aftermath of the Civil War to the social turmoil of the 1930s, a warm, intimate epic tale of two remarkable women in a small Ohio town, and of their fellow members in the Waynesboro ladies' literary society. From girlhood to matriarchy, through wrenching battles for suffrage and prohibition, to images of distant battlefields and loved ones lost for ever, the result is a great, rich, satisfying read, already acclaimed as a classic of its kind.

G. J. Scrimgeour
A Woman of Her Times £2.50

A woman's story that every woman will live as if it were her own. Through three continents, two world wars, through marriage and motherhood, love and pain and betrayal, Elizabeth Wingate is a woman of her times: a dutiful wife in Ceylon; a socialite in 1920s London; penniless and alone in 1930s Hollywood – journeying through decades in search of a destiny only time can reveal.

'A remarkable book . . . great style, scope, masses of colour . . . Elizabeth Wingate's story touches the heart' BOOKSELLER

Patricia Roberts
Tender Prey £1.95

Only Mary James's daughter Ali suspects that her new 'daddy' is not all he seems. When he disappears with her ten-year-old sister Junie, Ali's worst fears are sickeningly confirmed. Then, ten months later, a horrific 'gift' arrives on Mary James's doorstep.

'A remarkable first novel: an extremely nasty story, powerfully narrated' THE TIMES LITERARY SUPPLEMENT

Zoe Fairbairns
Stand We At Last £2.50

'Quite splendid . . . a thoroughly intelligent and entertaining saga which follows five generations of women through the history of their emancipation' COMPANY

'Travels a long way in time and space . . . gives a résumé of the last hundred years of the women's struggle for emancipation while telling a rattling good tale' THE TIMES LITERARY SUPPLEMENT

Robert Perrin
Noonday £2.50

A passionate saga of a family with one great and undivided passion spanning two centuries and four generations. A vibrant, dramatic, epic story of hatred and bloodshed, devotion and rebellion, patriotism and pride. The love of men for their country and the struggle to secure it against the odds.

Tom Sharpe
Blott on the Landscape £1.95

'Skulduggery at stately homes, dirty work at the planning inquiry, and the villains falling satisfactorily up to their ears in the minestrone . . . the heroine breakfasts on broken bottles, wears barbed wire next to her skin and stops at nothing to protect her ancestral seat from a motorway construction' THE TIMES

'Deliciously English comedy' GUARDIAN

Wilt £1.95

'Henry Wilt works humbly at his Polytechnic dinning Eng. Lit. into the unreceptive skulls of rude mechanicals, but spends his nights in fantasies of murdering his gargantuan, feather-brained wife, half-consummated when he dumps a life-sized inflatable doll in a building site hole, and is grilled by the police, his wife being missing, stranded on a mud bank with a gruesome American dyke' GUARDIAN.

'Superb farce' TRIBUNE

'. . . triumphs by a slicing wit' DAILY MIRROR

Vintage Stuff £1.95

'When Tom Sharpe turns his attention to a very minor public school with assault courses for over-active underachievers, cold showers and beatings, the result is predictably savage. Hoaxes, chases, car crashes, shootings, and general mayhem. Wicked riotous humour'
                                                DAILY TELEGRAPH

'A roar of derring-do, misunderstandings and catastrophes . . . a knickerbocker glory of a plot features a model pupil who takes literally every word he hears. "Turn over a new leaf" has Peregrine in the camelias in a trice . . . Needle-Sharpe . . . vintage stuff all right'
                                                THE TIMES

Unity Hall
Secrets £1.95

Les Hirondelles – the mansion where three generations of the de Courtenays gather under the Mediterranean sky and languish amidst wealth and luxury. Three generations of secrets: the father's passion for an Algerian masseuse; the eldest son and his illicit love of his own half-sister; the daughter's insatiable sexuality schooled by her father; the granddaughter a hireling of the sensuality of pain; and Anne, the outsider looking for a man to free her from twisted lust . . . Amongst them walks a stranger of powerful wealth – the man who knows the biggest secret of all . . .

But Not for Long £1.95

Ingrid Pallia's life is a whirl of cars and coke and kicks, like bedroom tangles with the voluptuous Monique and the two pretty boys from the bars. In the movie world of dollars and deals she is a superstar with a past; her next scandal will be the publication of her true confessions. Her next movie will be with the paedophile director Bellino. And it's all happening in Rome, city of kidnap and terror.

The White Paper Fan £1.95

Jade had just made love in the jacuzzi in Aspen, Colorado with the big blond American when she got the phone call. The man who'd always been her father, who'd adopted her and Poppy when they were just tiny Chinese baby girls, had been killed in a hit-and-run accident. He bequeathed them not only money, but many unanswered questions. Who were those names in his address book? What did the clippings from the Hong Kong newspapers mean? And who were Poppy and Jade, anyway? The answers lay in Hong Kong, in a labyrinth of drugs and death, sinister Triad connections and dark secrets – hidden behind the white paper fan.

Daphne du Maurier

Frenchman's Creek £1.95

While the gentry of Cornwall strive to capture the daring Frenchman who plunders their shores, the beautiful Lady Dona finds excitement, danger and a passion she never knew before as she dares to love a pirate – a devil-may-care adventurer who risks his life for a kiss . . .

'A heroine who is bound to make thousands of friends, in spite of her somewhat questionable behaviour' SUNDAY TIMES

Jamaica Inn £1.95

The cold walls of Jamaica Inn smelt of guilt and deceit. Its dark secrets made the very name a byword for terror among honest Cornish folk.

Young Mary Yellan found her uncle was the apparent leader of strange men who plied a strange trade. Was there more to learn? She remembered the fear in her aunt's eyes . . .

'An exciting brew . . . for a late evening's reading' SATURDAY REVIEW

The House on the Strand £1.95

Dick Young was lent a house in Cornwall by his friend, Professor Lane. During his stay he agreed to be a guinea-pig for the Professor's new research drug – a drug which transports him from the house at Kilmarth back to the fourteenth century. There, in the manor of Tywardreath, he witnesses intrigue, adultery and murder . . .

Arthur Hailey
Hotel £2.50

The scene is the St Gregory Hotel, New Orleans. Through this totally
fascinating novel move vividly drawn characters involved in robbery
and blackmail, a near-disastrous orgy and a take-over battle . . . There
is courage too, and a love story that will remain etched on the reader
mind.

Overload £2.50

His latest, greatest bestseller.

Nim Goldman, vice president of GSP&L – the corporation feeding
power, light and heat to kilowatt-hungry California. He's got a big job
and he's got all the women he can handle. But Nim knows the crunc
is coming: soon, very soon, power famine will strike the most
advanced society the world has known . . .

'3,200,000 kilowatts, OPEC, terrorists, power thieves, hypocrisy and
paralysis in high places . . . chaos for power-guzzling California . . .
another blockbuster' OBSERVER

The Moneychangers £2.50

The genius of Arthur Hailey combines money, people and banking in
an absorbing story of the financial and personal crises seething behin
the dignified bronze doors of a major US bank. Interwoven with the
dreams, passions, rivalries and guilty secrets are currency and credit-
card frauds, embezzlement, a prison gang-rape, Mafia torture and th
call-girl sex that sweetens irregular business deals.